# THE HORRORS WE HARBOUR

EMILY COOPER

solstice

London · New York · Amsterdam/Antwerp · Sydney/Melbourne · Toronto · New Delhi

First published in Great Britain by Solstice Books,
an imprint of Simon & Schuster UK Ltd, 2026



1 3 5 7 9 10 8 6 4 2

Simon & Schuster UK Ltd, 7th Floor
199 Bishopsgate, Broadgate, London EC2M 3TY



www.simonandschuster.co.uk
www.simonandschuster.com.au
www.simonandschuster.co.in

Simon & Schuster Australia, Sydney
Simon & Schuster India, New Delhi

The authorised representative in the EEA is Simon & Schuster Netherlands BV, Herculesplein 96, 3584 AA Utrecht, Netherlands. info@simonandschuster.nl



A CIP catalogue record for this book
is available from the British Library

Hardback ISBN: 978-1-3985-3583-1
Trade Paperback ISBN: 978-1-3985-3584-8
eBook ISBN: 978-1-3985-3585-5
Audio ISBN: 978-1-3985-3781-1



Typeset in Baskerville by M Rules
Printed and Bound in the UK using 100% Renewable Electricity
at CPI Group (UK) Ltd

MIX
Paper | Supporting responsible forestry
FSC® C013604

*For my dad, who always keeps the light on.*

# PROLOGUE

*There's something sinister about the seas 'round Ynys Halen. Beyond the creatures that swarm the island each night, I mean. There's a rot beneath the waves. A pestilence. I'd sooner sail straight into a whirlpool than along that coast.*

—Quote from an unnamed sailor

They're waiting for me, down on the beach.

In the clotted dark, they look like splotches of paint drawn out too thin and long by a thumb. Their hair is black, their skin so pale it's almost translucent, like the bell of a jellyfish. If I get too close, maybe I'll be able to see their hearts beating through their flesh.

I don't know why I think the two girls are waiting, let alone for me. They're not looking at my tiny porthole up in the lighthouse. Their focus is trained on something suspiciously still, lying prone on the wet sand.

We don't go out past dark, but something bids me to push my bedroom door ajar. Down the corridor, Rhian snores gently. The lighthouse's fortified front door doesn't whine on its hinges like usual, almost as if it approves of my plan. I slip out into the night, my bedclothes doing little to stave off the cold. The stone steps down to the beach bite at my feet.

The ocean roars, every bit a monster as the creatures it conceals. Waves pound against the sand. A full moon hangs beyond the bay, drawing the tide into a frenzy. The girls are framed in a halo of sea spray, occasionally lit up by the glare of Point Beacon's beam. Their hair is perfectly still despite the wind. As I approach them, their heads turn to track me, moving as if governed by a collective consciousness. Their eyes are the same watery blue, rimmed in pink, like they're fighting back tears.

The girls mustn't be much older than my nine years, but I feel small and infantile in their company. They regard me the way adults do, with a quiet authority that's implicitly understood.

A toddler stirs in the arms of the shortest girl. It's a small, pale thing with a full head of dark hair and the same weeping blue eyes as the other girls. My gaze tracks to the Thing in the sand. The taller girl nudges it with her toe. She holds her feet like a ballet dancer.

She sniffs. 'Is it a seal?'

'No,' I say, quite decisively. 'It's a tidewraith.'

The tidewraith's lips have peeled back, revealing razor-sharp teeth. I'm struck by the urge to run my finger across them. Its thick, muscular tail reminds me of a conger eel's, with the frilled dorsal fin that runs down its length. The gills on its throat have swollen like bracket fungi protruding from a tree, and the talons attached to its front limbs look close to pulling clean off.

The smaller girl says, 'Why doesn't it look like one?'

'Because it's bloated,' I respond.

Bloat. It's a funny word. I think it sounds the way it looks. *Blow-t.* Waxy, blue-ish skin. Distended stomachs threatening to burst in a shower of sinew and viscera. Pruned fingertips. All things a girl of my age shouldn't really see, or so Rhian says. That doesn't stop her from entreating my help when she has to drag drowned sailors from the shallows.

'Bloated,' the eldest girl says, or almost hums. 'How horrible.'

'What killed it?' the shorter girl asks. Her lips are almost blue.

I shrug. 'Might be natural causes.' Most tidewraiths are just as vulnerable to time as the rest of us.

She shifts her bare feet in the sand. 'Do you think it suffered?'

'What a strange thing to ask,' the other girl replies.

Out in the bay, a tail slaps the water. My pulse spikes. 'Why are you down here?' I ask, eyes darting between them. This is *my* beach. *My* responsibility. 'You know it's dangerous at night.'

'There's a storm coming. Can't you tell? Look at the cumulonimbus.' The elder of the dark-haired girls levels a finger out at sea. The horizon is stacked with menacing, flat-topped clouds. 'We mustn't be here when it breaks.'

It's as if I never spoke. The taller girl turns, tracking a path towards the steps up from the beach. The other girl lingers a moment longer. In her arms, the toddler stares back at me with a knowing far beyond its age.

'Do you think it suffered?' she asks again.

'I don't think they *can* suffer. They're monsters,' I respond.

She shakes her head; the toddler shakes with her. 'Mother says suffering *makes* monsters.'

'Suffering makes Gods on Ynys Halen,' I say. 'That's how Llyr ascended to Godhood.'

'Suffering, cannibalism, martyrdom.' She recites the prerequisites of Godhood with a soft lisp. More words Rhian says aren't fit for a girl my age. I told her if that's the case, she shouldn't make me go to Sunday service. It's the only argument with her I've ever won. 'Do you really think Llyr did that? That he *ate* people?'

I consider it for the first time. There are etchings of Llyr on the walls of the church – this towering wave of a man with a beard down to his chest and blue eyes rendered in sea glass. I recall the image of him with blood smeared across his lips, sinew between his teeth. A violent shiver chases through me.

'He must've,' I concede.

'Would you eat a person if it meant you'd become a God?'

'No,' I snap. 'I'm a good person.'

'I never said you weren't.' She looks at me strangely. 'You're odd.'

I jut out my chin. 'You're odd, too.'

She smiles, or at least I *think* it's a smile, before she turns and disappears the way she came. I'm left alone on the beach, wondering if I'm still dreaming.

# CHAPTER I

*Suffering, cannibalism, martyrdom. Through my research, I've discovered these are the conditions which transform a human into a God. With my sacrifice, I will inherit the power needed to protect Ynys Halen from its monstrous seas. I will not let anyone else endure the same fate as my Bronwen.*

—Llyr, God of Sea and Storms,
before his ascent to Godhood

Most lighthouses are a promise of sanctuary. *My* lighthouse is a threat.

Tonight, it perches on the cliff with teeth bared and bloody. Wind howls through cracks in the watch room windows. My throat stings, assaulted by the stench of kerosene. A bone-white ray of light beams out from Point Beacon, swinging in even circles around the shallows.

I cup my hands against the glass. My hurried breaths fog the window. The ocean beyond swells ominously, rippling like a swathe of black silk. Each pass of the light illuminates dark shapes coiling beneath the surface. They gather in droves, tangling just short of Point Beacon's reach. Tidewraiths are nocturnal, kept at bay by light. The lighthouse beam is the only thing that prevents them swarming our island when darkness falls.

'It's not enough,' I shout above the gale. 'They're going to make it to shore!'

Rhian knows I'm right, but she doesn't vocalise it. Our symbiosis demands that she is the optimist.

'It's going to be okay,' she calls down from the lantern room. 'Check the other beaches!'

I throw open the door to the widow's walk – the small, rusted walkway that encircles Point Beacon's watch room, just beneath the lantern room. The wind wrestles for control over my limbs as I bring a pair of binoculars to my eyes. There's not been a storm this fierce since the one the sisters predicted, all those years ago. A decade has passed since then, but even at nineteen, thunder fills me with dread.

I steady my hands, hold my breath, and begin my assessment. Point Beacon's light illuminates the coves on the eastern face of the island. There is no evidence of tidewraith activity in the crystal-clear waters. It's a small mercy. I let the beam pass by twice more before switching my attention to the island's northern beach: a long, sandy stretch of coast whose furthest reaches I can only just discern. The light turns the dunes a ghostly white, but there are no wraiths in the water. Something must have drawn them here tonight.

Shivering, I dart back inside the lighthouse. 'The other beaches are clear.'

'We might make it to sunrise yet,' Rhian calls down. 'How many are we dealing with?'

I pull my cloak tighter around my body and dash back onto the walkway. This time, I turn my binoculars to Sawtooth beach – *our* beach. It feels as if each time I blink, more eyes are staring back from the surf. Some are inky black, only visible when the lighthouse's beam catches them just right; others are cat-like with vertical pupils, glinting teal as the light hits them; a few are milk-white, miniature moons floating atop the waves.

My mouth dries out as I retreat indoors. 'There's too many.'

'*How* many?' Rhian calls down.

I swallow, wincing at the tension in my throat. 'Hundreds.'

The wind screeches. Rhian's lack of response tells me everything I need to know.

A dark, serpentine shadow – bigger, *much* bigger than the rest – surges towards the reef. We often see whales off the coast, and this rivals even the largest of the humpbacks. I know, in my bones, what it is. The leviathan: the first tidewraith. Bigger and hungrier than the rest.

What looks like a jagged ridge of coral emerges from the water as the leviathan surfaces. A sailor would be forgiven for thinking they'd spotted a strangely shallow reef, but the branches of bony, antlered material are in fact fused to the leviathan's spine. Its thick, silver tail breaks the water.

The leviathan's arrival whips the smaller tidewraiths into a frenzy. When a wave rolls across the bay, they use the opportunity to dart across the serrated claws of the rocky reef. Dark clouds of blood bloom in the water, drawn by jagged shards of stone. But for each wraith slowed by the reef or deterred by the light, more make it past. Each time the beam arcs away from the bay, they use the beat of darkness to surge towards shore.

'They're going to make land.' My realisation hangs in the air.

Rhian descends the ladder from the lantern room two rungs at a time. When she spins round to face me, her furrowed brow gleams with sweat, curls of silver hair stuck to the skin. 'I need to go down. I'll light one of the ley lines. Stop them getting to the village.'

The ley lines are our failsafe – clay trenches hidden beneath the sand, filled with a stream of kerosene. We top them up every time there's a storm, knowing how the tidewraiths use big swells to cross the reef. The trenches lay in wait until we ignite them with a flame – a wall of fire between the tidewraiths and the village.

'You can't go down there tonight,' I protest. 'There are too many wraiths. Let me fetch help.'

'No,' Rhian snaps. 'This is our burden. We can't let the islanders know Point Beacon is fallible.'

The islanders see the lighthouse as an unerring sentry. Most of the time, it is: Point Beacon has kept Ynys Halen safe from tidewraiths for centuries. But there are nights where it all hangs in the balance – tidewraiths lunging at the shore, barely staved off. Rhian says we're not to tell anyone about those nights. It shatters the illusion.

'Set aside your pride!' I plead. Rhian derives her entire self-worth from being the lighthouse's keeper. She sees it not as a duty, like I do, but as her *purpose*. 'There's no shame in asking for help . . .'

'You think that's what this is about? *Pride?*' She shakes her head, and the disappointment on her face bleeds through me. 'It's not about shame. It's about what will happen if the islanders find out we can't protect them.'

I push sodden strands of blonde hair away from my face. 'What do you mean?'

Her usually ruddy cheeks blanch. 'I need to go, Guin. Stay here. Keep an eye on the flame.'

My heart sinks like an anchor in my chest. It digs in somewhere vulnerable. My voice is barely audible above the gale as I murmur, 'Please don't go down there.'

'I have to,' she insists. 'They'll overwhelm the island if I don't do something.'

We exchange a tense look, punctuated by the rotting windows rattling around us. She's waiting for my approval. She *needs* it. Not because I'm her superior; in fact, she is mine. It's her other role that she's wrestling with. She may be my grandmother, but she raised me like I was her child.

I want to throw myself down and beg her to stay. To tell her that I *can't* lose her – that without her, I'll be alone in this lighthouse on the edge of the world, and I don't want to be alone. Not again. But women with jobs like ours don't get to be selfish. Our failure tonight could see Ynys Halen overrun, its tenuous relationship with these violent seas blown to smithereens.

I turn my back before tears spring to my eyes. Rhian says crying does us no good – that we lighthouse women were born with salt inside us, and purging it through tears is a waste. Through gritted teeth, I force out, 'Go.'

She grasps my head from behind and plants a kiss in my hair. 'Be good, Guinevere.'

Her footsteps shake the watch room floor as she descends the stairs. Two at a time, like usual. The door swings open, granting entry to a frigid gale which races up the stairs, then slams shut behind her.

It will take her three minutes to reach the cove. One to navigate the winding path which leads to our lighthouse; one to traverse the headland between Point Beacon and Sawtooth beach; and a final minute to descend the rocky steps onto the sand. After that, all she needs to do is find the kerosene ley line beneath the sand and light it up. I count the seconds aloud, desperate for some semblance of control.

Just as my throat constricts, the beam glances over Rhian's hunched form. She slips down half the steps to the beach, but holds her lantern steady. Waves spill onto the shore. There's more than just seaweed hiding amidst the foam. Glistening, scaled fingers shudder free from the water. Talons claw into the sand.

The first tidewraith slithers onto the beach. Its tail moves in serpentine coils, propelling it forwards. Its torso is scarred, riddled with barnacles. Like all tidewraiths, its face is the approximation of a human's: eyes, nose and mouth all where they should be – but the pupils are slitted, reptilian; the nose is flat, and the lips hide rows of sharp teeth.

Three more creatures follow, dragging themselves up onto shore. To see them, you'd imagine they must have as much grace as a seal on land – all flopping, fumbling. But the tails that enable them to dart through the water confer disturbing speed on the shore . . . and they're making a beeline for Rhian.

'Rhian!' I screech, though there's no logical way she can hear me over the storm. 'They're here!'

One of the creatures is faster than the rest. I make it out in hideous flashes of the lighthouse's beam. FLASH – reptilian eyes that reflect Point Beacon's light straight back at it. FLASH – a muscled tail that drags across the sand. FLASH – a gallery of razor-sharp teeth, wet with something viscous. FLASH – Rhian, mere feet from the beast, hair plastered to her face and eyes widened in panic.

Darkness.

It takes an eternity for the beam to swing around again. I pound on the watch room windows with my fists, as if that will make it progress faster. Finally, it lights up the cove. All I can make out is a crimson slick across the sand before darkness falls again.

My chest aches. I scrabble desperately at the window, nails screeching across glass. Then, amidst the gloom, there's a spark. Rhian's lantern flickers before curving across the sky. It hits the ground and shatters, letting out a puff of flame . . .

The ley line hidden beneath the sand should roar to life, the lantern's flame catching on the kerosene beneath the sand.

It's not working.

It's not *working.*

It's not . . .

An invisible line explodes across the sand. Fire bursts across the beach, sparking an infernal wall that separates the sea from the shore. Triumph soars and dies within my chest. The intensity of the blaze illuminates the scene in excruciating detail: the monsters retreating to the ocean, one with its tail ablaze; Rhian lying in a halo of red.

My next movements come and go in the blinding flashes of Point Beacon's light. The front door to the lighthouse swinging open; the stairs to the beach disappearing beneath me; wet sand compressing beneath my boots.

Rhian lies on her back, blinking up at the stars. There is something serene about it – a dreamlike quality that would bid me to paint, if I had the talent. The violence of the wound at her throat robs me of that inclination. Her spine glints like a string of pearls, hidden in the oyster flesh of her throat. Rhian brings her hand to cover the injury. She must realise the futility when her fingers trace its cavernous expanse.

'Rhian,' I sob, throwing myself down beside her.

The tidewraith that killed Rhian observes my grief from the shallows. It wears her blood like lipstick – a scarlet smear against a grimace of sharp teeth.

Rhian attempts to speak, air rushing through the open hollow of her throat. She clamps her hand over the wound.

'Listen to me, Guin,' Rhian rasps, her voice a garbled mess.

I lean in closer, the violent heat of her blood radiating outwards. 'What is it?'

She wraps calloused fingers around my wrist. 'Don't let them hurt her. Leave this island if you have to.'

'Hurt who?' I'm struck by the urge to take her by the shoulders and shake the answer loose. 'Who is "them"?'

Her eyes lose focus. A rattling breath inches past her lips. I feel her slipping away, drifting beyond my reach.

'Rhian,' I whimper. 'Please, Rhian.'

Rhian is silent. She does not breathe, nor blink. Her heart does not beat. I know that without needing to feel for a pulse. Whatever she intended to tell me stays locked behind her bloodied lips.

The howling on the other side of the fire wall grows louder. More ravenous. Drawn in by my desperation, the tidewraiths haul themselves onto land. Past their ranks, the leviathan watches me from beyond the reef. The flames that separate us have put up a valiant fight against the wind and rain, but they're failing. They sputter out with a hiss.

I position myself in front of Rhian's cooling body, arms spread wide. 'Come on, then!' I shout. 'Let's have you!'

Rhian's killer slithers across the doused ley line, poised to strike. A sliver of molten gold peers over the mainland. It glances off the sea, bouncing to the rocks, grazing the lighthouse, spilling across the beach. The tidewraith wails. It retreats into the ocean, rejoining its horde. The other dark shapes beneath the waves recede across the reef, out into the open sea.

Dawn chases away the storm. The rain subsides; the wind dies down. In its wake, dread grips me in a vice. In one fell swoop, two certainties about Rhian have been shattered: that she and I had no secrets, and that she was never scared.

Rhian *was* scared. Scared of someone, or something. And I don't know what.

# CHAPTER 2

*I think she was a bonny lass, though I wasn't seeing straight*
*I'd been drinking whiskey since that morning at eight.*
*We met on the beach, under moonlight's pale glow*
*She had a strange scent and eyes white as snow.*
*When she showed me her teeth, I tried to have faith*
*Now that I'm sober, I wonder: was she a girl, or a wraith?*

—Folk song popular
on Ynys Halen

The waves wash away Rhian's blood, a cat lapping milk from a saucer. There should be something cathartic in it. But there is no sense of closure, nor the feeling that she has found rest in the place she most loved. There is only the sharp-edged hollow in my chest, and the sense that my life has changed irrevocably on a scale I cannot yet comprehend.

For centuries, Point Beacon kept back the tidewraiths. There were close calls, but never to the extent of spilled blood. Never like last night. As I stare down at her cooling body, Rhian's words echo between my ears: *It's not about shame. It's about what will happen if the islanders find out we can't protect them.*

Amidst my grief, one thing is clear: I need to make this look like an accident. If concealing Point Beacon's failings – *our* failings – was important to her, it should be important to me.

I wince as Rhian's head snags on a rock beneath the water, neck snapping back with a grim crunch. If nothing else, I think she'd find macabre humour in this spectacle. *Should've laid off the cake*, she'd say in that gravelly tone of hers, always on the verge of laughing. *Would've made it easier for you to drag me out to sea.*

When the waves swirl around my chest, fear grips me by the throat. I cannot swim. None of the women on Ynys Halen can. They used to say that our wombs would be sucked out by underwater currents. When a woman fell into the cove and emerged with her womb presumably where it should be, there was a subtle revision of history. Now, we cannot swim because the tidewraiths might be lurking, and we do not have the strength to fight them off. There is a whole world on my doorstep, blue and beautiful, yet I'm not allowed to explore it. Chest-deep in the water, the injustice hits me urgently.

Fear convinces me that the leviathan is lurking beneath the waves. The knowledge that no tidewraith comes out when the sun is up, and that the water here isn't *nearly* deep enough to conceal such a colossal beast, does nothing to still my quivering heart. Each tendril of seagrass that brushes my calves must be a hand; each sharp shell trodden underfoot a set of hungry teeth.

Limbs stiffening with the cold, I use my leg to probe the ocean floor. A few years ago, an anchor washed up in the bay. From my window, on a still day, I can see the rope looped around the wooden stilt. It snares my ankle; I lift my foot until I can take the rope in my hand. I tie it around Rhian's middle, looping around her neck, and then her legs.

Adding to the sense of desecration, I scoop handfuls of rocks from the seabed and stuff them into her pockets. Eventually, she sinks to the ocean floor. Her fingers claw at the surface. The last bubbles of oxygen slip past her lips, rising like moon jellyfish.

Despite their desperation for her flesh moments ago, the tide-wraiths won't touch Rhian now. Their appetite doesn't stretch to the dead. When her body grows bloated, she might re-emerge – but on her trip back to shore, the reef will wound her badly enough to disguise her real cause of death. A bite to the jugular, delivered by jaws too sharp to be human, and too numerous to be a shark. I'll tell everyone it was a freak wave. Crashed right up against the cliff surrounding Point Beacon, and took Rhian back into the sea with it. No one will question it: we all knew the ocean would take her eventually.

'Goodbye, Rhian.' My voice cracks, and I am glad no one else is around to see it. 'I'll look after Point Beacon.'

It feels as if there's more I should tell her – that I will spend the rest of my life trying to live up to her legacy, that I'm sorry for the times I was unkind, that I'm sorry I spent so long wishing my mother back to life rather than appreciating the one I had in front of me. Instead, I wade away, the water clinging to my legs like treacle. Something soft scrapes my ankle – her hand, or perhaps her foot. I pause, smile, and add, 'I'll look after Persnickety, too.'

I take in the scene for a minute longer, not yet ready to leave her. Burnished light caps each wave, illuminating golden fronds of seaweed beneath the surface. A shoal of silver fish dart around my calves, glinting like coins. At times like this, I struggle to believe that the ocean can be so cruel by night. That is the paradox of Ynys Halen: the ocean gives, and the ocean takes away. It delivers a kiss and rips out our throats with the same full lips.

Point Beacon blinks down from its cliffside perch, steadfast as ever. Rhian's death should've ruined this place, but even when tidewraiths have rent my world in two, the lighthouse persists. It must. The cliff could slide out from beneath it, and Point Beacon would land on its feet like a cat. Just as well, given that it's the only thing standing between us and certain death each night.

It wasn't always that way. Llyr used to stand between us and the tidewraiths: centuries ago, he used his dominion over storms to bring down forks of lightning that would drive the tidewraiths back. Kerosene seems a small price to pay in comparison to the tithe Llyr demanded.

The remnants of last night's storm rush into our living quarters as I shoulder through the front door. It whines, harmonising with the howl of the wind. Rhian had been telling me she'd oil the hinges for the past two months. I suppose she never will. Persnickety meows as I sling my coat onto its hook. When he notices I am not Rhian, his next meow is more of an accusation than a greeting.

'She's not coming back, Percy,' I tell him. 'The sea took her.'

Persnickety blinks orange eyes back at me. After a moment's consideration, he pulls back his lips and hisses. We only tolerated each other for Rhian's sake. Now that she's dead, I'm not sure where that leaves us. He stalks into the kitchen, tail twitching.

The lighthouse has a preternatural sense for predicting exactly what I need, and it does not fail me today. A fire roars in the kitchen range. When I turn on the tap to scrub the blood from my skin, hot water streams out, even though I did not light the heater.

The lighthouse's quirks are inexplicable, and I no longer think to question them. It's always been this way. Will always be this way.

I swap my sodden, bloodstained clothes for the first garment my fist closes around: a summer dress, totally unfit for weathering the remnants of the storm. Beneath the sandy linen, my skin is blinding red, ringing with the cold.

As I leave the lighthouse, Mackerel, the grey mare Rhian bought me as a tenth birthday present, whinnies pleasantly. On another day, we might amble into town together – but for now, the thought of her rocking-horse gait makes me want to retch. I rub her broad forehead and resolve to walk.

My feet are leaden, unable to navigate the dirt and stone path without snagging. It feels as if I've staggered into an alternative plane of existence I can't escape from. The colour has bled from the island – purple fronds of heather turned grey, bursts of yellow gorse no more than a monochrome smear. Hardy grasses bent by the sea breeze stretch in an endless, colourless slick. My field of vision swells and recedes like the tide.

The desolation of it all reminds me of the name our island was given at its birth. *Ynys Annuwiol*: godless island. The mainland was rife with ancient Gods – mortals who found a way to swap their humanity for Godhood. As these Gods warred for control over strips of the mainland, our island lay unclaimed by all but its people. When Llyr became a God, it was renamed Ynys Halen for our salt harvests – but there is an air of forsakenness that lingers. I feel it keenly today, staggering through the monochrome landscape.

The island grows around me. Cottages hewn from dark stone seem to emerge from the earth. They're built low, hunkered close to the ground like sheep bracing against the wind. Smoke curls from their chimneys, filling the air with the sweet hint of burning wood.

Ynys Halen's thoroughfare stems from a central square which forms the stage for the island's solstice festivals, and otherwise acts as a congregation point. A slope stretches from the heart of the island to the harbour, where our few ships are docked – sailed by the tidewardens at the Halenprophet's behest. We're led to believe they're only used for the purposes of fishing or retrieving goods from the mainland, but I've heard of unwed mothers being given passage to 'maternity homes' on the mainland.

The deluge has turned the slope into a river. Water cascades over the rim of my boots as I march down the hill. There's barely anyone else out, save for a few scrappy children ferrying goods to Meyrick's greengrocer. Halfway down the hill, I stall outside a glass-fronted building. Elegant white script twists across the window: 'Morgan Mortuary.'

The part of me that feels utterly alone in the universe recedes. The hardened version of me – the one who lost her mother, and her grandmother, the one shaped by the tide and the wind, all her softness eroded – takes the front. A bell chimes as I push through the door.

Dylan smiles from behind the counter. It's not unusual for me to be here – whether visiting Cat, or bringing news of a bloated corpse washed up on Sawtooth. But once Dylan takes in the sight of me – my not-fit-for-purpose dress, my red-raw skin, the absence in my eyes – the warmth evaporates from his face. Wiry brows knit together in the middle of his forehead.

I clear my throat and tell him that the worst has happened. He takes off his silver-rimmed spectacles and sets them on the counter between us. His skin wrinkles around his fists as he scrubs at his eyes.

'Rhian is dead?'

I nod, wondering if he is going to make me say it out loud.

'Dead,' he repeats, though it isn't a question this time.

'It was only a matter of time.'

Rhian rarely let me heat the living quarters at Point Beacon. She said that if I did, the cold outside would bite twice as hard. I applied the same logic to my treatment of her – always keeping her at arm's length, because if I didn't, her inevitable death would break me permanently. I spent my entire life loving her less than I should have, all because I knew she was impermanent. More so than most; Rhian owed the ocean its dues.

Dylan gathers himself, a paternal concern sweeping across his features. He reaches out, almost as if he's about to draw me into a hug, but falters at the last second. People think I'm as steadfast as Point Beacon – all brick and mortar.

'I'm so sorry, Guinevere.'

I smile through gritted teeth. 'You've nothing to apologise for.'

He runs a hand through his silvery hair – sparser than it was this time last year. 'You could stay with us, you know. There's a spare room. It's ever so quiet here: Ffion's moved out to the library; Liliwen is always at the apothecary. Cat would love to have you.'

'Someone needs to look after the lighthouse,' I reply.

Dylan sighs. For a moment, I think he might insist, and I think I might let him. I imagine handing Point Beacon to someone else, prising my wrists free of its shackles. What must it be like to have a *normal* job? One where bad days are allowed, because they don't spell death; where illness means a day off, not labouring over the flame while you're sick as a dog; where your colleagues are *people*, not the roiling mass of the ocean.

Instead, he asks, 'Is there a body?'

I swallow my disappointment. 'She'll wash up soon enough. I'll send for help with the stretcher when she does.'

He winces before he can stop himself. 'I'll ready the paperwork.'

Dylan slips away into the back room. I arrange myself awkwardly on the leather loveseat beside the window. My stomach twists. A grandfather clock ticks in the corner. My skin suddenly feels too tight. Sweat beads at my nape, trickling down my spine.

'Guin?'

I startle at Dylan as he re-enters the room. 'Yes?'

'I just need your signature, as her next of kin.'

My legs hum with static as I cross the room. When I gaze at the paper Dylan has laid on the counter, all the words blur into one. I stare and stare until they separate, but then all I can see is the word 'DEATH' in bold script at the top, and Rhian's name beneath it.

My fingers curl around the counter, nails digging into the wood. Although my breaths come thick and fast, I cannot drag enough air down my throat. I'm suffocating. I'm going to die . . .

Hands fasten around my shoulders. The room blurs and shudders as I'm steered back into the loveseat.

'Breathe.' This voice – a new voice – reminds me of the ocean's swell. Hushed but powerful. 'In –' there is a deep intake of breath, '– and out.'

I struggle for control over my lungs. *In* . . .

My throat closes. Darkness fringes my vision, eating away at my sight the way caterpillars destroyed Rhian's cabbages last summer.

'Four things you can see,' the voice commands. I open and shut my mouth, a fish out of water. 'Come on, Guin. Tell me four things you can see.'

With my vision narrowed to a pinprick, all I can see is her eyes. 'Blue,' I choke out. 'Blue eyes.'

The blue eyes wrinkle at the edges. 'Three more things.'

Light gnaws away at the darkness. 'Grandfather clock, chandelier . . .' I pause, scanning what little I can see. A vase full of trumpeting yellow flowers. 'Daffodils.'

'Good,' she murmurs. 'Three things you can hear.'

'You,' I croak. 'Your voice.'

'And who am I?'

'Catrin Morgan.' Her name is a hymn upon my lips.

'Good.' She takes my hand. Rubs her thumb over my knuckles. 'What else can you hear?'

'Clock ticking.' I pause, listening. 'The wind.'

'Two things you can smell.'

I inhale, and this time, the air clears my windpipe. My lungs expand, my mind swimming with sweet and earthy notes. 'Sage and . . . blackberries?'

'My new perfume.' She laughs. 'One thing you can taste.'

I press my lips together. The answer is always the same. 'Sea salt.'

There is a moment of silence where all I can hear is the clock tick, tick, ticking and the wind groaning outside; all I can smell is blackberries and sage; all I can see is those blue eyes staring back at me.

'Would you look at that?' There's a smile in her voice, an intonation that only comes with upturned lips. 'You're breathing all by yourself now, Guin.'

'She's gone,' I say, the words flat and clumsy on my lips. 'Rhian is gone.'

# CHAPTER 3

*Though Llyr no longer lives among us, we feel His presence across the island. We show thanks for His years of protection through proper Salting. Salt communion is taken each Sunday; babies are baptised in saltwater; and salt plays a vital process in funeral proceedings.*

—Excerpt from 'A Child's Guide to Worship'

The rest of the afternoon passes in a sickening blur. Forms I barely read before scribbling a spider web signature; faces twisted up with concern; grief writhing inside me like an octopus. The room surges and swells. Catrin vanishes briefly, then returns to take me home. We stagger across the island, blown off course by wind and shock alike.

Point Beacon's windows glow like hot coals. Silhouettes hang suspended between the net curtains – haunting daubs of pale skin and dark hair. Anger surges in me then: Rhian's body is barely cold and already, people have taken to ransacking the lighthouse.

I shrug free of Catrin's grip. The lighthouse door whines open for me before I've had the chance to ram my shoulder against it. Chest pounding, I follow the sound of activity to where it simmers down the hall.

My anger snuffs out. Ffion scrubs my discarded clothes in the sink, working away the blood; Liliwen cooks currant-studded griddle cakes in a pan suspended over the fire. Nutmeg and cinnamon cut through the lighthouse's stale scent. Their heads snap up simultaneously.

'Guin.' Their words are a harmony, a chorus, a prayer.

Behind closed doors, the island calls them the Coven. Not out of affection, mind. Most of the time, I can't remember why I found them so haunting when we met. Other times, they all say the exact same thing at the exact same time, and it makes my stomach clench. I think whatever preceded their washing up on Ynys Halen changed them.

Since the day I found them on the beach, I've managed to worm myself into their ranks – an unofficial fourth member. I feel a desperate need to keep myself there. My lack of blood relation feels like something I must compensate for.

Us falling together makes sense. They were outcast for their own strangeness, and the suspicion that they hailed from the mainland; whereas I was outcast for my mother's 'sins'. We'd all been shunned by the island, so we made our own pack. Catrin – unarguably the most beautiful of the sisters, even though they're near identical – managed to claw her way up the social hierarchy, owed to her aforementioned beauty.

They encase me in layers of their arms, hearts beating against my skin. Catrin must've told them what happened. I sag, my body relaxing into the familiar shape of our bond. It's a space hollowed out by the tide of shared experience, shared trauma, shared dreams.

Cat's blackberry scent winds through the others. Her hand finds mine. Someone steers me into a chair. Percy comes screeching off it, loath to accept my intrusion even in the depths of grief.

'I'm so sorry, Guin,' little Liliwen murmurs. She's the heart of the sisters – full of empathy and innocence. 'I don't know what to say.'

'I once read that a death at sea is the sign of someone pure of heart,' Ffion says, her voice somehow faraway.

A laugh comes bursting out of me. Rhian's heart was black as coal. She swore like a sailor, drank like a fish, and was prickly as a sea urchin. Ffion and her bloody reading. If Lili is the heart, then Ffion is the brain. She devours books like berries from the hedgerow. She has a quote for every situation, an answer for every question, an explanation for every quandary.

The sisters glance at each other, once again giving the impression of a hive mind. Luckily, whatever information they exchange doesn't encourage them to fuss over me any further. Lili returns to the griddle cakes, whose edges have begun to catch; Ffion resumes her battle with the bloodied clothes. Persnickety sits beside the range, warming his flanks. At least he's having a good day, spiteful little creature.

As the sun slips beneath the horizon and the ocean becomes a dark, clawed beast, I light up Point Beacon. My nights are punctuated by my hand-cranking the tank, which needs to be done every two hours or thereabouts lest the island be plunged into darkness.

Still, I'm happy to play pretend. The sisters and I pile into my bed. When it becomes quite clear we can't all fit comfortably,

Ffion drags in Rhian's mattress. It still smells like her – salt spray mixed with something sharp and hot, reminiscent of whiskey.

The others fall asleep quickly, baby rabbits tucked into the safe recess of their warren. I've never quite adapted to their casual, platonic intimacy, but I pretend it comes naturally to me. Pretend that sleeping in a tangle of stirring limbs and fluttering mouths is a joy. Sacrificing my own comfort for theirs is an easy choice.

Still, as Cat's sweet breath whisks across my face, I'm possessed by dread. It pools in my stomach, filling me with nausea so intense I have to extricate myself from the web of limbs and spit out the window.

I can hear the leviathan out beyond the reef. It makes this eerie sound Rhian and I used to call 'lumming' – not quite a hum, because it has a distinct 'l' sound at the beginning, but similar in resonance and tone. It sets me shaking to my bones.

'Shut up,' I hiss from between gritted teeth. 'Shut *up*.'

Each time I close my eyes, Rhian's panicked face is burnt into my retinas: the red blur of her lips, a smear of pale skin, punctuated by dark brows. Her final plea: *don't let them hurt her*. How can I do that when I don't know who she means, or who I'm supposed to protect them from?

'Hey,' Catrin whispers.

I startle, surprised she's awake. She's propped up on her elbows, strands of hair stuck to her forehead. Her eyes catch the moonlight streaming through the window.

'Hey.' My response is hoarse, numb.

'Can't sleep?'

I shake my head. 'I can't stop thinking about it.'

Cat lays silent for a minute, chest rising and falling softly.

'What really happened?' she asks, tentative in her delivery. 'To Rhian, I mean.'

I knot my fingers together. 'A wave swept her from the cliff.'

Catrin stares at the web of my fingers. 'You always do that when you lie.'

My breath flutters like a moth trapped in my chest. Rhian's dying words beat against my ribs. She begged me not to tell anyone, but I feel as if the secret's poisoning me from the inside out. I need to purge before it rots me.

Cat's the other half of my brain. We share everything but a body. If I'm going to divulge this to anyone, it has to be her.

'It was a tidewraith.'

'*Tidewraith?*' Catrin hisses. Liliwen stirs beside her. She slaps a palm over her mouth at my glare. 'Sorry. I just – I thought Point Beacon kept them back?'

I drop my voice to a whisper, barely audible above Lili's gentle snores as they resume. 'There were hundreds of them last night, all gathered around Sawtooth. The leviathan was there, too.'

Catrin stiffens at that. Some on Ynys Halen think the leviathan is a fabrication. An overinflated piece of folklore, the product of hazy eyes or drunken observations. There's plenty of whales around our coast, but I'd never mistake one for the leviathan.

'It stirred them into a frenzy. They came across the reef. Not even the beam could stop them. Rhian went out to make sure they didn't make land . . .'

And now I don't have a grandmother anymore. I've seen what Rhian's insides look like. Now, I'm the sole custodian of Point Beacon. My fortress on the edge of the world is starting to feel more like a prison. An inescapable life sentence.

When Catrin doesn't reply, I whisper, 'You can't tell anyone.'

Catrin frowns, a furrow appearing between her eyebrows. It reminds me she is Dylan's daughter, through and through. 'Why? If the wraiths are getting out of control, we should tell the Halenprophet. Maybe the tidewardens can do something about it?'

When Llyr communes with the Halenprophet through spilled salt, it is the tidewardens who carry out his bidding. They are stewards of not only the church, but the island itself. They bear sole responsibility for our small fleet of ships, as well as underpinning law and order. When a rabid dog made itself a scourge, it was the tidewardens who put an end to it; when old man Cecil shot his son, it was the tidewardens who brought him to justice.

Feasibly, they *should* be able to help – but I cannot ignore Rhian's final plea.

'Rhian made me promise,' I say. 'She was scared. Told me I couldn't tell *anyone* what had happened, because of what they might do.' The full detail of what Rhian said echoes between my ears. *Don't let them hurt her. Leave if you have to.*

Cat's entire body stiffens, all the way down to her lungs. She sits perfectly motionless, as if she's hewn from stone. I'm reminded again why people find the sisters so eerie. In the pale moonlight, she looks utterly spectral.

I'm almost about to snap my fingers, if only to break the spell that has settled over her, when Cat's voice cracks like lightning through the quiet. 'What *would* they do?'

I flinch. The motion jolts fresh tears from my eyes. 'I don't know. And it's not as if she's around to tell me. But if Rhian was scared . . .'

Cat nods silently, the weight of Rhian's fear strung between us like an anchor.

Pulled by their respective duties, the sisters leave at first light. Cat kisses me on the cheek before the sisters set off across the heath. I touch the space her lips grazed, skin still flushed.

With the lighthouse extinguished, I climb into the lantern room and buff the lens until it shines. I have to stand on the widow's walk afterwards; the lingering kerosene gas bites at my lungs. Across the writhing channel of the ocean, the mainland is beginning to wake. Pretty, white-sailed boats leave their harbour, bound for rich waters far from our coast.

In her right mind, Rhian would never suggest I leave Ynys Halen behind. I told her once – and *only* once – that I wished I'd been born on the mainland. I've never seen her so angry. She went rattling around Point Beacon, slamming doors and stamping her big old feet.

I remember asking her why it was so wrong. She asked if I had no sense of duty; if I cared not a jot for the fact everyone – every*thing* – we knew was on Ynys Halen; if I'd considered the impossibility of finding a home on the mainland, without money or goods to trade. I think I must have started crying, because I also recall her apologising, which she rarely did. She told me to think of it logically: the tidewardens control the boats, and they're not in the business of gifting their own islanders to the mainland.

All I wanted was a life without the ever-looming threat of tidewraiths. Rhian told me they're no different from the wolves that lurk in forests on the mainland. I understood, but it never stopped me from wanting. I can want and want and want, but that's no contest for the fact that this island is baked into my bones – that its fingers coil around my heart like ivy, sea salt woven into my flesh.

So in her dying breaths, why did Rhian tell me to leave? To forsake our lives' work, and flee to the mainland she'd always detested? I can't even begin to untangle it, let alone understand who I should keep safe. *Don't let them hurt her.* Hurt *who?*

My reverie is shattered by someone banging on the door. After I take the one hundred and thirty-three steps down the tower, I pull it open to find Mrs Llywelyn with a bunch of flowers in her arms. She taught me from the ages of five until eight, at which point Rhian pulled me from school – a decision driven by her need for an understudy.

'Rhian was . . .' She struggles for the right sentiment. Rhian was a lot of things, few of them complimentary. 'She cared about you very much.'

I've never been any good with sincerity, so all I can muster is, 'Thank you.'

Mrs Llywelyn smiles. 'I've got to see to my granddaughters now – I've got a whole gaggle of them! – but don't be a stranger.'

No sooner than she's left, a cart trundles across the heath and pulls up outside my door.

Old Mr Meyrick parks up beside the garden gate and hops down from the carriage. White paint on its side reads 'Meyrick's greengrocer'.

The stoop to Mr Meyrick's back doesn't stop him from dressing like he's got somewhere important to be, with buttoned shirts and cravats in every colour imaginable. He doffs his woollen cap, revealing a dusting of grey hair. 'Afternoon, Miss Wyn,' he says, grinning. 'I've got a delivery for you.'

Rhian used to be responsible for arranging our food deliveries. I'd often find her hunched over the kitchen table, trying to optimise the paltry stipend we are given by the Halenprophet to keep Point Beacon running.

Mr Meyrick waves off my concerns that I've not paid for the delivery, and begins unloading crates. He offers to help me carry the perishables down to the cellar, but I insist on doing it myself. Our bulk shipments of kerosene from the mainland are stowed in the back room of the basement. Rhian always cautioned me against going in there; a miasma of kerosene hangs in the air. When Rhian came up, she'd have to sit in her room with her head bowed against her knees. She said it made her feel sick to be down there too long.

'This should see you through the next couple of weeks,' Mr Meyrick says, dusting off his hands. 'But after that, I want you to come and see me at the grocers. Don't keep yourself cooped up, you hear me? Bring that grey mare of yours – Mackerel, isn't it? – and I'll sort you out.'

Heat creeps across my cheeks. I rub the back of my neck.

'It'd make me feel better,' Mr Meyrick says. 'You'd be doing me a favour.'

Now, favours are something I can deal with. Mr Meyrick retreats back down the garden path before trundling off on his cart. Mackerel calls longingly after the cart-horse.

Osian, the earnest, brown-eyed shepherd from the neighbouring farm, arrives at the door an hour later, a paper-wrapped leg of lamb clutched beneath his arm.

'I thought I could make you lunch,' he says, running a hand through his russet hair. 'You've never been much of a cook. I can't imagine grief has changed that.'

I snort. 'Talk about kicking a woman while she's down.'

Osian hovers by the front door, as if he didn't spend half his weekends here growing up – our friendship the product of Rhian and his mother's conspiring. When Rhian said there was a neighbouring boy coming to play, I was distraught. All I knew of boys was that they played roughly. But Osian was gentle, conscientious. He spoke in soft tones and treated my scant belongings with tender care.

As we grew, our friendship was cemented in fleeting conversations, my elbows braced on the drystone walls between our land, a flock of sheep meandering by.

Osian follows me into the kitchen and makes himself busy. Any islander walking in on this tableau would be discomforted: a woman sitting with her legs up on the kitchen table while a man sweats over the stove. Osian's never been the type to pay much heed to gender roles.

He tells me that his brother, Arthur, has officially become a tidewarden. I've no fondness for Arthur; he used to tease Osian relentlessly, and pulled at my hair whenever he came to collect him.

'You're not planning on following him, then?' I ask.

Osian flashes me a scathing look. 'Even if I didn't have a fundamental disagreement with the prospect of an all-male cohort, I'd sooner throw myself from the bluffs than sit and beg for the Halenprophet like a well-trained collie.'

I laugh. 'Most men hate submission, unless they're submitting to another man. What – you don't want to help him dress in the morning?'

'I do not want to dress him, nor feed him, nor sew up his clothes,' Osian mutters.

I've always found it funny that the tidewardens derive so much pride from the same duties they disparage their wives for. Almost as funny as me lamenting women's denigration while I sit with my feet up, watching Osian slave over the range.

He goes on a tangent about his new sheepdog pup. They're supposed to be working dogs, kept outside in cages – but somehow the whelp has wormed its way into the Vaughan home. It sleeps beside Osian in bed. I imagine him tangled in the sheets, hair mussed with sleep, one strong arm curled around the pup. I'm suddenly compelled to pick at a splinter protruding from the kitchen table, redirecting my mind.

'This'll go lovely with some mint sauce,' Osian says absentmindedly, checking on the lamb where it roasts in the range.

I think, suspiciously, of the fresh bunch of mint Mr Meyrick just delivered. 'I don't have any mint.'

Osian straightens. 'Yes, you do . . .'

He falters, his hand revealed. A pink blush creeps across his cheeks.

'Osian,' I groan. 'I can fend for myself.'

Half the Vaughan flock had to be culled last winter on account of some communicable disease. They've been struggling for money ever since. I can't stand the thought of Osian spending his meagre profits on me.

'It was nothing, really. Mr Meyrick owed me for the last lot of mutton I gave him. And besides, you know I'm forever dropping in for tea. It's only fair I contribute.'

Osian busies himself wiping the range clean, even though it's spotless. The blush on his cheeks has spread to his nape, his throat.

'Osian,' I murmur.

He looks up with a whelp's eyes.

'Thank you. Truly.' I hope the sincerity of the sentiment expresses itself in my voice. 'Now, for both our comfort, let's never speak of this again.'

He grins, nodding eagerly.

Once the lamb's cooked through, Osian serves it with a cluster of roasted potatoes and a thick sauce made using the mint he paid for. It's the first proper meal I've eaten since Rhian died, and I can feel it fortifying me with each mouthful.

With the food demolished and plates cleaned, Osian makes to leave. He stands beside the front door, dark eyes glinting even in the dark of the hallway. I hang back in the kitchen doorway at arm's length. I'm always slightly scared he'll do something that breaches the floodgates between friendship and something more. I'm not sure if I'm scared because I don't want that to happen, or because I do.

'I'll be seeing you, then,' he says softly.

I shrug my shoulders. 'Not if I see you first.'

He smiles back at me, and steps out into the fresh air. I watch him retreat down the garden path, shaking his head as he goes.

# CHAPTER 4

*Tidewraiths bear resemblance to myriad species. Their teeth are similar to those of a blue shark, with a muscular tail not unlike that of a conger eel. Their forearms are almost humanoid, while their talons most closely resemble an osprey. In the past century, their numbers have stabilised following a period of exponential growth.*

—'Classifying the Range and Behaviour of Tidewraiths', from the *Journal of Coastal Ecology*

As the one who stands to inherit Ynys Halen's mortuary, no one's better placed to organise Rhian's departure than Catrin. All I need to do is turn up on a rainy Wednesday morning.

The island's church is perched beside the bluffs – sheer, crumbling cliffs that stretch along most of our coastline, looking out across the sea. It's a modest building, in keeping with the island's architecture: drab, grey stone, a slate roof, and a simple bellcote.

In lieu of acknowledging the mourners around me, I crane my neck at the macabre paintings that line the walls, detailing Llyr's ascent to Godhood. The first shows Bronwen, Llyr's wife, ripped apart by the leviathan. Llyr raged, feeling that if the Gods had not forsaken Ynys Annuwiol, perhaps they could have saved Bronwen. If no God would claim the island, he would become one himself.

He pored over books, studying how mortals on the mainland seized divinity. Their paths differed – some through suffering, some through cruelty, some through martyrdom – but all shed their humanity in the process. From this, Llyr shaped his own formula: suffering, cannibalism and martyrdom. Together, they would forge his Godhood.

Llyr had already suffered, but began to self-flagellate to cement his pain, illustrated in scarlet wounds crossing his skin, and when the islanders saw how dedicated he was to their protection, they began to revere him. And so when Llyr requested a sliver of human flesh, a tribute came forward: a girl of eighteen years, willing to part with the soft flesh of her thigh. The painting shows him with meat between his teeth, eyes crazed.

At Llyr's behest, the islanders drove a stake into his heart – and watched in awe when he awoke the next morning. His transformation could not come soon enough. Shoals of tide-wraiths swarmed the island – alike the leviathan in all but size. The final painting shows Llyr driving them back with flashes of lightning and urgent currents.

Mourners continue to pile into the church, faces slick with rain. Cat welcomes them in, the perfect host. I hate every second of it – the way they all lay claim to my grief. They didn't know her. Not the way I do. Not the way I *did*.

A well-meaning woman peers around my hair and instructs me to find solace in the fact that Rhian died in the place she loved best. Internally, I'm screaming, *She died with her windpipe ripped from her throat! What solace is that?* But Lili is standing beside me, and I want to be a good influence, so I just smile and smile and *smile* until the woman grimaces and walks away.

Ladies dab at their tears with neatly embroidered handkerchiefs; men lament the passing of one of this island's greats. It's funny, because you could count on one hand the number of people on this island Rhian genuinely liked. Lots of them sucked up to her – she was afforded a certain amount of renown as the island's protector – but whenever that happened, she'd turn to me after and say, 'They're never getting an invite for dinner.' Prickly old beast.

Halenprophet Lewys comes shuffling out of the sacristy, flanked by his tidewardens. We all walk in a slow procession to the graveside, pretending not to feel the rain. The Halenprophet's off-white robes drag through the mud, staining the hem. His pretty, red-haired daughter, Rhosyn, walks behind him, wearing the grey robes of Halenprophet-in-waiting. When old Lewys croaks, she'll take up the mantle – using spilled salt to commune with Llyr, guiding our island's faith. Her honeyed eyes meet mine, and she offers a brief smile.

I've never known how much stock to place in Halenprophecy. One summer, Halenprophet Lewys predicted our crops would die. People were beside themselves, hoarding food and turning on their neighbours – but the harvest was richer than ever. There were other times, though, where his predictions were eerily accurate; he foretold old man Davies' death, trampled by a cow; he pre-empted the inferno that would've taken half our wheat, if not for the fire break he oversaw.

Maybe if he'd divined Rhian's death, I'd have been able to prevent it.

The Halenprophet stands beside me at the grave. I stare down into the yawning pit, and briefly consider throwing myself into it. Cat squeezes in between me and Lili, twining our fingers together. She anchors me above ground.

'I'm so sorry about your mother, Genevieve,' the Halenprophet says.

'Guinevere,' I correct. 'And she was my grandmother.'

Lewys has a bumbling sort of charm, which I find far less endearing today than I usually would. He used to call up at the lighthouse every few months, keen to check on Rhian. Together, they'd go down to the cellar, and emerge discussing the next kerosene shipment. I was never allowed to join. It was one of the few realities of life at Point Beacon Rhian shielded me from.

'Of course.' He nods, his scant smattering of grey hair flapping. 'Guinevere.'

Rhosyn glances at me around his withering frame and mouths an apology.

A handful more tidewardens emerge from the church, a wicker coffin held between them. They're wearing their ceremonial garb: shirts and trousers the same ominous blue as the ocean, complete with buttons made of salt. They'll want to hurry up, lest the rain melt their buttons. That'd be a spectacle.

'Breathe,' Catrin murmurs.

I glance at her, ready to mutter that I'm doing just fine – but then I scan over the tidewardens once more and realise what sparked her instruction. Aledd has his filthy hands on Rhian's coffin. He flashes me a smile. If anyone deserves to be buried, it's *him*.

I knew he'd be here – he's one of the Halenprophet's favourite tidewardens, after all – but I didn't think he'd have the nerve to carry her fucking coffin. He *hated* Rhian. It was because of him that I never saw her growing up. That didn't stop him from thrusting me into her care after he'd killed my mother.

The crowd goes tense and quiet as they lower the casket into the grave. Aledd holds my gaze the whole time, the corners of his mouth twitching. If Rhian was actually in there, she'd reanimate just to take him by his loathsome little face and make him feel the fear he instilled in my mother.

I know what they all say: it was an accident. The islanders paint her as the architect of her own demise, and there's no grounds for it except his word. He told everyone she begged for his hands around her throat. That he was absolutely beside himself when he realised what she'd made him do. Funny, that, because I remember him leaving the house in a hurry, not a tear on his face. He left her there for me to discover. Went about his day, and remarried not a month later.

Now, as my mother lays rotting, his slate has been wiped clean. How does he get to carry on, when my mother was robbed of the chance? When he stole the breath from her lungs?

Halenprophet Lewys begins the parting rites with all the conviction of his younger years. Meanwhile, I'm practically vibrating with rage – hatred oozing from every pore. Aledd presses a handkerchief to his eyes and it's all I can do not to choke him there and then.

Cat curls her arm around my waist. I focus on the pressure of her fingertips, the heat of her body. If I don't, I'll end up in the gaol, blood caked beneath my nails.

Halenprophet Lewys finishes up the closing rites and delves into the pocket of his robe, producing a fistful of salt. It's the island's most holy resource, used sparingly in religious ceremony. Salt rains like sleet from the Halenprophet's fist, glancing off the coffin with a gentle hiss.

# CHAPTER 5

*Tidewraiths are endemic to Ynys Halen; they are not found anywhere else in the world. They are apex predators, and while they can be killed like any other animal, their main weakness is to light. Sunlight and Point Beacon's beam impact the wraiths in equal measure. Torchlight is too weak to provide a real deterrent.*

—'Classifying the Range and Behaviour of Tidewraiths', from the *Journal of Coastal Ecology*

Too soon, dusk calls me back to the lantern room.

Shoving aside my grief, I focus on the practical things – the things I *can* control. The length of the wicks, the strength of the flame, the clarity of the glass. I clamber up to inspect the Fresnel lens which I spend half of my life polishing. Today, it only requires a quick buffing before I'm satisfied. It gleams in the sun's fading light, though the splendour is nothing compared to how it shines in the dark.

The lens functions something like a magnifying glass, but instead of being a solid piece, it's made up of concentric rings, like a bullseye. The rings bend and focus light, allowing the lens to capture and intensify light to the extent that Point Beacon's beam can be seen from thirty nautical miles away.

I hold my breath and pour kerosene into the tank. The hand pump whines as I pressurise the tank. I've done this enough times that I can *feel* when the pressure is just right, but I check the gauge anyway. The kerosene hisses through a series of tubes, heated by burning alcohol, and eventually emerging in a gaseous state which I ignite with a match.

The flame roars – unbridled, incandescent – then seems to remember where it is, growing steady and focused. Point Beacon surges to life. It casts light out around the shallows. Muscular tails breach the surface, fleeing in response.

Our lighthouse hasn't yet caught up with the technology of the mainland. We have to hand-crank the tank to keep the flame burning. Overnight, someone must turn the handle every two hours lest we plunge the ocean into darkness. Rhian and I used to take shifts, enabling us to sleep through half the night. Now, my only choice is to snatch disjointed slivers of rest in between hand-cranking the tank.

*You can sleep when you're dead,* Rhian would say.

'Easy for you to say, you old cow,' I mutter.

Once Point Beacon's alive and purring, I lurch down the stairs and throw myself into bed. A short-eared owl causes a racket somewhere out on the heath, its rasping alarm call mimicking the beats of my heart. I fall asleep to the dull rumble of the ocean crashing against the cliff.

I wake with a start, having slept more deeply than I intended to. Usually, the threat of the lighthouse going out keeps me from anything more than superficial rest. I feel more invigorated than I have in a long time; my skin is criss-crossed with lines where I've pressed myself into the quilt, and there's a glisten of saliva trailing from the corner of my mouth.

The lighthouse is utterly still. The ocean hushes outside. A few restless gulls caw, their calls carried away by the wind. Everything is okay. *Go back to sleep, Guinevere,* I tell myself.

But I can't shake the feeling that something is wrong. My stomach clenches. I sit upright, fingers curled around the quilt. Darkness has fallen so thickly tonight that I can barely see through it. It clings to my eyelashes like frost. It's dark and quiet. Dark and quiet. Dark and . . .

Oh, *fuck.*

I toss the covers aside and thunder up the spiral staircase, the sepulchral dark hounding each of my steps. My pulse matches the frenzied tempo of my feet. Sweat moistens my palms; I lose my grip on the handrail. I do not have time to pause and steady myself. The entire island is in peril.

The lantern room still hums with the heat of the flame. It can't have been long since it went out, but even thirty seconds is enough for the tidewraiths to invade the beaches. Maybe they're slithering up into the village now. Perhaps they've found the mortuary, found *Catrin,* lured by the scent of slowly rotting flesh . . .

*Focus, Guinevere.*

I've always thought I could do this in the dark – but now, with my trembling fingers and breaths shuddering out of me in rapid succession, I cannot figure out the mess of metal before me.

I can almost hear Rhian say, *Check the fuel.*

Finally, my knuckles collide with a familiar *clang*: the kerosene canister. I lift it, biceps shaking, and pour. An acrid tang fills the air. Droplets of kerosene splatter to the floor. Rhian would have my head for that. I close the reservoir.

*Light the wicks.*

My clumsy fist knocks a box of matches to the floor. I sift through the detritus. Strike the match. Light the wick. The flame roars; the beam blinks to life. I hold my breath as it swings around. Finally, as my lungs start to ache, it illuminates the cove.

Sawtooth beach is empty.

Mercifully, *impossibly*, it's empty.

Half-convinced my eyes are deceiving me, I hurry out onto the catwalk that hugs Point Beacon's upper level. Wind tangles its fingers through my hair, pulling me towards the ocean. I cling to the decaying handrail, rust peeling beneath my fingers.

Again, the beam lights up the beach. Again, it is empty.

I don't allow relief to take root. Instead, I wrench my binoculars from their perch and fling myself back onto the widow's walk. The cold is so bitter that my skin sings with it. I cast my gaze across the dunes east down the coast, the village harbour. The lighthouse's flame has burned white-hot shapes into my retinas; I can't see the dunes nor the pier with enough clarity.

Taking the stairs two at a time, I fling open the lighthouse door hard enough that it rattles on its hinges. I barely have time to stuff my feet into boots before sprinting to Mackerel's paddock.

She whinnies, startled by my imposition.

'Sorry, Mack,' I pant. 'I need your help.'

She somehow senses the urgency and doesn't resist when I lead her over to the drystone wall. I spring onto her back, her bare flanks hot beneath my calves. There's no time for a saddle, nor bridle. I knot my hands in her mane and squeeze my heels against her sides. She leaps into a gallop.

The night air drags each breath from my mouth, plumes of hot vapour left in our wake.

Fortunately, the moon is full and swollen. It casts just enough ivory light across our path that Mack can dodge the potholes. We gallop east along the bluffs, only slowing to descend onto the dunes at the foot of the Williams' farm. Shingle clatters behind us, followed by the hiss of sand.

Using my calves, I steer Mackerel to where the tide laps at the sand. We patrol the shoreline twice. While eyes blink at us from deeper in the water, there are no tidewraiths on the beach itself. It's almost enough to bring tears to my eyes.

I still need to check the harbour. The tidewraiths rarely drag themselves up onto the boardwalk, preferring the easy slope of our sandy beaches – but tonight, I can't afford to be complacent.

By the time we've clattered to the village and down to the pier, Mack is breathing hard, her flanks slick with sweat. I'm expecting I'll need to explain myself to a member of the tidewardens, since there's usually one stationed beside the pier to stop people from venturing onto the boardwalk at night – but thankfully, I'm the only soul awake.

Ynys Halen's meagre fleet bobs on the rising tide. I wait to see tidewraiths dragging themselves up onto the pier, but all I find is a colony of seals. They consider me with inky eyes, whiskers twitching.

'We made it, Mack.' My voice quakes with disbelief.

The sun breaks across our backs as we trot back up the slope and across the heath.

*

I shut the lighthouse door behind me and collapse against it. It doesn't make sense. I am as attuned to the hiss of kerosene as I am to the beat of my own heart. I could be at the bottom of the ocean in a coma, and I would *still* be roused by the absence of sound and light.

But I wasn't. I slept through near disaster.

I'm not sure how long I sit with my back pressed against the door, guilt coiling in my stomach. When I come to, there is a soft weight in my lap. My eyes are so firmly glued to the wall in front of me that I feel out the weight with my fingertips. It's warm, thick with downy fur.

The surprise is enough to wrench my eyes from their resting place. 'Percy?'

He looks at me, orange eyes drawn wide, and springs off my lap. Persnickety cavorts down the corridor to Rhian's room. I hear him leap up onto her chest of drawers.

The ginger tomcat has never shown me even his most lukewarm acceptance. Clearly, we were both startled by his sitting in my lap. My head spins as I dish up his breakfast. He doesn't come to collect it.

I might ponder his uncharacteristic attention were it not for the secret of my failure lodging in my chest like a thorn. It digs into my cardiac muscle with each guilty beat of my heart. I cannot help but feel that I have failed the island, failed myself, and worst of all, failed Rhian.

But no one got hurt. No one is even *aware* that the light went out. They were sleeping soundly in their beds, comforted by the belief that someone else was working to guarantee their safety. My guilt is a weight to carry, and nothing more.

*

Three mornings after Point Beacon dimmed, a bell rings across Ynys Halen.

It echoes through the village, across the heath, and pounds on my door. A pit opens in my stomach, dread unfurling from its depths. The church bells are used sparingly; any chiming outside of their typical use is a plea for the islanders to congregate.

My guilt hounds me all the way to the church. I arrive on wooden limbs, stomach seemingly tilting inside my abdomen. Apparently, the Halenprophet failed to attend Sunday service, and no one has seen him since. Osian and the sisters have fed me daily updates, not understanding that I've twisted each morsel of information to fit my narrative: that this is *my* fault.

There's no evidence to suggest the Halenprophet's absence has anything to do with Point Beacon going out, but that doesn't stop me feeling nauseous on the way to the church. It looks as if I'm the last one to make it here; all of Ynys Halen gathers in and around the graveyard, their eyes trained on the church door. A gale moves restlessly between tall grasses and crooked headstones. The wrought-iron gate whines. Silhouettes shift behind the church's arced windows.

It doesn't take me long to find the sisters; they stand in a regimented line, their dark hair swept back across their shoulders, pale fingers held loosely at their sides. I stand next to Catrin, who greets me with a ghost of a smile.

'What's all this about?' I ask.

Ffion's eyes dart to meet mine. 'Nobody knows. People are saying something's happened to Halenprophet Lewys.'

I inhale shakily, lungs filling with the clean sharpness of salt air, the sweet note of lichen and moss.

At that moment, the church's iron-studded door groans open.

Three men dressed in ceremonial tidewarden garb walk towards us, their salt buttons glinting in the morning light. My father is among them. The rage I repressed at him carrying Rhian's coffin comes pounding back up my throat.

A hush falls over the crowd, but not for long.

'Will you tell us what all this is about, Aledd?' Mrs Llywelyn calls. 'We've not seen the Halenprophet in days, with no word on his welfare!'

Aledd dips his head. He's a pathetic creature, with a weak jaw, stooped shoulders and thinning hair. He's followed by Arthur Vaughan – Osian's older brother – and Owain Meyrick, of Meyrick's fame.

'Hey, Arthur.' I recognise Osian's voice above the rising din. 'Has the Halenprophet taken ill?'

Arthur fixes his brother with the same look he wore as a spiteful child, all lowered brows and puckered lips. After a brief discussion, Aledd emerges as the spokesperson for the trio of wardens – shoulders squared, chin set at a defiant angle.

'On Sunday morning, we found Halenprophet Lewys deceased.'

My vision blurs; my heartbeat grows to a crescendo, thundering in my ears. *Deceased.* The word feels strange in my mind. It's the same as when I saw 'DEATH' in ornate script at the top of Rhian's certificate. Like when you say a word over and over – *died, died, died, died* – until it no longer makes sense.

There is a collective intake of breath around us. It's held deep in our chests, the tension growing and growing until we cannot help but let the breath free. Cries go up from the crowd. People protest, claiming this can't have happened, that it can't be real. I clutch at my heart, but it's not mourning that drives me to do so. It's guilt.

I glance at the sisters, keen to read their expressions, but my eyes snag on the way their hands have instinctively found each other. They're like a line of paper dolls, inextricably bound to one another. I brush my fingertips against Cat's; she tangles our hands together.

'Where is Rhosyn?' someone shouts. 'She should be guiding us through this transition.'

Aledd swallows, a motion that jolts his worthless body. 'Rhosyn is also deceased.'

My heart leaves its cradle in my chest, instead lodging in my throat. My knees buckle. I stagger backwards. Someone catches me just before I hit the floor. Catrin links her arm around mine, holding me upright. Grief explodes through the crowd – hands trembling, sobs tearing from throats.

'Rhosyn was Lewys's only daughter.' I recognise Mr Meyrick's voice, even when it's raw with grief. 'And in the event of his death, she would have become Halenprophet.'

The implication is clear; we are without a figurehead for our faith, and we've no hope of a new one emerging. Halenprophecy is passed through the Blythin family line – an ancient art which awakens into the flesh of Blythin children once the old Halenprophet passes. It's thought that the Blythins descend from the girl whose flesh turned Llyr into a God, and he gifted her with the art of Halenprophecy in return. Without a Halenprophet, Ynys Halen is adrift.

'What happened?' Ffion asks, her voice brash. I want to take her by the shoulders and tell her to be quiet, because I don't think I'm ready for the answer. 'What could've taken both Halenprophet Lewys and dear Rhosyn in one fell swoop?'

Aledd's eyes track to me. It's only for a split second – and could easily be missed – but it feels like an axe to my neck. He knows. He *knows.*

'As some of you may know, the Halenprophet and Rhosyn enjoy taking exercise in the early hours of the morning. It's believed that during their walk, they strayed too close to the edge of the pier. We discovered . . .' Aledd pauses, swallowing uncomfortably. '*Most* of their bodies, floating beneath the pier. From the nature of their injuries, we can only conclude they were pulled into the water and killed by a tidewraith.'

Killed.

By a tidewraith.

The creatures *I* am supposed to keep at bay.

My body suddenly weighs too much, and my lungs are too narrow. The collective gaze of the crowd swings around like Point Beacon's beam, landing squarely on me. I feel myself illuminated in excruciating detail. Every part of me – every guilty sinew, every shadowed crevice – is laid bare, ripe for inspection. For *judgement.*

If the Halenprophet and Rhosyn were at the harbour in the early morning, I would've seen or heard *something.* Them walking on the pier, or else the frenzied sound of tidewraiths feeding on their bodies. They couldn't have been there any later, either; the sun would've been up, and the tidewraiths recede to the depths during the day.

'Point Beacon is supposed to keep them away,' Owain Meyrick says. 'Did the lighthouse falter, Guinevere?'

There are a hundred pairs of eyes pinned to me, and I know I need to say *something* – to either admit my guilt, or claim my innocence. Cat's hand squeezes mine; I grip her so tightly my joints ache.

'It's okay,' she whispers. 'It's all right, Guin. Tell the truth.'

She stares at me so intently that everything else fades to irrelevance – the tidewardens, the islanders around us, Ffion and Liliwen and Osian. All that exists is me and Cat, her blue eyes the centre of my small universe.

'Point Beacon went out.'

My admission is barely a whisper, but it has the same effect as a gunshot. The crowd grows frenetic, like a shaken jar of wasps. The combination of mourning and fear is a dangerous one; people press closer together without meaning to, shoulders jostling, toes trodden by neighbouring boots. The quiet grief working its way through the crowd densifies, sharpens.

'How could you?' asks a sorrowed voice from the crowd. 'How *could* you?'

'Your mistake cost us our faith,' another adds. 'Our island is rudderless. *Faithless.* Without a conduit for Llyr to speak through, we're as good as *Ynys Annuwiol.*'

The villagers' anger bears down. As the crowd contracts, the sisters form a barricade around me, their long fingers braided together. I think that small action is all that stands between me and the island's wrath.

Aledd holds up a hand, as if calming a spooked horse. 'All hope is not lost. Halenprophet Lewys had a son. His mother gave birth on the mainland.'

Cat intakes a sharp breath. It's an unspoken truth that unwed mothers are often the cargo on our fleet's rare voyages to the mainland, swept away like ash from the hearth, but I didn't know one of them was swollen with the Halenprophet's child.

'We have spent the past days arranging his safe return to Ynys Halen,' Aledd says.

'A *mainlander?*' someone yells, their voice twisted with disgust.

'This won't do,' Mr Meyrick shouts. He looks crueller than I've ever seen him, brows lowered and pupils narrowed. 'A mainlander cannot act as a conduit for Llyr.'

'Guinevere Wyn failed in her duties,' a man snaps. 'That doesn't mean we'll tolerate a mainlander becoming our Halenprophet.'

'A mainlander with Blythin blood and salt in his veins.' The voice comes from the church's innards, somehow gentle and commanding at once – the quiet authority of a shepherd.

Our new Halenprophet steps into the light. 'It was not Guinevere's hand that caused Point Beacon to falter. It was Llyr's.'

# CHAPTER 6

*Llyr imparts the Halenprophet with the ability to scry the future in spilled salt. His hand guides theirs; their hand carries out His will.*

—Excerpt from 'Spilled Salt', a guide to the origin of the Halenprophet

Everyone thrusts forwards at the same time, jostling to get an eyeful of the new Halenprophet. I'm caught between relief so potent it almost makes my knees buckle, and disbelief I struggle not to show on my face.

I felt, deep in my bones, that I had not miscalculated on the night Point Beacon went out. Waking to hand-crank the tank is as natural as breathing itself to me. But I was faced with an unignorable reality – the beam *did* falter – and I had no choice but to attribute it to the only person in the lighthouse that evening.

But what could Llyr have to gain by snuffing out the beam? And *why?*

I push onto my tiptoes, desperate to dissect the sincerity of our new prophet – but the woman directly in front of me has a beehive of hair piled up onto her head, and I can't see past it. Murmurs ripple through the crowd – half directed towards my failure, half towards the new Halenprophet.

'Can you see him?' I ask Cat, who's a good head taller than me.

She shakes her head. 'Lil, let me boost you up.'

In one practised movement, Cat drops to her knees and Liliwen clambers onto them. She peers above the crowd, neck craned. Her eyes widen.

'What's he like, then?' Ffion insists. 'A foppish mainlander?'

Liliwen leaps down from Cat's knees. I pull Catrin to her feet, our hands tangled together.

'Worse,' Lili says gravely. 'He's gorgeous.'

A laugh explodes past my lips, despite everything.

'Good morning,' the Halenprophet says, his voice a rich, earthy bass. 'Thank you all so much for gathering here at short notice. I only arrived last night, but I couldn't wait to meet you all. My name is Taliesin, and I am your new Halenprophet.'

Entranced by the melody of his voice, the crowd stills. I find a sliver of unobstructed space, the Halenprophet's form silhouetted between the backs of the islanders' heads. Lili wasn't wrong; he has a sort of beauty which is rarely found on the island. Thick eyebrows frame tender, warm eyes; dark waves of hair cascade to his shoulders; his complexion is rich and warm, the same brown as a guillemot's back.

Whoever his mother was, he's certainly taken after her. There's almost nothing of Halenprophet Lewys to be seen.

'Well,' Cat whispers. 'That's just . . . absurd.'

I feel a discomfort in the pit of my stomach. It's not that I think

Cat's affection should be reserved for me. My own heart wanders, sometimes veering towards Osian when he rolls his sleeves up or hums beneath his breath. Still, it pains me that I must do so much to earn her focus. Occasionally, a man will come along and capture her attention for an hour, or a day, or a week, and all I can think is *why him?* What makes him so special?

In this instance, it's not hard to understand. Our new Halenprophet is remarkable.

Ffion leans in and whispers, 'I'd not say no to a ride on that pony.'

I stifle my resulting laugh behind the web of my fingers. We wait with bated breath, hungry for more of the Halenprophet's words. He can't be much older than me – mid-twenties, perhaps – but he speaks with the quiet authority of a man twice his age.

'I know many of you are worried about the future, but I want to reassure you that my mother did everything she could to teach me about Ynys Halen. Being here . . .' Taliesin pauses, drawing in a deep breath. 'It feels like a homecoming.'

I glance at the faces around me – not just the sisters, but the islanders at large. In their faces, I see opinions begin to shift. Furrowed brows soften; clenched fists unfurl.

'I have studied your history extensively. I understand the sacred role Halenprophecy plays in communing with Llyr.' He runs his tongue across his lower lip. 'I felt my father had passed before I received the news. I woke with the urge to spill salt, and when I did, I saw myself on Ynys Halen. The art of Halenprophecy has awoken in me. It would be my life's delight to wield it for this island's betterment.'

'God, he's good,' Ffion whispers.

I can hardly tear my eyes from him. I'm not one to go all soppy over a man, but something about the way he speaks is hypnotic – his cadence, the way his eyes find specific faces in the crowd and focus on them, the open sincerity.

'I am looking forward to getting to know you all over the coming weeks, months, *years* – but today, I'm afraid I bear ill news.'

The pit that appeared in my stomach this morning tears open like a scab.

'As you heard, it was a tidewraith that took my father and half-sister.' His eyelashes flutter, as if tears are threatening to spill over. 'I spilled salt to commune with Llyr, to understand why such evil befell my family – and he answered. It was he who snuffed out the lighthouse that night. He orchestrated their deaths.'

Gasps ripple through the crowd. A panicked voice asks, 'Why would he do that? Has Llyr forsaken us?'

'On the contrary,' Taliesin says. 'It is we who have forsaken him. I read my father's journals. Page after page of grief at the empty pews on Sunday, at salt wasted in kitchens instead of on the altar, at our young people forgetting the God who shielded this island. Llyr is resentful. And can we blame him?'

The crowd murmurs, heads bowed with shame. I wonder if it was Llyr who drew the tidewraiths to Sawtooth the night Rhian died. Did our lofty God see our absence at church, and decide to take matters into his own hands?

Taliesin lowers his voice, almost tender. 'I don't want you to worry. I'm here to guide and protect you. But we all must renew our efforts to praise Llyr.'

A bleating voice asks, 'If we all attend church, will it be enough to regain his trust?'

Taliesin gives a noncommittal bob of his head. 'Llyr wishes for us to devote ourselves to him as we did in former times.'

If there's a disturbing ambiguity in his response, I seem to be the only one who feels it. Around me, people nod eagerly.

'If we commit wholeheartedly, Llyr will allow Point Beacon to shine,' the Halenprophet says.

Ffion clears her throat before asking, 'And if we fail?'

Her question elicits a rumble of discontented whispers, glares directed her way as if to vocalise the possibility of failure makes it more likely.

Taliesin raises a hand, and the congregation falls silent once more. 'Llyr is a loving God, and as such, he has offered us three chances to better ourselves, each marked by a portent. The first was the darkening of the lighthouse. If we fail to appease him, the second portent will materialise: the ocean will become barren. If we continue to displease him, the third portent will be unignorable. The sea will run red. If that ever comes to pass, it will indicate that Llyr is about to abandon Ynys Halen for good.'

'Portents?' Catrin hisses. 'What is he talking about?'

Ffion whispers, 'A portent is an event that foreshadows something disastrous . . .'

'Yes, I know what a portent is, Ffion,' Cat snaps.

'Abandon us?' Lili's quavering voice rises above the sisters' murmuring, the harried mutters of the crowd. 'What does that mean?'

The Halenprophet finds Lili, his eyes softening. 'Even without exercising his power, Llyr's presence functions to moderate the tidewraith population. Without him, we will see tidewraiths swarm the island in numbers greater than ever before – to the extent that Point Beacon will no longer be able to protect us.' I swear Taliesin meets my gaze directly. 'I do not intend to let it get that far.'

Towards the front of the crowd, a child begins to cry. It's a high, keening sound, not dissimilar to the wails Percy lets loose when he patrols the lighthouse at night. Taliesin stoops, and when he straightens, he has taken the child into his arms.

The little girl – I see, now, that it's one of the Williams' grandchildren – wraps her arms around Taliesin's neck. Our new Halenprophet smiles as she rests her head on his shoulder, her small body jerking with quietening sobs. I've never seen a child so comforted by a stranger – much less by a strange *man*.

Around me, the women are moved. They wear soft smiles, or touch hands to their chests. I've not a jot of maternal instinct, but even I am moved. How a man treats those weaker and smaller than him is the surest mirror of his soul.

Taliesin strokes the back of the girl's head and smiles out at the crowd. 'I wish I could have spared you the weight. But I want to be honest with you all, in the hopes that one day, you will grow to trust me. And I do not wish for my arrival to be tainted by sadness and fear; I want this time to be a happy one.'

The Halenprophet hands the girl – now asleep – back to her mother.

With a soft smile, he says, 'Let us show our worship through joy. Together, we can save Ynys Halen from ruin.'

I've never had much faith in Llyr. Anyone willing to eat a young woman's flesh earns my distrust. And besides, despite Point Beacon and Llyr's lightning both functioning to keep the tidewraiths at bay, I've always seen us as opposing forces. The stone and mortar reality of Point Beacon versus the intangible God.

But even *I* find myself shaken by the threat of his abandonment. No one knows that tidewraiths overran Sawtooth the night of Rhian's death, and if they gather in even greater numbers, I dread to think what will happen. The sisters and I mull it over on the walk back to the village.

'Do you believe it, then? Portents and the like?'

I've no idea why Liliwen directs her question at me, aside from the fact I'm the token heretic, what with my regular failure to attend church. It earns me less scrutiny than it would any other islander.

'I've no way to explain the lighthouse going out *other* than it being by Llyr's hand,' I murmur, wary of the steady stream of congregants around us. 'So I suppose I have to believe.'

'You sure you didn't just oversleep?' Ffion teases.

I bristle at the accusation – largely because I spent nights believing it was true. 'The last time I overslept, I was in my mother's womb.'

An image of her surges to the forefront of my mind: blonde and lithe and smiling. I shove it down. That's the worst part of the way Aledd stole her. He didn't just take *her*; he took her memory, so I could never imagine her without purple bruises on her throat.

'We'll see if it's true soon enough,' Cat muses. 'I can't imagine the uproar if the ocean runs barren. What'll we do without my Friday fish stew?'

Lili grimaces at me. Cat's a terrible cook, but none of us dare tell her. She's manufactured this routine where we all sit around the mortuary dining table on a Friday night and tell her how delicious it is. Not even Dylan is spared.

'I think your fish stew will be the least of our worries if Llyr decides to abandon us,' Ffion snips.

'*If* he abandons us,' Lili says carefully, as if speaking of it with too much certainty will make it a reality, 'what would that mean?

Does he leave and go elsewhere? Or does he just . . .' – she lowers her voice to a whisper – '*die?*'

'I don't think Gods can die,' Ffion says. 'Or at least, they can't be killed. I've read of Gods having their organs stripped out, their heads lopped off, their blood drained by humans from opposing religions – but it doesn't kill them. Only a God can kill a God.' She whistles, long and low. 'What I wouldn't give to be a spectator in a battle like that.'

Lili murmurs, 'What a horrible thought.'

I look over at Cat, waiting for her to make a biting remark, but she's just . . . *staring* at me. She doesn't stop, even when I catch her.

'What?'

Cat links our elbows and marches me ahead, out of earshot. 'Why didn't you tell me about the lighthouse?'

I think about it for a moment. My guilt wasn't solely focused around the potential harm; it was also my failure in the line of duty. Rhian's body was barely cold, and I'd let standards slip with disastrous consequences.

'I thought you'd judge me,' I reply.

She clucks her tongue. 'In over a decade of friendship, I have never judged you, Guinevere.'

'You did when I had that fling with Gethin Thomas.'

She wrinkles her nose, probably remembering Gethin's tendency to explain the mechanics of the lighthouse to me, or his signature scent of clothes that should have been washed sooner. I barely even *liked* the lad, but Cat was busy entertaining the advances of some hopeless boy from the village, and Osian had started courting the Davies' youngest daughter. I'm not sure what mattered to me more: keeping pace with them, or distracting myself.

'True,' Cat laughs. 'You deserved it, though. He was horrific. And ugly.'

Some girls would express polite interest in their friend's trysts. Not Cat, though. She's never been one to mince her words.

She lowers her mouth to my ear, hot breath dampening my skin. 'Never hide things from me again.'

'I won't.'

Catrin jerks to a stop. She places her hands on my cheeks, forcing my gaze upwards to meet hers. Her pupils are dilated, swallowing up the blue of her iris.

'*Promise* me,' she demands.

Shakily, I reply, 'I promise.'

A smile lights up her face – so radiant I almost feel the need to shield my eyes. 'Good.'

The island's fresh devotion takes root. Little shrines spring up along the village's roads, marked by effigies of Llyr whittled from driftwood. People leave offerings of gold and silver, posies of coastal flowers, jars of pickled seaweed, bottles of whiskey and mead.

The Sunday after Lewys was found dead, I attend Sunday service for the first time since I was a child. I don't like to be beholden to people, and feel I owe our new Halenprophet a certain amount of repayment for clearing my name.

Cat invites me to her home to get ready, which is how I learn that she treats church as her personal pageant. She sits at the dressing table, humming beneath her breath. I don't think Cat's bedroom has changed a jot in the past decade. It's cloyingly feminine: all pink, plush cushions, stuffed animals, trinkets collected from markets and pining boys. Anyone else with a room like this would be accused of being infantile. Cat escapes all that, as she does most things. Her beauty affords her a grace many aren't lucky enough to receive.

Beneath all the perfectly combed hair, the rosebud lips, the sloping nose, the sapphire eyes – beneath all that, if you're foolhardy enough to dig down, there's a different side to Cat. Most of the time, she's a cloudless day, a newborn kitten, a dove's call. Other times, she is absolutely monstrous. I've watched her strike fear into the heart of girls who dared to speak ill of her; I've seen her plant seeds of gossip to earn her revenge; I've ached as she encouraged boys she had no interest in to invest in her love with jewellery, gowns from the mainland, custom-made shoes.

I could never hold it against her. Cat gives back what she gets. If you are kind and fair, she is kind and fair. If you are wicked, she will be ten times worse. She has a keen sense of justice, and it swings both ways: benevolence and malice delivered by the same hand.

I watch her in the dressing table mirror as she teases her hair into a bun. She catches me staring; I avert my eyes like a guilty thief.

'Creep,' she teases.

She's not wrong. Sometimes, I have these dreams where I'm standing over Cat as she sleeps. There's no context to it, but a certainty festers in my bones: I can either be with her, or be her. The decision is so excruciating that I always wake before I can make it. I feel that tug now – the urge to kiss Catrin as she applies pink stain to her lips, and the warring desire to climb inside her mouth, down her throat, until I'm more her than I am me.

My cheeks flush with shame. Cat, oblivious to the obsessive nature of my thoughts, daubs my lips in the same shade of peach. Her finger tastes like liquorice.

I can never tell where I stand with Cat. Or maybe I can, and that's just a comforting lie I tell myself. We're friends. Friends who once shared an aching kiss and never spoke of it again. We'd taken turns at a bottle of whiskey, and that night seems so impossibly beautiful in my mind that surely it didn't exist. A scarlet sunset, a turquoise sea, the keening call of an oystercatcher. A kiss that was over before it'd really begun.

I'm still thinking of that kiss as we walk to the church together. Men stare at Cat as she passes, their eyes practically popping from their heads. Women, too, find something in her worth investigation, but their glances are surreptitious. To the untrained eye, she appears totally unaware of the effect she has – but I register the twitching of her lips, the way she throws her shoulders back each time we're set to pass someone.

We slide into one of the church pews, her thigh pressed up against mine. My memories of the church are punctuated by bone-aching cold, coats staving no chill; macabre murals staring down from the walls; adults almost trampling me underfoot, as if I did not exist at all.

Either my memory is hazy, or the new Halenprophet has changed the fabric of this place. Candles glow from sconces on the walls; children play with wooden toys at the back of the church. From his roost at the lectern, Halenprophet Taliesin gazes down. He has donned his white robes and wears them better than Lewys ever did, broad shoulders filling out the pale fabric. I could swear he looks straight at me and smiles – picking my face out of the hundreds stuffed into the pews.

'Am I mad,' Ffion says in the seat beside me, her voice low, 'or is he staring at me?'

Heat chases up my chest. Maybe he just has that effect on us.

Halenprophet Taliesin begins his sermon in earnest. I'd planned to attend with the sort of reluctant irritation Rhian might display, but I find myself enraptured. Taliesin is a dynamic preacher, walking to and fro as he speaks. The islanders' faces turn to track him, our eyes glued to each of his movements.

He speaks of Bronwen – something I cannot recall Halenprophet Lewys ever mentioning. Taliesin asks us to imagine how fiercely Llyr loved Bronwen. Her death made him grieve so fiercely that he forsook humanity itself. This, the Halenprophet tells us, is how we should love one another. How we should love Llyr himself.

'Without Bronwen, there would be no Llyr,' he states. 'Because Bronwen died, Llyr became a God – and because he became a God, our island was kept safe from tidewraiths for many years.'

'All for the paltry price of one woman each solstice,' Ffion mutters beside me. I dig my elbow into her ribs.

Just as Point Beacon guzzles kerosene, Llyr needed fuel. The islanders' offerings of bread and meat failed him. His power dimmed, and the tidewraiths multiplied.

The first sacrifice was not planned: a woman consumed by sorrow flung herself from the cliffs. Her blood slicked the water. Llyr stirred. That night, he shaped currents that pulled the tidewraiths far out to sea, and beckoned down lightning that chased them to the depths. The price of his protection was implicitly understood: flesh and blood.

Over the years that followed, the islanders learned that his hunger would peak every six months on the solstice, when the veil between our world and the Gods' is thinnest, and that not all sacrifices could sate him. He liked women. *Pretty* women. It's thought they reminded him of the wife he'd lost. Each Salt Queen was selected specifically for her beauty, the same way the fattest cow is chosen for slaughter.

It was a price worth paying – a sentiment more keenly felt by the islanders at large than the Salt Queens themselves, I'm sure. My ancestor – so far removed that I've forgotten the number of 'greats' – was the one to put an end to it. After her daughter was crowned Salt Queen and fed to Llyr, she discovered Point Beacon's beam drove back the wraiths just as well as Llyr's lightning. No more Salt Queens needed to be sacrificed. We still worship Llyr, the Halenprophet acting as a conduit for our devotion, but no more blood needs to be shed.

We've grown since then. Ynys Halen's women are prickly as gorse, stiff as a December breeze. None of us would walk willingly into the sea, and I doubt the men would dare to ask us. The last remnant of the practice rots in Sawtooth bay: a slender, wooden pole driven into the sea floor. That's where they'd string her up. I give it the middle finger sometimes.

'For too long, women's voices have been decentred in our faith. And why?' Taliesin shakes his head. 'Llyr does not love women less than he loves men. In fact, it was his love of a woman that drove him to Godhood in the first place.'

Taliesin glances around the church, head lowered as though humbled. I glance sideways at Cat. She watches him with a tentative smile, her fingers curled around the lip of our pew.

'I find that one can judge a society's success by how it treats women. And in that interest, I would like to encourage the women of this congregation to speak with me, one on one, following today's sermon.'

I'd half-expected him to announce that women were finally to be made tidewardens, so the announcement of a women's circle falls slightly flat. But my disenchantment isn't reflected elsewhere. A contented murmur goes up from the women around me.

The same can't be said of the men. Ynys Halen's men could never be accused of joviality, but this announcement seems to push them further towards reticence. Mr Meyrick frowns up at the Halenprophet; Arthur Vaughan shakes his head surreptitiously. The men stand up to leave, abandoning the women in the pews.

'I thought he was about to announce women could become tidewardens,' I say to the sisters, my voice low.

'Now that'd be a fine thing,' Ffion says. 'A bunch of sailors who cannot swim.'

'It's hardly a lost art, Ffion,' I mutter. 'I'm sure he could teach us to swim, *and* teach us to sail.'

'He can teach me to swim, all right,' Catrin says, a scandalous purr to her words.

'Why do you think he wants to speak to the women alone?' Lili asks, all the innuendo lost on her.

Ffion shrugs. 'I reckon he's looking for a wife. Someone's got to pop out those Halenprophet babies.'

'I can think of few fates worse,' I mutter.

'Oh, come on, Guin,' Cat says, smiling. 'I think you're safe. You're already married to the lighthouse.'

I roll my eyes. She's not exactly *wrong*, but it smarts nonetheless.

At that moment, Osian passes our pew. He quirks his eyebrows at me. 'Have fun,' he says. 'I'll come round for tea soon?'

I give him a small nod in return, loath to give Cat anything substantial to pick over.

Once he's out of earshot, Cat sneers, '*Have fun!*'

'Don't be such a toad,' I snip. 'He's nice.'

'Oh, I bet he is.' Cat wiggles her brows salaciously. 'Men can pretend to be all sorts of things when they want a chance in your knickers.'

I give up speaking to her, sensing that she's in one of her moods. Osian isn't like that, but I don't dare tell her so, knowing she'll mock me for it. I fold my arms and turn to the side.

I keep expecting Cat to vie for my attention and claw me back, but she doesn't. Lili and Ffion chat between themselves; Cat wanders over to join the queue which now stretches from the sacristy to the door, talking to a couple of girls who work in the bakery. I watch from the corner of my eye, stomach churning.

The line dwindles. Each woman who comes out of the sacristy has a dreamy expression on their face, a sheepish smile that can't be hidden.

'What the hell's he doing to them in there?' I ask.

'Helping them see God, by the looks of things,' Ffion says.

I snort.

'What do you mean?' Lili asks.

'You know,' Ffion waves her hand. 'Dipping the wick. Giving the cliffs a good battering. Going for a roll in the heather.'

'You're as bad as a man,' I mutter, still laughing.

Ffion shrugs. 'I look better doing it.'

Cat looks over and catches us laughing. *Good*, I think, under the misguided belief she'll come scuttling back to see what's so funny – but she doesn't. All I'm spared is a glance over her shoulder before she ducks through the door.

After a span of minutes, Cat emerges, a furtive smile curving her lips. She saunters back down the line and pauses beside us.

'He's even more handsome up close,' she declares.

'Did you get a sense of what he wants with us?' Lili asks.

'He didn't ask for my hand in marriage, if that's what you're asking.' Cat's blue eyes dart to mine, sparkling with mischief. 'But if he had, I'd have struggled to say no.'

I resist the urge to roll my eyes again. Cat juts out her lower lip and drops down onto my lap, her legs kicked astride my knees. She pulls me in close, her arms around my nape.

'Did I upset you, Guinny?' she whispers, lips tickling my ear. 'I didn't mean what I said about you being married to the lighthouse. Any man would be lucky to have you.'

I sit very still, taking in a lungful of her blackberry scent. I can never be cross with her for long. 'I'm not sure they'd agree.'

As a child, I thought about marriage extensively. I mean, as extensively as a young girl can, and in no more detail than the shapes and colours: a white dress, a cake, a posy of gorse and heather. When I met Osian, I inserted him into the fantasy – my kind and gentle groom. But then I grew introspective, and questioned whether it was really what I wanted, or what I *should* want.

I asked Rhian about marriage, and she said the only good thing her husband – my grandfather – ever did was die. She said I ought not to worry myself, because few men are strong enough to live as we do, and that I'd be better off taking a male concubine. I didn't know what that was, and she wouldn't tell me.

'That's just as well,' Cat murmurs. 'Because you're mine.'

My heart stutters. She pulls back, grins, and trots out of the church.

'Guinevere Wyn.' A smile – a *genuine* smile – spills across the Halenprophet's face. The way my name rolls from his tongue makes me shiver. 'I've heard so much about you. Please, sit down.'

Taliesin gestures towards the desk that dominates the room.

His sacristy is scantly furnished, with two rickety chairs and a basin of salt. It smells like parchment: earthy, slightly sweet. The macabre murals that once hung in the church are now stacked against the wall.

I sit delicately, hands folded in my lap. I'm not sure I like the positions he's placed us in: him above, me below. As if sensing my displeasure, he takes the seat opposite me.

I clear my throat. 'Good things, I hope.'

'The best,' he assures.

A pregnant quiet hangs between us. I feel viscerally aware of each shift in my body, and how he might interpret it.

'Some say you're in search of a wife,' I venture.

He smiles again, but it doesn't touch his eyes. 'Do they.'

I puff out my chest and straighten my shoulders. 'If that's the case, you won't find one in me. I have my commitments, and I don't have the time nor inclination . . .'

'You think that's what this is? That I'd ask this island's women to parade before me like cattle at the market, so I can pick the finest specimen?'

Taliesin appears genuinely hurt – his brown eyes rounded, lips pursed.

Picking over my words, I say, 'I can't imagine why else you'd want an audience with only women.'

Taliesin blinks down at me. His eyelashes are distractingly long. 'I've found that the many strands of faith on the mainland tend to find themselves at odds with women's emancipation.' He swallows, throat bobbing. 'I won't have that be the case here.'

Hearing a man speak like this is quite unprecedented. Ffion whispered of books from the mainland detailing women living in matriarchal societies, or else freeing themselves from the shackles of domestic servitude. It was a tantalising idea to the sisters, all of whom want children and must, therefore, take a husband. I suppose *I* must have one, some day – a little Wyn to keep the lighthouse manned. The thought makes me shiver.

'If there's anything you want to speak to me about, I'm all ears,' Taliesin adds.

I give him a guarded smile. 'I'll bear that in mind.'

He leans forwards, bracing his elbows on the desk. I force myself not to retreat.

'Catrin Morgan spoke very fondly of you,' he says.

A warmth spreads outward from my heart. 'She's a good friend of mine.'

Taliesin nods slowly. 'Did you grow up together?'

When we first met, I asked Cat who her mother was. It was a dreadfully insensitive question, really, but I was a child who could not understand the concept of a father raising children without a woman's labour to lean upon.

Cat said she didn't have one. That she came from a mermaid's purse – these thick, leathery sacs that wash up on the shore. I spent the next day ranging across the strandline, saving the horned pouches from the surf. I didn't find any babies inside them, mind.

Rhian told me the truth: that Dylan found the girls in a rowboat, washed up onto shore. Lili was a newborn, Cat not much older, and Ffion the eldest. They're so striking in appearance that it would've been easy to pick out their mother if she lived on the island. How did the girls end up in that rowboat, bobbing across the sea towards Ynys Halen? Maybe it was an accident – three girls playing in the boat when it suddenly set adrift. Maybe it was purposeful. An act of cruelty.

Still, they landed on their feet with Dylan.

'Yes, we grew up together. For the most part. Why do you ask?'

He pauses, then answers, 'I sensed a certain ... sadness in her. I wondered if that was a recent development – if anything happened to make her withdraw.'

I ponder on it, considering everything I know about Catrin. In truth, I think she's caused more sadness than she's experienced. It's not that she's cruel, necessarily, but she has a certain way of treating people – like they're pawns in a game she's playing. She's broken plenty of boys' hearts, and sent a slew of girls into social isolation.

I'm not sure what Taliesin sensed in her, but I can't imagine it was sadness.

'Cat's the hardy sort,' I say, finally. 'And if she was suffering, I'd know about it.'

'That's good. Perhaps I was mistaken.' He drums his fingers on the lectern. 'I'd love to visit you up at the lighthouse one day. This Tuesday, if you'll have me.'

I'm not sure I'm in any position to deny the Halenprophet, and he's intrigued me enough that I'm happy to welcome him at Point Beacon. At least then we'll be in *my* territory. I'll have the upper hand.

'Certainly.'

'I'm sure you've plenty to attend to. I've kept you long enough.'

Sensing a dismissal, I retreat through the sacristy, my footsteps echoing. Just as I reach the door, Taliesin's voice cuts through the quiet.

'Oh, Guinevere?'

I stop in my tracks. When I turn, I find Taliesin standing, though I did not hear him move. The hairs on my arms stand on end. With the gentle smile on his face, he's the picture of benevolence – but his eyes have changed. Hardened, maybe; brown deepening to black, brows slanted.

The Halenprophet crosses the room, boots clicking neatly against the tiles. When he reaches out to take my hands, I do not stop him. His palms are soft and uncalloused, like the polished bowl of an oyster shell.

'I know it was you,' he murmurs, holding my gaze. It feels absurdly intimate – our hands tangled, his lids slightly lowered, the gentle metronome of his breath hot across my cheeks.

'What was me?'

A gentle smile pulls at his lips. 'You let the light go out.'

My heart makes one urgent beat against the cage of my chest, then stills entirely. Taliesin's grip tightens along with my throat. All the guilt I thought I'd released comes surging back, almost overwhelming in its intensity.

'How did you know?' I whisper, my voice brittle.

'You *radiate* shame,' he says. 'It was a guess. Thank you for confirming my suspicions.'

My flapping mouth will be the death of me. 'You said Llyr snuffed out the light.'

'Gods like Llyr are not so patient as to offer *three* portents.' Halenprophet Taliesin swallows; I watch his throat rock. 'The two he foretold were a convenient shroud for your misstep.'

I try to pull my fingers away, but he holds firm. 'Why would you protect me?'

'Believe it or not, I have your best interests at heart.'

Usually, I can tell when a man is lying. They get this eagerness in their eyes, like they can't quite believe how easy it is to claim the upper hand. Halenprophet Taliesin stares back at me with a practised composure.

'And what are my best interests, Halenprophet?'

He rolls his shoulders. 'Survival at any cost.'

We study each other, and I wish I could even out my breaths the way he does. As it stands, my chest is heaving, pulse hammering against my throat. The stale, paper-sweet air in the sacristy feels too dense, as if inhaling too much might cause my lungs to pop. Beyond the window, the ocean hisses as it crashes against the bluffs.

The Halenprophet tips his head back and laughs. 'Don't look so scared. Your secret is safe with me.'

Part of me wants to believe him; the other wants to run. He releases my hands, and I'm left to wonder if he ever really gripped them at all. There's no relief in it, though – no sense of escape. Only prolongment.

Halenprophet Taliesin opens the door and beckons me through it. 'Just remember, Guinevere,' he says, 'my confessional is *always* open.'

# CHAPTER 7

*If you smile at the ocean and it smiles back, run for your life.*

—Island superstition

Every time I see the Halenprophet walking about the village with his soft eyes and blinding smile, I feel I am being chased by a rabid dog. He's given no indication that I ought to distrust him. In fact, he's been ridiculously thoughtful. Without any pomp, Taliesin has increased my monthly stipend from the church, in light of my 'steadfast dedication to Ynys Halen'. Similarly, Ffion says he offered to increase the library's allowance for shipping books over from the mainland, and Lili said he bought a whole shelf of stock in the apothecary when she told him it had been a quiet week.

It's not just when people are watching, either. I spend a lot of time quietly observing the island. It's my way of pressing my palms up against Ynys Halen's windows – the warmth of their homes reflected on my face. From the widow's walk, I witnessed Halenprophet Taliesin rescue one of Osian's lambs from a ditch. He tucked it inside his coat and walked it all the way to the farmhouse.

Cat does little to soothe my unease. Whenever the sisters speak of Taliesin, Cat gets this sly smile, as if she knows something we don't. Occasionally, she'll dangle pieces of information in front of us – remarking on how buttery soft his robes are, or the smell of his skin, or the hazel ring around his pupils. Things one couldn't know unless they'd been afforded a certain closeness.

I know she's trying to provoke me. She wants me on my knees, begging to know how she got close enough to see the ring around his eyes. Cat loves me jealous. Sometimes, I give in and let her have it, if only to see her smile.

Halenprophet Taliesin continues his tradition of the weekly women's circle, inviting us to commune together or privately. The men *hate* it. I hear them grumbling in the greengrocer's. They call Taliesin the Boy Prophet, lamenting the way their wives speak of him with reverence. I think, privately, it is a strange amount of vitriol to harbour towards a man whose only verified crime is listening to their wives.

I've never been one to enjoy communing in any form, but I find myself compelled to join – wary that if I don't, I'll be left behind. He encourages us to find ways of maintaining an income when we marry, even if our husbands protest it; to nurture our female friendships, even if they are considered frivolous.

These ideas are radical, really. A married woman with a job would be considered a failure of all parties. But Halenprophet Taliesin delivers the messages so casually that we're almost lulled into thinking it's *normal.* He speaks of retaining independence, of setting boundaries within the marital bed, of the division of household labour.

In the quiet warmth of the church, I can believe it's possible. But then I watch Mrs Beddoe, encouraged by Taliesin to seek employment at the tailor's, trailing after her husband like a beaten dog with a blackberry stain around her eye. And I realise this island will never change.

That night, clinging to the railings of the widow's walk with my binoculars held aloft, I watch a storm petrel defend its burrow out on the heath. The tiny, black-feathered bird is hardly bigger than a swallow, but the grunts and purrs it gives off are enough to scare away the fox stalking through the heather. I watch the fox as it goes, white-tipped tail slung low. It trots across the heath, towards the village.

My binoculars catch an unusual smudge of light dancing by the pier. It takes me a few breaths to understand what I'm seeing: flames licking across the deck of our largest fishing boat.

Inhaling through my teeth, I scan the foot of the pier. There should be a tidewarden stationed there, but even with the consistent flashes of Point Beacon, it is too dark to discern anything outside of the glowing flames. I wait for a span of breaths, praying I'll see someone leap into action and douse the inferno with buckets of saltwater – but nothing happens.

The raft of flickering light grows.

The last thing we need is our boats going up in flames. I swear as I throw myself down the stairs, slinging a cloak over my shoulders before I leave the lighthouse. It's cold as a widow's bed, with a nasty sea breeze that needles its way beneath my layers of clothes. An owl patrols the heather now, hooting softly.

Mack startles at my sudden imposition, her nostrils flared. I mutter my apologies as I ease the bridle over her head and leap onto her back. We gallop all the way across the heath, wind tangling in her mane, the sweet scent of hay buffeting my face. By the time we reach the downward slope to the harbour, her flanks are hot and sweaty against my calves.

As the pier comes into view, two things are immediately clear: the fire is still raging, and there isn't a tidewarden stationed by the harbour.

The amber glow of flames stains the night. I throw myself off Mackerel's back and tie her to the railings outside the greengrocer's. Only when the bare soles of my feet slap against the wooden boardwalk do I realise I forewent shoes in my rush to leave the house.

The night is cold, and the sea spray even colder. My breath coils out in vaporous plumes. I rush past the first two skiffs, their white sails folded down like a gull's wings. The burning ship sits furthest out in the water, its bow like the curved chest of a humpback. Moonlight spills across the water, intermittently competing with the flash of Point Beacon's beam.

I wait for the earthy tang of woodsmoke to fill the air, but all I can smell is seaweed and saltwater. In its absence, I interrogate my other senses. I can *see* the flames, but if there was a fire burning unrestrained, I should be able to feel its heat – to hear the hiss and crack of wood bending, *burning*. But all I can hear is the slap of waves pushing up against the pier, the occasional gull's call, and . . .

Whispers.

Reflexes kicking in, I throw myself down onto the wooden boardwalk. I'm not even sure why I do it – only that something inside is screaming to make myself small, unobtrusive. I crawl on my belly towards the ship, hiding in the shadow cast by a stack of crab traps.

Ynys Halen's men gather on the boat, their meeting illuminated by torches in the tidewardens' hands. They stand in regimented lines, all facing towards the prow of the boat. Most of them are positioned so I cannot see their faces, but as I crane my neck, I pick out Arthur Vaughan's ruddy face, Aledd Williams' crooked nose, Mr Meyrick's cravat. What are they all doing out here, in the dead of night?

Standing at the front of the crowd, Halenprophet Taliesin speaks with clipped words, his back straight. Flame and shadows dance across his face, illuminating the sharp line of his jaw, the slant of his brow.

No matter how I strain, I can't make out what he's saying. I sidle closer, crawling along the boardwalk . . .

In my haste, I knock a crab trap askew. It clatters off the pier, landing in the water with a crescendo of noise. All the whispering ceases. I press myself tighter to the wood, praying they will not see me. Point Beacon's traitorous beam glances across the harbour, shedding light on my feeble attempt at hiding.

I hold my breath until my lungs ache. Until my body *demands* to breathe.

The whispers resume. Achingly slowly, I shimmy my way back down the boardwalk, keeping close to the shadows that Point Beacon cannot reach. Only when I feel dirt beneath my knees do I straighten, making a beeline for Mackerel where she waits outside the greengrocer's. My fingers tremble as I undo the knot in her reins.

'Guinevere.'

The voice comes from behind, sharp as a cracking whip. I

turn slowly, cloak pulled tight around my body. Halenprophet Taliesin stands between me and the harbour, his face unreadable in the shadows.

'I thought there was a fire.' My explanation comes out panicked. 'But I'll be going now . . .'

The Halenprophet closes the distance between us in one of my breaths. 'No. You won't.'

I stagger backwards, colliding with the soft heat of Mackerel's hide. She whinnies anxiously, the sound reverberating across her ribcage and through my own. Taliesin advances, illuminated briefly by the lighthouse. His pupils are narrow as pinpricks.

'No one else knows how to operate Point Beacon,' I whisper. 'And if you harm me, the island will be lost to tidewraiths long before Llyr can make up his mind . . .'

The Halenprophet holds out his hands, as if steadying an anxious animal. 'I'm not going to harm you. I just wanted to explain.'

The quiet between us is permeated by Mack's snorting breaths, waves breaking against the pier.

'The ocean has forsaken us,' he says. 'For the past three days, our boats cast out their nets in search of fish. Each time, they came up empty.'

'The second portent,' I say, my mouth numb. Fear spreads its tendrils through me.

Halenprophet Taliesin nods.

'And you only thought it pertinent that the *men* know.'

'I wished to spare the women unnecessary fear.'

How noble. 'And when they cannot find fish at the market, what will you say?'

'That the ships are undergoing maintenance,' he says, a practised response. 'Everything will be back to normal soon.'

'Our displays of devotion haven't shifted Llyr's temper, then,' I venture.

The Halenprophet exhales, his chest deflating. He glances across his shoulder at the harbour, where the torches still burn brightly.

'No,' Taliesin murmurs, 'but I have a failsafe.'

'And will you tell me what that is, or is my womanly brain too feeble to comprehend it?'

His jaw twitches. I think I've struck a nerve. Before I can question him further, a low groan rises from the waves beyond the harbour. I'd recognise that sound anywhere. The leviathan. Goosebumps rise along Taliesin's throat.

'Get back to the lighthouse,' he says, each word clipped. 'You don't want to risk it going out again.'

As I vault onto Mackerel's back, the leviathan's hum increases in volume. When we reach the top of the slope, I glance across my shoulder. Taliesin's still standing there, his eyes fixed somewhere out at sea.

The women find out anyway, as women do.

The fishmonger's stall is barren, save for some limp piles of samphire, a scattering of cockles and a pile of whelks. The women don't accept the Halenprophet's explanation, conveyed through the fishmonger's mouth.

Distrust spreads among the islanders. We've plenty of food, just no fish – but people start to hoard what they have with no regard for their neighbours. It's a mental thing, I think. The animal part of our brain perceives scarcity and reacts impulsively, without sparing thought for logic or rationality.

Devotion becomes a competition. Who can spend the longest

in church? Who can lay the most opulent offerings at Llyr's new shrines? If Llyr is pleased by these cutthroat displays of faith, he does not show it; each morning, the fishing boats pull up empty nets.

Amidst it all, the Halenprophet is a shining beacon. He invites us into his church, and he *listens.* Just last night, when Lili could not sleep for her worrying, she wandered to the church and found him sequestered there, praying for our salvation. He absorbed all her doubts. She said she slept better than she has in months.

Taliesin recruits a flush of new tidewardens. I'd half-expected him to announce a handful of female tidewardens – a performative gesture, designed to further endear and mollify the women of Ynys Halen – but the new cohort is all-male, as standard. They are taught to sail, allowing all our fleet to leave the harbour at once, scouring our waters for fish.

They needn't have bothered. When I wake for Sunday service, the tide that laps at Sawtooth is blinding scarlet.

# CHAPTER 8

*Ynys Halen's seas, despite their notoriety, are our most precious asset. We enjoy bountiful catches all year long, resulting from plankton-rich waters that surround our shores. Even when stocks on the mainland falter, our seas provide!*

—Excerpt from a poster in the window of Ynys Halen's fishmonger

'The third portent has materialised. We stand on the cusp of imminent demise.'

Collective emotion overwhelms the congregation. People slide from their pews, landing on their knees; others begin to sob, the sound echoing through the church.

I went to find Cat the minute I saw burgundy foam spilling onto the shore. She was pacing around her living room, Dylan trying and failing to console her. Now, she sits beside me and trembles.

'But all hope is not lost,' Halenprophet Taliesin assures, his white-clad arms spread wide. 'There is a way forward. We have a chance yet to save Ynys Halen. It will not be easy, and it will not be holy, but it is our only chance of survival.'

His words drone between my ears, as if I'm hearing them but not really understanding what they mean. Beside me, Lili whimpers. I draw her against my side, and use my other hand to grasp Cat's.

'I have wrestled with this. I have tried *desperately* to think of another way – but each time I spill salt, Llyr makes himself clear.' Taliesin sucks in a strangled breath. 'He wants another Salt Queen.'

For a heartbeat, no one moves. Taliesin's words hang over us like a suffocating fog. Ffion sucks in a breath.

I think of the pole in Sawtooth bay, of all the women whose lives ended there. I think of Mrs Bennion with her plum bruise, my mother's crushed windpipe, the Halenprophet's claims that we women should demand *more*.

Fury rises certain as the tide inside me. My fingers curl around the back of the bench in front, nails chipping at the wood. Rhian's warning sits heavy in my chest. *It's about what will happen if the islanders find out we can't protect them.*

Slowly, a ripple passes through the crowd. Sharp intakes of air, insistent murmurs, whimpering cries. One of the girls from the bakery shoves to her feet.

'I'd sooner slit my throat than drown that way,' she says, her anger fractured with fear.

'A woman fed to the sea like chum?' Mrs Llywelyn's voice cracks. 'After all these years . . .'

Halenprophet Taliesin lets out a cry, bending at the waist. He clutches at his head, jaw gritted so firmly I think his teeth might crack.

'Please,' he breathes. 'Llyr is listening.'

I knew Llyr communicated with the Halenprophet through spilled salt; I *didn't* know he had the ability to invoke pain. Arguments bloom and die, stifled by the threat of Llyr's retribution. The collective sense of disgust and fury gutters.

Halenprophet Taliesin straightens, face still twisted with pain. A bead of sweat rolls from his forehead to his temple, before dripping from the ledge of his jaw onto his robes.

'When I met with this island's women, I prayed to feel *nothing.* I hoped it would give me evidence that Ynys Halen's solution does not lay in sacrifice – but it cemented that fact. I spilled salt that evening, and my suspicions were confirmed.'

Dread infests my body. I glance at the faces around us, hoping to see my horror reflected there – but instead, I notice something else. A distinct absence of the navy-clad stewards of our faith. Aledd is the only one present.

'Among all the women of this island, there was one who stood out. One who would stand to sate Llyr – her beauty unparalleled.'

Every muscle in my body stiffens. I know what he's going to say before he says it.

'It's Catrin. Catrin Morgan. I'm so sorry.'

All the air flees the church in one singular motion. I thrust to my feet, tearing my hands free of the sisters on either side. My fingers curl into fists, if only to hide the way they tremble.

Across the church, Dylan shoves to his feet and howls. I can't piece together his words – only that they're thick with grief and anger.

'No.' I shake my head. 'No, it isn't. It isn't Catrin, because we're not feeding *any* of the women on this island to the sea.'

'Guinevere,' Mr Meyrick pleads. 'Lower your voice. He's listening.'

'Oh, is he?' A laugh tears out of me. I throw my arms wide. 'Well, how's this? *You're not having Catrin Morgan!*'

White light explodes through the room, like when Point Beacon ignites. The islanders shriek, jostling against one another as if they're expecting to be cut down where they stand. Trembling, Dylan sits back down. I try not to let my terror show.

'What was that?' Liliwen bleats.

I glance down, loath to tell her I do not know. The only explanation I can conjure is that it was a rogue lightning strike. Something only Llyr could concoct. My stomach churns; I feel my breaths coming faster, much as I try to control them.

'He's angry,' Taliesin whispers. 'And he won't calm until we agree to sate him.'

The Halenprophet's eyes lock to Catrin where she sits stiffly beside me. For the briefest second, he smiles. It's not an apologetic smile; it's a taunt.

Aledd steps forwards, his hateful little face screwed up in an approximation of pity. 'Catrin will be treated with the utmost care, leading up to her sacrifice on the solstice, when the veil between us and the Gods is thinnest . . .'

'Are you mad?' I shout, my eyes volleying across the crowd. 'You're not having her.'

'Please, Guinevere.' Taliesin braids his hands together. 'Don't make this any harder than it needs to be.'

'It's a false solution!' I shout. 'You think Llyr is going to take one woman and be satisfied? No. It's going to be just like it was back then – a woman sacrificed every six months like clockwork.'

I turn my eyes to islanders cowering in the pew around me. 'That's *you*. Your daughters, your wives, your mothers. Are you prepared to open that floodgate?'

'Without sacrifice, tidewraiths will overrun this island . . .'

'Then build another lighthouse!' I throw up my arms. 'Get me a new lens for the lantern room, and new windows so the light can shine brighter.'

'Llyr has made himself clear,' Halenprophet Taliesin says, flinching as he invokes our God's name. 'He wants a Salt Queen, or we will revert to being a Godless island once more.'

I turn again to the congregation. 'Does that sound like love to you? A God who demands women's blood, else he'll leave us to the wraiths?'

They blink up at me with wet eyes, trembling lips. Not one of them stands in my defence – *Cat's* defence. Not even Osian. I stare at him across the pews, willing him to intervene. He casts his eyes to his lap.

'We're leaving,' I announce.

I hear Ffion and Lili push to their feet beside me. Cat remains seated, her body frozen like that of a prey animal.

'Get up,' I whisper.

Catrin blinks at me, her eyes wide.

'I said *get up*.'

Cat staggers to her feet. I grip her elbow tight enough that she begins to whimper. Breathing hard, I lead her out of the pew, the sisters trailing behind.

I turn to the congregation again. 'Now, we're going to leave, and no one's going to follow us. Tomorrow, once you've all slept on it and realised how fucking *monstrous* this idea is, we can put all it behind us.'

A hundred pairs of eyes stare back at me, unblinking. From his position at the lectern, Taliesin cracks his knuckles. I rest a hand on the church door handle. The metal grows clammy beneath my hands.

Breath straining against my lungs, I push the door open. Outside, a wall of tidewardens ready their rifles. I falter, stuck between the fear of the islanders and the intent of the tidewardens beyond.

I glance over my shoulder at Taliesin. He smiles softly, looks to his congregation, and whispers, '*Get them.*'

There is an explosion of movement – islanders flinging from their pews, grasping at Catrin, and, by extension, *me*. Dylan tries desperately to stem the tide, but it's futile. His silver-rimmed spectacles are crushed underfoot as the congregation surges towards us. They're pulling at her hair. Her clothes. Fabric snags and tears. Her pale skin is exposed.

The sisters worm in between hungry, snatching hands. The appearance of them flanking Catrin – their haunting cohesion – stymies the crowd, but not long enough. Ffion alternates between jabbing at people with her elbows and trying desperately to reason with them; Liliwen is howling. None of it is enough to stop them wrenching Cat's hair from her head.

Outside the church, the tidewardens are closing in. We're fucked either way.

There is a thunderous snap, and for a moment, I think lightning has struck. That Llyr, God of Sea and Storms, is making himself known the only way he can. The crowd snaps to attention, retracting and gasping at once. I look over their heads to see the smoking barrel of a rifle pointing directly at one of the church's windows, wielded by Osian's firm hands. All the glass is blown out. I've watched him use the same gun to defend his sheep from hungry hounds a hundred times. Our eyes connect – the sliver of his pupil meeting the saucer of mine.

*Run,* he mouths.

Without pausing to thank him, I do.

I take Catrin by the elbow. Yank her free of the grabbing hands, even though I know it must hurt. I *feel,* but do not see, the sisters behind us. We vault through the now vacant window, shards of glass crunching underfoot. I'm running blindly through the graveyard, then beyond its bounds, heading for nowhere other than *away* – but if I'm to keep Cat safe, I need to think.

There's only one place on this island where I can protect her. A stronghold with a fortified door and reinforced windows, designed to weather the worst storms.

We leave the path, cutting straight across the heath. The noise of the crowd surges then fades, whipped away by the wind that blasts across the heathland. Spiny gorse and matted heather whip past, snaring our feet and arms. Point Beacon rises in the distance.

A glance across my shoulder paints a ghastly tableau. Catrin's white-knuckled hand anchored to mine; the sisters strewn out behind her, as if they are a kite, and I'm the flyer; the swarm of islanders intent on stopping us. Intent on crowning Catrin. The tidewardens are the navy cap of their wave, flintlock rifles kicking back against their shoulders. Bullets whistle past, never striking true, but threatening.

'What the fuck are they doing?' I shout back. 'They're going to kill us all!'

'Less shouting,' Ffion pants. 'More running.'

Point Beacon towers before us, proud and tall. The lighthouse door swings open without my provocation. We file through, throwing ourselves across the threshold. The fortified door slams shut behind us, violent enough that the walls shake.

The sudden, portentous silence is only permeated by our ragged breaths. I count them, the same way I did the night Rhian died. It's the only semblance of control I have. One, two, three . . .

Fists slam against the door. The metal rattles, hinges vibrating. I throw my weight against it, as if that alone will stop the mob outside. The pounding continues, growing fiercer, more layered. And then, loud enough that my hands fly to cover my ears, a glottal moan cuts through the noise. It comes from Point Beacon itself – ancient mortar shifting, metal distorting.

The banging stops. The lighthouse falls silent.

Ffion's pupils are narrow pinpricks. Catrin and Lili are pressed so tightly against the wall I think it might absorb them. I push to my feet, fingers tightening instinctively around the bolts in the lighthouse door. My ankles shake as I prop myself onto tiptoes, eyes focusing through the tiny porthole. The crowd's still there, but they're utterly still. Their faces are tilted upwards – not focused on us, but the lighthouse itself.

Again, Point Beacon groans. It's not unusual for the lighthouse to make odd sounds – I've grown up with its night-time mutterings as a lullaby. But this is different. The islanders sense it, too. I pick out individuals amidst the crowd: Arthur Vaughan, whose face is pale, totally absent of its usually ruddy flush; Mrs Llywelyn, who stands away from the crowd at large, her grey brows pitched together; Mr Meyrick, who takes off his cap and clutches it to his chest.

I'm not sure if it's reverence or terror that widens their eyes, sucks the blood from their faces. A gale whips through their ranks. Miss Davies from the dairy over by the bluffs barely reacts as it lifts her skirts up to her knees, and the Blayneys' youngest boy doesn't even flinch as it lifts the cap from his head and whisks it off across the heath.

Their retreat begins as a trickle: Mrs Llywelyn tiptoeing away, as if trying to avoid the attention of a particularly vicious dog. Arthur Vaughan follows her, and then the rest of the Vaughan brood. The Griffiths go next, then the Bennions with their litter of children, then the ageing Williams.

Eventually, all that's left is a handful of men. Tidewardens. A prick of white stands amidst their sea of navy. Halenprophet Taliesin.

My fingers tighten around the bolts, blood draining from my knuckles. I feel the reverberations of Point Beacon's voice – a howl transmitted through the bricks, the metal beneath my hands. The tidewardens turn paler still.

All at once, they turn and walk back the way they came.

# CHAPTER 9

*Manon Wyn coaxed the defunct lighthouse back to life. She discovered that its beam staved off tidewraiths. After a period of unrest, the tradition of crowning a Salt Queen was abolished. Her descendants tend the beacon, a purpose they will fulfill indefinitely.*

—Excerpt from 'The History of Point Beacon', an unpublished novel penned by Rhian Wyn

'Did – did the *lighthouse* just save our skin?'

Ffion looks between us incredulously. Point Beacon's groaning is the least of my concerns.

'It sounded like a monster,' Lili murmurs.

I say, 'It's just Point Beacon's old bones.'

That's what Rhian used to tell me when I first moved here. The lighthouse's incessant sighing used to keep me awake. She said, 'If you're not scared of my old bones creaking when I get up from the dinner table, you shouldn't be scared of Point Beacon's, neither.' But the islanders haven't slept in its confines, and don't know how the lighthouse likes to grumble. I lay a palm against the bricks and convey my gratitude for its good timing.

'Shook them up well enough,' Ffion says. 'Now, if only we could train it to do that next time . . .'

Her voice trails off like a petering gale. Next time. Because there *will* be a next time, and we all know it. They're not going to stop here. They will stop at nothing to get Cat. That knowledge lingers between us, and none of us dare address it.

'They want to kill you.' Liliwen stares at Catrin with round, glassy eyes. 'To string you up and let the ocean take you.'

Cat purses her lips. 'Thanks for that reminder, Lil.' She appears no more affected than on a typical day, her pale skin the same shade as ever. How can she seem unmoved when I feel as if my world is tilting on its axis?

'I can't believe that just happened,' Ffion says, her lower lip trembling. She jerks her finger towards the door. 'I mean – we grew up with those people. They *know* us. How could they disown Cat so readily?'

Cat shrugs her shoulders. 'Fear'll do that.'

'I've been scared before, but I'd never do that,' I mutter.

She finds my gaze and holds. 'You're only saying that because it's me.'

'I don't want them to hurt you,' Lili whispers.

'I don't much fancy being hurt either,' Cat snaps.

Liliwen begins to whimper softly. Percy, despite typically being averse to noise of any description, comes trotting out from the kitchen and settles himself in the cradle of her lap. It doesn't stop her, but it gives her something to do with her hands. She strokes the length of his back.

Unable to process the scale of what just happened, I set about preparing the lighthouse. There's a fire in the range I know I did not light. It must've been Point Beacon. I've never understood the lighthouse's near-sentience – its ability to predict and respond to my needs – but today, I appreciate it more than ever. I pat the chimney breast affectionately and place a pot on the hotplate. Yesterday morning, I made enough lamb and potato *cawl* to last me all week. It should make a fine enough lunch for the four of us.

The place always felt fit to burst even when it was just me and Rhian. Point Beacon has two small bedrooms. Mine has the best view: a tableau of the beach, which is either haunting or idyllic depending on which day you catch it. Still, I resolve to give that view over to the other girls, moving myself into Rhian's room. The thought of someone else sleeping in her bed, touching her things, rearranging her wardrobe – it makes my chest tighten.

I gather my few possessions: clothes, books, and the stuffed humpback whale Rhian gave me when I first arrived at the lighthouse, imaginatively named Whaley. The girls have moved to the kitchen now, and as such my shameful clinging to childhood relics remains a secret. When I throw my effects onto the bed in Rhian's room, I fail to notice that Persnickety has extricated himself from Liliwen, and is now napping on top of the quilt. He yowls, indignant.

'The sisters'll be staying,' I tell him. 'Try to make a good impression.'

Percy manages to scowl, despite having no eyebrows. He rearranges himself on top of my clothes, kneading the fabric furiously. I tuck Whaley underneath the pillows.

'What are you hiding?'

Cat stands with one shoulder braced against the door frame, a lazy smile at her lips. She's so at ease, as if we've returned from a day at the beach, not her near sacrifice.

'Nothing,' I mutter.

She brushes past me, rummaging beneath the pillow. Cat grabs and cradles Whaley with all the tenderness of a mother. 'You stuffed him under a pillow!'

I snatch Whaley back from her. 'How do you know it's a he?'

'Isn't it?'

'Well, yes, but . . .'

'How long have we been friends now?' She briefly considers her own question before settling on, 'Too many years. And you've hidden him from me all this time!' The amusement drops from her face. She cocks her head and asks, 'What else have you been hiding?'

'I'm not *hiding* anything,' I mutter, placing Whaley back on the bed. Visible, this time. Persnickety sniffs at him disdainfully. To hide my embarrassment, I give myself the task of sorting through Rhian's clothes, searching for things that'll fit each of the girls. 'And I see no sense in talking about my stuffed whale when you're facing death, Catrin.'

'Don't use my full name.' She yawns, cat-like, canines flashing. 'It makes me feel like I'm in trouble.'

Sometimes, Cat is so brutally open that I wish she'd keep some things to herself. Other times – like now – she snaps shut firmer than a mussel's shell; trying to extricate anything real becomes painful, and leaves us both frustrated. I pull dresses from their hangers with more force than necessary.

'Come on,' I groan. 'Give me something to work with.'

'Oh, sorry.' She huffs out a breath and flops down onto the bed. 'Next time I'm condemned to death, I'll consult you about how I should behave in the aftermath.'

'There are good people on this island.' On reflection, I add, 'Some of them, at least. If we can just get through to them, I'm sure we can . . .'

'Did any of those "good people" actually *do* anything when the Halenprophet suggested drowning me?'

'Your father did,' I say quietly. 'And Osian.'

Cat kicks her legs against the side of the bed frame. 'Oh, your darling Osian. Sorry, Guin, but I don't think he's going to make much of a difference when everyone else on this island wants me dead.'

I stare back at her, not rising to the bait. She's always trying to provoke me into defending Osian.

'You of all people should know it was only a matter of time before something like this happened,' she mutters.

The muscles in my shoulders tighten. I think of Rhian's warning. 'What's that supposed to mean?'

'Aledd fucking Williams,' she says. 'He killed your mother.'

'I know.' The words come out blunt, forced through gritted teeth. 'Where are you going with this?'

'He *killed* her, whether you believe it was an accident or not, and where were the consequences? He was Halenprophet Lewys's favourite tidewarden. A holy man, by all accounts.' Cat bounces her leg restlessly. 'He comes to church every Sunday, stands there in his finest. Your mother was collateral damage. The same old shit plays out over and over.'

I clear my throat, wondering which way I can respond that'll leave her suitably vindicated. I've spent long enough stewing on the injustice of what happened to my mother. Most days, I can say I've reached a point of acceptance – except for when I see Aledd's hateful face and want to drive my thumbs into his eyeballs.

'It's the way Ynys Halen is,' I say.

'That's exactly what I mean!' She thrusts to her feet, pacing back and forth. 'Men are presumed innocent at all costs. Women are learning opportunities for them – dolls to use and abuse and discard and then . . . *oh*, don't worry, it was just a mistake!' Cat runs a hand through her hair. 'What I'm saying is that the precedent is already set for this, Guin. Women are disposable here. If you think it's a surprise that they're willing to sacrifice me, you've not been paying enough attention.'

Shame sits heavy as a bowl of Rhian's rock-hard porridge in my stomach. My shoulders sag. When Cat looks at me, she must see something worth empathy, because her expression softens a fraction.

'It's written into our scripture, for God's sake,' she murmurs. 'Bronwen's death as a footnote in Llyr's story. This island's been rotten from the start. Anyway,' Cat huffs a humourless laugh. 'I've always felt that my life was destined to end in sacrifice.'

I flash her a scathing look. 'As if I'm going to let that happen.'

'It wouldn't be the worst thing in the world,' she muses. 'At least things would get back to normal.'

I swear she says things just to provoke me. It's as if she wants to see how far she can push before I snap. 'You're *so* right, Cat. It'd be totally normal, except you'd be dead. There'd be water in your lungs, and salt in your eyes, and the tidewraiths would take anything the sharks didn't.'

I throw the piles of clothes onto the bed, narrowly missing Percy, who screeches off into the hallway, pissed as ever.

'You take everything so seriously.' The bed whines as Cat shifts her weight. She gestures for me to sit, and I can't be bothered to deny her. Cat's hands find mine, braiding our fingers together. 'Are you scared? Is that what this is?'

The question hits me straight in the chest. 'It's not about me. It's about *you*, Cat.'

'I'm not worried.' She shrugs her shoulders, our bare arms grazing. I wonder if she's as aware of that as I am. 'Really, I'm not. There's no one else I would trust to keep me safe.'

'So that's my job now, is it?'

'We're dissimilar in a lot of ways, but I know there's one thing we have in common. We'd both bleed to keep the people we love safe.'

*Love.* To me, that word is a tidal wave. It's so loaded. So meaningful. Cat throws it around like any other verb. To like, to enjoy, to love – it's all the same to her. On my sixteenth birthday, she told me she loved me, and it robbed the breath from my chest. Then I overheard her tell another girl she loved her, too, and I realised that Cat and I don't love in the same way.

Maybe my understanding of love isn't really love, either. A chimeric beast of worship and obsession and tenderness and frustration and lust.

'What if they come to take you?' My voice breaks. The tears I've been trying to suppress pound against my eyes. 'There are only four of us. What if we can't stop them?'

Her eyes soften from ice to warm water. She squeezes my hand. 'Ffion got into a fight with a man twice her size when he tried to steal a book from the library. She won. Liliwen poisoned a boy in her class so expertly that he died in his sleep and never showed a single symptom.'

My eyebrows shoot up at that. I can't imagine soft-faced Lili intentionally harming a *fly*, let alone a boy.

'Okay, well the story about Liliwen is hearsay.' Catrin laughs, eyes sparkling. This is when I love her most. She's so beautiful it makes my teeth hurt, like keeping honey in your mouth too long. 'But you, Guin, are the strongest of all.'

'The kerosene tanks aren't even that heavy,' I protest. 'And anyone could haul sailors out of the shallows. Once you get the knack, it's . . .'

'Living on a cliff edge and dragging bodies from the sea isn't the only way to be strong, Guin,' she says, exasperation lingering at her brow. 'I mean internal strength. Life dealt you a rough hand. I mean, your mother, and then your grandmother. But you persisted. You're still here. You've never let it rot you.'

I'm not so sure about that. On the cusp of sleep, I often daydream about snuffing out Aledd's life. Instead of counting sheep, I imagine myself lodging a blade in his chest over and over.

I wave Catrin off. 'You're going to make me big-headed.'

'Let me compliment you.' A wicked smile curves her lips. 'It's my final wish.'

'Not funny.'

She uses her free hand to press my nose up into a snout. I choke out a laugh, swatting her away.

Her walls are coming back up – any softness, any vulnerability, covered and sealed off. I need to impart the dire reality of our situation as well as I can before she shuts down completely.

'We can't live like this for ever. Cooped up in the lighthouse, the islanders baying for your blood.'

Cat flops back onto the bed. 'The Halenprophet said I'd be

sacrificed on the solstice, when the veil between our world and the Gods' is at its thinnest. That's in two months, and change.'

'And?'

'If we can resist that long, maybe they'll pick another girl,' she says darkly.

It reminds me of an argument I once had with Rhian. She taught me self-defence so I would not meet the same end as my mother. She said I had to be faster, scrappier, than the other girls. In learning to defend myself, all I was really ensuring was that men with bad intentions would choose another girl.

'*Or*, if the solstice comes and goes without sacrifice, the islanders will see the Halenprophet for the fraud he is,' I mutter.

'How do you know he's a fraud?' Cat asks.

'Because Llyr would never threaten to abandon us. We're all he has.'

Whatever paltry worship we have to offer is the most Llyr can hope for. What would he do otherwise – go to the mainland, which is already bloated with Gods? Find a foreign land where no one has ever heard of his name or his sacrifice?

'What if the Halenprophet is telling the truth? What if Llyr *does* abandon us?'

I shrug. 'If the cost of Ynys Halen existing is placating a bloodthirsty, misogynistic God, then let it drown.'

Point Beacon quakes. A painting falls from the wall, clattering to the flagstones.

There's a knot in my stomach I can't untangle. Sitting with the reality of what we're facing, bile singes the base of my throat. Silence winds its way between us, thick and heavy.

Eventually, Catrin says, 'We should go and live on the mainland once this is over.'

I glance over at her, half-expecting to see a teasing expression – but she's sincere. She studies me intently, eyes flitting across my face.

Sometimes, in the bleak hours of the morning when I'm hand-cranking the tank of a decrepit lighthouse to stave off horrors untold, I wish I'd been born on the mainland. It's one of my guiltiest perversions – praying I could extricate myself from this life, this *duty* that has been imposed upon me. Rhian bore the weight with pride.

'You and me,' she breathes. 'Can you imagine it? We'd have a little cottage somewhere in the woods. A donkey, a handful of chickens, and some goats.'

'You'd really do that?'

She exhales, stirring the scent of her own perfume. 'With you, I would. There's few things I wouldn't do with you, Guin.'

It knocks the breath clean from my lungs. Cat's drawing little circles on the quilt, utterly oblivious to the fact that what she's just told me is the most intimate thing I've ever heard.

# CHAPTER 10

*Point Beacon has marked Ynys Halen's coast for centuries. In former times, it alerted passing cargo ships to the coastline. Shipping routes no longer pass Ynys Halen, save for those which go directly to the dock on the island's northern side. Some allege this is due to the fear of tidewraiths.*

—Excerpt from 'Maritime Ynys Halen'

By the time we've heated up the leftover *cawl*, the sun has dropped behind the mainland. It casts the ocean in a strange, pink light. Ffion pilfers a bottle of whiskey Rhian had hidden in the pantry.

Once the dark outside grows truly suffocating, Ffion and Lili take to fighting over the other bedroom with great vigour. It's implicitly understood that Cat and I will share. She doesn't mind that I'll be a poor bed mate, what with needing to rouse every two hours to hand-crank the tank.

Liliwen pouts so badly at the prospect of sharing a room with

Ffion that we eventually clear out one of the storage cupboards and make a bed out of old pallets and blankets. It reeks of paint and the metallic tang of cleaning supplies, but Lili says it's preferable to withstanding Ffion's snoring.

Once the others are settled, Cat and I retreat to Rhian's bedroom. We haven't slept in the same bed – just us two – for years, but it's comfortable as anything, like slipping into a well-loved jumper as summer draws to a close. I lie with my back to her, counting each of her breaths. She draws on my back with the tip of her finger. I did not ask her to, nor do I ask her to stop.

The night passes slowly, as it always does. My last sleep of the night is deathly deep. By the time I wake, sunlight filters through the window. Cat's space in the bed is cold and vacant. When I push out into the hallway, I notice the trapdoor in the middle of the floor has been propped open. We pulled the curtains closed on the windows last night, and despite the slowly rising sun, it's too dark to see well. My eyes strain against the darkness.

'Cat?' My voice echoes through the gloom.

There's a flurry of activity – the scraping of metal against wood, or something similarly grating. Footsteps scurry across the cellar, pausing at the bottom of the stairs. In that brief moment of quiet, an unsettling thought strikes me: what if it's *not* Cat? I'm not usually one to let fear fester like that, but since Rhian died, I've begun to imagine ghosts where there are none, monsters in shadowed spaces.

I rear back from the trapdoor. Footsteps pound up the stairs, so fierce I feel the wood must be splintering underfoot. Cat bursts from the opening, staggering up into the hallway.

'Guin,' she says, clutching her chest. 'You frightened me.'

'*You* frightened *me*,' I accuse. 'What're you doing messing around down there?'

She scowls, a divot appearing between her brows. 'Taking stock of our supplies. We ought to figure out how long we can survive without provisions from the village.'

A familiar smell hits me: the biting tang of kerosene. I wrinkle my nose. 'You didn't go in the back, did you?'

Cat looks at me strangely. It's the same expression I used to give Rhian when I felt she was asking too many questions. 'No, *Guinevere*, I didn't go in the back.'

I groan. 'Don't call me Guinevere.'

'Well, don't be so stifling,' she says.

The trapdoor snaps shut behind her without provocation. She leaps as if scalded, nearly knocking me to the floor.

'That's Point Beacon telling you to be nicer,' I say drily. 'I'd listen, if I were you.'

'I'm *very* nice,' she insists. 'So nice that I've made my ungrateful friend griddle cakes for breakfast.'

I follow her into the kitchen, where Ffion and Lili are sat at the table, the image of a contented family. Percy blinks up at me from Liliwen's lap. Suck-up.

Cat tends to the pan. Based on the smell, I'm almost certain the hotcakes have begun to burn, but I don't mention it.

Ffion asks, 'Did you light the fire this morning?'

'No,' I admit. 'The lighthouse does that sometimes.'

Ffion's brow furrows. 'You talk about it like it's alive.'

'It is,' Cat interrupts, talking around a mouthful of hotcake. 'Tell them what it does, Guin.'

The other sisters look at me like I'm mad. Maybe I am. I push dried currants around my plate as I tell them about the lighthouse's quirks: doors opening without me needing to push them, fires lighting themselves, hot baths drawn after storms. Even Liliwen looks unconvinced. You know it's bad when lover of whimsy, believer of superstition, will-agree-just-to-save-you-looking-stupid Liliwen pulls a face.

'It must just be a combination of wonky plumbing and … strong winds, or something,' I mumble.

Admitting what I truly believe – that there is a spirit inside this lighthouse – seems a bad way to build their trust in me. I don't mean a spirit in the 'translucent, hovering three feet above ground' sense, though we've plenty of those on the island if old wives' tales are to be believed. It's more that I think this lighthouse has a … a *soul*, or whatever it is that grants us sentience. My lighthouse is a beast of its own.

'And here I was, thinking Lili was the batty one,' Ffion mutters.

She doesn't know the half of it. I talk to the lighthouse sometimes, too. The only response I get is the creak of a door, or the sputtering of flames in the range, but it's nice to feel heard. Rhian used to do the same. She pretended she didn't. Laughed at me for daring to think this place had a heart. But sometimes, when she went to fetch kerosene from the basement – the one place she had any semblance of privacy – I'd hear the muffled chorus of her whispers from behind the trapdoor.

I thought she was a mad old cow until I started talking to the lighthouse as well. By the end, we were both as bad as each other. God, I miss her.

'What's the plan for today?' Liliwen asks, holding up her plate for Cat to deposit hotcakes onto.

Only when silence falls do I realise she was asking *me*. Cat looks expectantly over her shoulder. Our conversation from last night is still fresh as a daisy in my mind. I want her to trust that I can keep her safe. That I can keep us *all* safe.

'The lighthouse is fairly well fortified, but it could do with some reinforcements.' Suddenly, the glass expanse of the kitchen window – the view I've spent years enjoying – looks awfully vulnerable. 'Maybe we could put slats across the windows. Just in case.'

Liliwen pales. 'You think they'll break the windows to get to Cat?'

'Better to be safe than sorry,' Ffion says, spearing a clump of food from Lili's plate.

I gesture to Cat with my fork. 'How's the pantry looking?'

She looks at me blankly.

'Will it last until the solstice?' I elaborate.

Cat exhales noisily through her nose. 'Absolutely not. I wish you'd kept fuller cupboards.'

Ffion cocks her head. 'The solstice?'

Cat explains her theory absentmindedly, shifting hotcakes around the pan with fluid motions of her wrist. Either we pass the solstice with Cat intact and find the Halenprophet to be a liar, at which point the islanders will – presumably – realise the error of their ways, or Llyr *does* abandon us, and we'll have no use for food what with our demise at the tidewraiths' hands.

Ffion takes to the concept of fortifying the lighthouse like an albatross to a sea breeze. She's read *hundreds* of books with predicaments like this, she tells us. A scrap piece of parchment serves as the blueprint for her machinations: a meticulous arrangement of trip wires, broken glass installed along each windowsill, a configuration of wooden slats across the glass which will allow light in but keep people *out*.

She digs a pitfall trap in the front garden, which I think probably isn't the best idea, but don't dare tell her that on account of her frenzy. Once that's done, she starts cutting pieces of scrap wood, hoarded by Rhian over the years, to the correct length for each of the windows.

Unwilling to intrude on Ffion's feverish efforts, the sisters look for other ways to keep busy. Liliwen joins me in the lighthouse's wind-battered garden. Rhian liked us to be self-sufficient, at least to a degree, but I've let the vegetable beds fall into disrepair since she died. If I'd known what was yet to come, I might've forced myself to develop a green thumb.

Fortunately, Lili has more of a knack for it than I do. She sets to weeding, pruning and watering the tattered remnants of Rhian's efforts: waxy broad beans, prickly gooseberries, leafy new potatoes. In the shed, she finds tubers and seeds Rhian had the good sense to store. Most won't sprout until after the solstice, but neither Lili nor I address it. Better to be safe than sorry, I suppose.

Suppertime brings an uncomfortable realisation: even if our crops are successful, we won't be eating decadently for a while. Cat whips up a decent enough *cawl* with hunks of carrot and potato, but it's not rich like one made with lamb or beef. Particularly when the potatoes are still partially crunchy.

'If I'd known I'd had my last oggie yesterday, I might've savoured it more,' Ffion laments.

There's a woman who sells oggies down on the harbour every Sunday. I can just about smell the buttery pastry – can almost *taste* the lamb and leek mixture stuffed into each crescent-moon casing. My stomach rumbles at the thought.

'At least we've got the ocean at our fronts,' I suggest. 'Nature's pantry.'

'If the tidewardens had no luck with their ships, I doubt we'll fare any better,' Cat says.

My defiant spirit forces me out onto the shore at first light. Cat protests my leaving – I'm only in bed for two hours at a time, and I'm not sure what she resents more: my absence, or my constant coming and going – but I'm too restless to stay still any longer. I take Rhian's old rod down to the shore and cast it wide, a scrap of bread hanging from the hook.

I stand there for long enough that my fingers go numb. Nothing bites.

Eventually, Lili comes out to join me. The sisters always have this strange look on their faces – the same one they wore the day I met them, as if they've not long stopped crying. It's emphasised on Lili's face today. Her eyes are red, her lips swollen.

She stands just short of me, scuffing the sand with the toe of her boots. I know she's scared, and I know there's something I should say in this moment – something elder-sisterly, tender and wise. I've never been good at all that, though. Rhian wasn't either. I remember one time I came home crying after some boy had kissed me as a dare, and Rhian stared at me like I was a riddle she didn't know how to solve. She took me up into the watchtower and asked for my help repairing one of the panels.

'Here.' I hand Lili a penknife tucked into a loop on my belt. I rarely come down to the beach without one; you never know when you'll need a sharp edge. 'Scrape some cockles from the rocks, would you? We can have them for breakfast.'

Lili looks briefly disappointed but sets to prising the hard-shelled critters from their perches. She stuffs them into the pockets of her dress, which probably isn't the most hygienic solution, but I don't dare mention it.

As the tide rolls in, it deposits all manner of detritus. We always get various sorts of odd sea creatures washing up on Sawtooth. Flat-backed rays which soon get picked apart by gulls; small, mottled catsharks; bizarre, misshapen critters whose gills were the only thing that enabled me to identify them as fish, which Rhian said must've come from the 'dark deep'.

The strangest was a minke whale which stranded itself on the beach. All the islanders came down to try to push it back in the water, but it died before we could get it there. Not wanting its life to be in vain, some sought to butcher and eat it – but it was an awfully hot summer, and the meat rotted before anyone could taste it. Over the course of a week, it baked beneath the sun, its belly filling with gas – until suddenly, one Wednesday morning, it blew up and blasted the side of Point Beacon in offal. Percy *loved it.*

This morning, there's a whole bunch of jellies. If the ocean wished to showcase its abundance, I wish it would do so with something edible. There are milk-white moon jellyfish, barrel jellies with their mushroom-shaped bells. There's also an outlier – a creature with a translucent purple sail attached to a gas-filled body and long, wrinkled tentacles.

'What is that?' Lili asks, nose wrinkled as she nudges the creature with her boot.

'It's a man o'war.'

'That's a funny name for a jellyfish.'

'It's not technically a jellyfish,' I tell her.

She frowns. 'What is it, then?'

'It's called a siphonophore.' At the deepening of her frown, I elaborate, 'It's not *one* organism, but several. A colony.'

'Aw.' She smiles. 'Are they friends?'

I want to wrap her up in wool and keep her safe for ever. I'm simultaneously struck by the urge to smack her across the face and tell her to grow up. 'Uh . . . it's sort of like a factory. They all have their own role. You know – hunting, reproduction, digestion.'

Lili has already moved on, picking pink shells from the shore.

The weather takes a turn for the better – winds dropping to nothing, sun beating down. We spend the next days sat on the widow's walk, legs dangling over the edge. Ffion finds a battered palette of watercolours, shipped from the mainland at great expense – a present from Rhian for my birthday one year. We take turns painting on pages torn from moth-eaten books, much to Ffion's dismay. I hang our art on the kitchen walls.

One afternoon, Ffion reads our palms – an art she apparently perfected having read a single book on the topic. Lili braids our hair into increasingly intricate styles. Cat sings while we listen in hushed reverence. I explain how to tell an auk from a puffin, a Manx shearwater from a guillemot, a harbour porpoise from a common dolphin.

We take our meals on the widow's walk, too, chatting as we survey the heathland for any sign of life. Our pantry's essentially bare, but the island provides. Catrin scrapes whelks and cockles from the rocks; Liliwen gathers armfuls of antlered pepper dulse before it dries out in the sun; Ffion picks golden sea buckthorn berries, vibrant as jewels. Percy, in a rare act of self-preservation, catches his own dinners: mice and rats, whose guts he deigns to leave outside my bedroom door so they squelch between my toes when I go to hand-crank the tank.

There's a gentle camaraderie to our routine. I wish we'd found this rhythm in better times. Why didn't I invite them all to move in after Rhian passed? We could've had all this without death breathing down our necks, even if only for a matter of weeks.

One evening, we sit on the widow's walk, plates of laverbread and cockles braced against our bare thighs.

'This might not be so bad,' Ffion says, between a mouthful of food. 'We're pretty good at this survival thing, aren't we?'

'Oh, for fuck's sake, Ffion!' Cat shouts at the same time as I mutter, 'Don't bloody jinx it,' while Lili bows her head into her hands.

'Why would you say that?' Cat smacks her fork against the railings. 'You know you're tempting fate, don't you?'

Ffion's jinx hangs like a cloud above us. It bursts the next morning.

I'm knelt in the front garden with dirt up to my wrists, wrestling with a particularly stubborn dandelion, when I see them. The two walk in single file, ants in a procession. I'm not surprised, really. If anything, I'm *offended.* They think we pose so little threat that two tidewardens will wrangle us into submission.

As they near the lighthouse, I recognise their faces. I'm compelled to shove to my feet. Arthur Vaughan has eyes like a shark – dead and black. There's an unhealthy, ruddy sheen to his skin, and he walks like he's trying to keep something pinned between his legs. Beside him is Gethin Thomas – the boy I had a fling with several years ago. He's tall and thin, like a razor clam.

I brush myself off, trowel clutched between my fingers. The men's eyes linger on it as they walk the stone path to the lighthouse. They ease open the garden gate without invitation.

'Gethin, if you've come with hopes of rekindling our relationship, I'll need to stop you there,' I say drily.

'I'm here on rather more pertinent matters,' Gethin says. A flush creeps up his throat. 'Bring out Catrin, and we'll be on our way.'

'She always hated you.' I let out a breath. 'I can see why, now.'

'Oh, you wound me,' Gethin mutters. 'Come on, now. Go and fetch her.'

'Of course!' I smile, feet rooted to the spot.

They either do not read my sarcasm, or do not care to react. There's only two of them, but I'm vitally aware of how I'm outnumbered. Arthur's arms are thick with muscle, hewn from years out at sea; even lanky Gethin has grown broader. My own limbs feel like twigs in comparison. Snappable.

Gethin steps towards me. My subconscious drives me to hold the trowel in front of my body, as if it'll do any good should he decide to exercise his physicality against me. Still, isn't that the crux of being a woman? Always outmatched. Always pretending otherwise.

'I've got children now,' he mutters, voice dropped low enough that Arthur can't hear him.

I'm not sure what he intends to provoke in me – jealousy? 'Good for you.'

His eyes shutter. 'I'd tell my daughter the same as I'm telling you. Give us Cat. It's the best thing for you.' He blinks again. 'The best thing for *her*.'

'So if Halenprophet Taliesin stood up there and said your daughter was the one Llyr wanted, you'd be okay with that?' I sneer. 'You'd just hand her over, would you?'

He runs his tongue across paper-thin lips. 'If I knew it'd save my other girls, yes.'

'There's nothing quite like a father's love, is there?' I think of

Aledd, and how easily he transferred me to Rhian's care after Mother died. 'How is it that I care more for Catrin than you do for your own flesh and blood?'

Arthur and Gethin exchange a look, perhaps assessing the scale of the threat I present. A crow caws from the railings of the widow's walk. They eye it warily.

'And *you*,' I snap, pointing my trowel towards Arthur. 'Does your brother know this is what you've chosen to do today? Hunting down girls and trying to pull them from their homes?'

Arthur's forehead twitches. He mustn't be much older than twenty-five, but already his hairline has begun to pull back like the tide, leaving a shining expanse of forehead exposed to the sun, the skin red and tight.

'Osian's a shepherd,' he says. 'He knows better than anyone that a cull is sometimes necessary to protect the flock.'

I scoff. Last winter, I sat with Osian as he wept over the ewe he'd had to put down. It was diseased, and he'd spent the best part of the summer trying to cure it to no avail.

'Osian knows you try *everything* before you decide death is a fitting solution.'

'Well Osian's spending a little stint in the gaol along with Dylan Morgan to think about what he did, so his opinion is entirely irrelevant,' Arthur leers.

I shouldn't be surprised they imprisoned him – he was an accomplice in our escape. But guilt pulls at me nonetheless. I wonder if he still thinks it was worth it.

Father of the year takes another step forwards. I can't believe I ever let him touch me. 'Say your goodbyes. Make peace with it.'

'I've another idea – *you* can make peace with the idea of *this* in your gut,' I snarl, brandishing the comforting weight in my hand.

'You're going to stab us with a trowel?' Arthur grinds out a laugh. He always was a prick, even as a child. When I first arrived at Point Beacon, he used to send his dog after me each time I walked beside the Vaughans' fields. 'Oh, colour me scared.'

They close in. I try to stand my ground, but find myself stumbling backwards, pitiful. I ought to lure them into one of the pitfall traps, but I'm not sure how to manoeuvre myself. Sweat races to bead across my skin. How much damage am I going to be able to do before they attack me worse?

'Get the fuck out of here, you ghouls!'

Catrin stands silhouetted in Point Beacon's maw. The wind snatches at her hair, causing it to billow out around her in a cloud of onyx. She looks equal measures beautiful and terrifying, blue eyes sharpened to cut. In her arms, she cradles the flintlock rifle Rhian kept under her bed. The muscles in her forearms tense as she chambers a bullet.

'You touch a hair on her head, and I'll put a bullet straight through your eye.'

The hairs on my arms stand on end. Even when she's acting in my defence, my body reacts to her as a threat. Arthur and Gethin stutter out excuses. One reaches surreptitiously for his own rifle, but Cat's eagle eyes track every moment.

'I'll blow your hand off before you get the chance,' she snaps. 'Now get. *Out.*'

Arthur scoffs a laugh – but his hands shake at his sides. 'C'mon, Geth,' he drawls. 'We'll come back with reinforcements.'

Gethin looks at me, and his eyes turn almost tender. He must recall our tryst with more affection than I do.

'Don't let Cat drag you down with her,' he says, voice low.

My skin goes hot, and it feels like I've swallowed a fishhook that's dug in somewhere raw. They retreat down the path, not bothering to close the gate behind them. I glance back at Cat, and her eyes don't falter as she watches them leave across the heath.

*Don't let Cat drag you down with her.* The way it paints us makes me feel sick. As if she's a shark, and I'm the seal pinned between her teeth, too daft and too awed to realise what's going to happen next.

# CHAPTER II

*Do not whistle beside the ocean, for tidewraiths will mistake it as the call of their own and rise up onto the shore to claim your life.*

—Island superstition

The next days of our isolated existence excavate cracks in our foundations. Once the rebellion of what we're doing wears off, all that's left is the task of survival and the ever-looming threat of the Halenprophet. I have these vivid dreams where Taliesin is a giant, and he peels Point Beacon from the cliff the way I shuck whelks from the rocks. He pinches Catrin between his fingers, lifts her up to his mouth, and . . .

'I just want something *sweet*,' Liliwen moans from the kitchen.

She's been a pain in my backside all week. As the youngest sister, she's used to being perpetually spoiled, and takes the barren reality of our existence as a personal affront. There's food in the pantry, sure, but we must ration it. Meals are a matter of sustenance, not flavour or indulgence. She pouts something awful, and while she generally gets away with it because she's the baby, my patience is wearing thin. It cracks entirely when I catch her eating our only jar of honey with a hooked finger.

Cat, on the other hand, seems doggedly determined to ignore every facet of this new reality. She fixes the rips in my well-worn jumpers, sewing over the holes with embroidered wildflowers. I try – *God*, do I try – to engage her in a frank conversation about her condemnation, but she waves it off like the clouds of midges that congregate on the shore in summer.

'Let it go, Guin,' she mutters. 'Stop wasting time worrying. Everything will work out all right.'

I spend a lot of time on the widow's walk, watching the heath. I'm half-expecting a siege, but days tick by with nothing to report. At first, I think they've forgotten about us entirely – but then I realise I'm just not looking hard enough. A rustle in the heather; a head popping up from behind a boulder; a pair of binoculars pointing back from an upstairs window. The tidewardens are watching us. Biding their time.

One night, a fog drops across the island. I sit in the tower, propped up in the makeshift bed I've cobbled together. There's no sense going back downstairs to snatch a measly two hours of sleep – no matter how tempting the warm nook of Cat's body is. Out in the curling ribbons of grey mist, something stirs. I take up my binoculars and peer out into the haze, heart thudding fierce in my chest.

Someone's out there.

I hold my breath, keeping the binoculars as steady as my shaking hands will allow. Did I lock the front door? I *swear* I locked the front door, but now that I'm thinking about it, I don't know if I did. What if I left it unlocked, and whoever's waiting out in the mist need only depress the handle to slip inside? To take Cat?

A glance at the flame in the lantern room satisfies me that it won't snuff out in my absence. I take the one hundred and thirty-three steps two at a time, leaping down the last three. The front door is locked, just as I thought. It should be enough to reassure me, but curiosity forces my eyes up to the porthole window. There's a small light amidst the darkness, glowing like a hot coal. It moves closer, held at chest height. My grip on the door tightens.

Osian steps free of the fog, a torch held like a sword in front of his body. He wears a black woollen cloak, the hood pulled up. Curls of russet hair frame his face.

Hands trembling, I unlock the door. When I try to heave it open, it sticks, unwilling to budge.

I pause, my heart thumping from the descent. Surreptitiously, I whisper to the lighthouse, 'It's okay. It's just Osian.'

There is a groan from the lighthouse – the settling of ancient bricks and mortar. When I push my weight up against the door this time, it yawns open. I step out into the fog – even thicker than it looked from up in the watchtower. The door whines as I ease it shut behind me.

'Osian,' I hiss. 'They let you out of the gaol?'

He nods, hair bouncing around his face. 'Yes. Dylan's still in there.'

His throat bobs – a tic that grips him every time he's nervous. Osian committed a treasonous act when he helped us escape. I can't imagine the islanders, seized as they are by terror, would take kindly to his swift release.

'What was the price?'

Osian folds his arms across his chest, which draws my

attention to the way his buttons glint in the torchlight. I realise his cloak isn't black, but navy; that the buttons aren't horn, but salt.

I let out an incredulous breath. 'You're one of them.'

'In name only,' he argues. 'The Halenprophet said he'd release me and bring over new stock from the mainland if I agreed to join.'

'A few sheep and a key? That's all it took to forsake your lifelong oath to never join those – what was it you called them? – "self-important chauvinists"?'

'I'm still on your side,' Osian says. 'Just as I always have been. I could hardly help you from the gaol.'

'You're going to help us?'

His face twitches. 'I'm going to help *you*. I don't want you getting tangled up in all this, Guin.'

I stiffen. What is he suggesting – that I leave Cat to her death? Wash my hands of her? 'If you've not noticed, I'm already fairly enmeshed.'

Osian lets out a deep breath and wipes his hand across his face. 'It's not your job to keep her safe.'

It certainly doesn't feel that way. Just as Point Beacon has always been my duty, I've felt a responsibility to Cat since we first met. 'So you'll let an innocent woman die because a man tells you it's necessary?'

A flustered laugh bursts past Osian's lips. 'I mean, she's hardly innocent!'

Osian's not one for outbursts of emotion in any direction. His uncharacteristic incredulity makes heat flood my cheeks. My nails bite into the soft bed of my palm.

I square my shoulders, feeling an urgent need to defend Cat even in her absence. 'Oh, but you are? You, who pretended to be my friend only to turn around and join the very force you swore against?'

'I might've let you down, but she's not who you think she is, either.'

'Enlighten me, then,' I spit.

Osian's eyes dart nervously to the door behind me. He steps forwards, his voice lowered.

'Why do you think I've never pursued you?' he hisses. 'It was because of *her*. She threatened me. Said she'd lay down poison for my sheep and I'd never be able to prove it was her.'

The weight of his words almost forces bile up my throat. He's wanted to pursue me all this time, and *Cat* warned him off?

Trembling, I say, 'She wouldn't do that.'

Even as I speak the words, I'm not sure I believe them. Cat's as conniving as she is kind. But what drove her to see Osian off? Jealousy, because she hates it when my attention isn't on her – or jealousy because *she* wanted to be the one to pursue me?

'God.' Osian laughs bitterly, head in his hands. 'She's got her claws in you so deep you can't even see them anymore.'

Hurt booms inside me, though I can't pinpoint what pains me more: knowing Osian would have courted me, or not knowing why Cat put an end to it.

A metallic whine cuts through the air – Point Beacon's door swinging open. Fingers curl around my bare shoulder. I gasp, nearly spluttering on the cold air as it tunnels down my throat. I jerk forwards reflexively.

'It's just me, you daft girl,' comes Cat's sleepy voice. 'What are you doing out here?'

She peers around my body, one hand still splayed across my shoulder. I can sense the precise moment when her eyes land on

Osian; the sharp protrusion in his throat bobs, and Cat's body pulls taut behind me. Osian stares back, his eyes lighting up with each flash of the beacon.

'Osian,' Cat says, her voice almost a snarl. 'You look as skittish as your sheep. What brings you here?'

He exhales noisily – almost a laugh, but without any humour behind it. When he looks at Cat, his expression darkens. 'I'd best be going.'

And he does, vanishing into the fog without another word.

Cat pulls me into bed and curls her body around me. Her skin is hot and soft against mine – frigid to the touch, rough with the hairs the cold coaxed onto end. I tell her there's no sense me staying down here and interrupting her sleep, but she insists and I relent, as I always do.

'Just ten minutes,' she whispers. 'Until I fall asleep.'

I realise she's not asked me a single question about Osian, or what he wanted. Her disinterest is completely out of character. Whenever Cat sees me talking to someone outside the Coven, she picks over the details like a gull stripping bones clean. I thought she did it out of jealousy once, and I told her so. We didn't speak for a week after that.

Tentatively, I say, 'Aren't you going to ask what he wanted?'

She lets out a half-laugh half-sigh, as if the prospect of her being curious is ridiculous. 'What did he want?'

Maybe I'm being ungenerous. I suppose Cat has bigger things on her mind than Osian being here. It's not like the old days, where the biggest scandal in our small world was mine and Gethin's fling.

I run my fingers across the quilt. 'He said you warned him off me.'

Catrin's hot breath rushes up against my nape. I expect her to protest, or laugh it off, or give me the silent treatment the way she often does.

'Obviously,' she drawls. 'I want you all to myself.'

I'm struck by the violent urge to kiss her. I imagine our legs tangling together, our mouths finding each other in the darkness, our hearts beating in unison. A kiss whose meaning neither of us could misinterpret, because the hunger would speak for itself.

Before I can act on it, I sneak out of bed and annex myself to the watchtower. As the beam swings around, I wonder why her threatening Osian's sheep isn't enough to make me stop obsessing over her.

'Ffion! Guin!'

It's barely first light when Liliwen's wavering scream rattles from the hallway below. I bolt down the stairs, heart punching in my chest. Lili stands in the hall, blue eyes drawn wide, lip quivering, and the door . . .

The door is open.

Dressed in tidewarden garb, Arthur and Gethin push through, rifles lowered. At the shock on my face, the sheer *panic* on Liliwen's, they begin rattling out assurances.

'We only need Catrin,' Gethin says.

Arthur nods doggedly. 'Give her up, and we'll leave you alone.'

'Give her up?' I practically spit the words at them. 'Over my dead body.'

Arthur looks me up and down, lip held in a sneer. 'Hopefully it won't come to that.'

'Is that a threat?' I snarl. 'You trespass in *my* home and try to threaten *me*?'

'There's no need for all this,' Gethin assures, as if I'm being unreasonable. I wonder if they'd take so kindly to two men storming *their* home. 'We'll take her nice and easy.'

Ffion's voice is calm and clear when she says, 'You won't take her at all.'

She stands silhouetted in the doorway to my old bedroom, a blade poised between her trembling fingers – one of my myriad penknives, left on the nightstand. She gestures for Lili to come to her, which she does, darting away from the men like a tiddler in a rock pool.

The sounds of Catrin stirring leak through the ajar bedroom door: the soft pop of her joints as she stretches, the rustling of the quilt, then the sudden still when she hears the additional voices out in the hall. *Stay in there,* I think, hoping that if I do it desperately enough, she'll hear me. *Stay quiet. Stay still.*

But then she's padding across the room, her bare feet on the tiles. Arthur and Gethin glance at one another, something like triumph sparking in their eyes. Cat eases the door open wider. Arthur and Gethin's gazes slide to the right, landing directly on her.

'Cat,' I say, my voice low, 'go up to the watch room.' That puts the most distance between her and our assailants.

Her hurried breaths whisk across my cheek as she slinks past me. Each of her movements is slow and deliberate. Without turning her back on the watchers, she grabs the handrail, guiding one foot backwards until it meets the first step.

'Up the stairs, Lil,' Ffion says, her voice level.

Liliwen follows Cat. Ffion and I stand at the bottom of the staircase, a flesh shield against the watchers.

'Get out,' I tell them. 'And don't come back.'

'*Selfish*,' Arthur spits. 'You weigh her life above the entire island?'

'I weigh her life above the demands of some bloodthirsty God and his empty threats,' I snap.

'Does it make you feel good?' Ffion asks. 'Doing the Halenprophet's bidding, like a well-behaved little boy?'

'The Halenprophet didn't send us,' Gethin interjects. 'He wanted to wait you out. Said you'd come crawling back once starvation set in.'

So that's why they've largely left us alone. They thought we'd run out of food, and come slumping out of our burrow like rabbits out on the heath. I'm surprised the Halenprophet was willing to wait that long. The islanders are taken enough by him to do whatever he asks – including ransacking the lighthouse.

For Arthur and Gethin to risk going against his orders, Taliesin's grip must be faltering. Perhaps he hosted one too many women's circles for men like the ones in my home. Nothing rattles a man's faith more than watching his brethren grant women a respect he would never afford them. Doesn't matter that Taliesin's equalist preaching was clearly a ruse.

'We're tired of waiting,' Arthur snarls.

We continue slowly up the stairs, one backwards step at a time, our eyes pinned on the tidewardens. They advance towards us. The stairs whine beneath their boots. Ffion protests, knife held out at a stiff angle, but the closer she gets the more her grip loosens. The wardens cling to the handrail as they ascend the same stairs I can navigate in the dark, a tank of kerosene beneath each arm.

'Don't come any closer,' I warn. 'I'll . . .'

'You'll what?' Arthur barks out a laugh. He raises his rifle, braced against his shoulder. 'Think you'll find *we're* the ones in control here.'

'Give me the knife, Ffion,' Cat hisses.

Ffion casts an incredulous look across her shoulder. 'What're you gonna do with it?'

'Tickle them,' Cat snaps. 'What do you *think* I'm going to do?'

If we weren't currently at the barrel end of two men, I'd call her out for the casual way she suggests murder. I'd rather they believe she's serious. Who knows – maybe she is. I think there's little Cat wouldn't do to keep us all safe.

And then Arthur goes to take another step and loses his footing. He lurches forwards, the next stair not where his brain thought it should be. Time homes in on that moment: his grip slipping, the trigger depressing, and the damned thing is already cocked, and the flint is sparking . . .

Catrin lunges for the knife, but before she can take it, Ffion plants her foot square on Arthur's chest and *pushes.* His green eyes widen, fingers clutching for a handhold that he cannot find. The rifle cracks. It fires straight into the ceiling. Plaster and rock shower down. Arthur tumbles into Gethin, and they go careening down the stairs, heads clacking against each other like two conkers in a schoolchild's pocket. They form a mass of clawing limbs and flesh, bones or teeth clattering on each step.

After that, there is silence.

My heartbeat rings through my ears, the reverberations of the rifle pounding in my chest. Cat pants behind me. We stand perfectly still, statuesque. Ffion's knife rattles down the stairs, bouncing once, twice, three times. It skitters to a halt at the bottom, coming to a rest between the two men.

'Oh, that's perfect, Fi,' I mutter. 'Now they've got *two* weapons.'

'Shut up,' she snaps. 'Least I thought to bring something to stop them. What were you planning to do – stare them to death?'

'For God's sake,' Cat mutters. 'Be quiet and *listen*.'

We wait, barely daring to breathe, to see if the threat has been neutralised. There are no groans, no indications that the men are attempting to right themselves. There is only the low, sardonic laughter of the wind as it rattles through decaying windowpanes.

I tiptoe down the steps. Suck in a breath and hold it. I push Arthur with the toe of my boot, waiting for a sign of life. Instead, I find dark crimson liquid pooling beneath his head – a halo of scarlet. I curse under my breath. My fingers curl around the handrail, gripping tight even though I am perfectly balanced.

Catrin moves past me, each movement stiff and calculated. 'Oh,' she says, her voice hollow. 'Oh, shit.'

Liliwen makes a strange, strangled sound. Ffion draws her into a hug, clutching Lili's cheek against her chest. The next sound Liliwen makes is slightly muffled.

Gethin's blue eyes are half open, his pupils volleying up and down, up and down. Vomit bubbles up from his throat, spilling over the edge of his lips like an overfilled bath. I kneel down, wrenching him onto his side. I touch the back of his head gingerly, searching for blood matted through his hair. Instead, my fingers sink into a cavernous divot in his skull. Something soft and warm balloons beneath my fingers.

I lower him onto his back again, reluctant to let the sisters see the extent of his injuries. I'm not sure if I'm trying to protect the girls from the gore, or Gethin from their prying eyes.

'Fuck, Geth,' I whisper. 'We didn't mean for that to happen . . .'

'What are you pandering to him for?' Cat snaps. 'He would've killed us!'

But when I look down at him, all I can see is the hapless boy I spent half a summer messing around with. His hands, now curled into claws, once held mine; his blueing lips once grazed my forehead; his pupils once dilated at the sight of me.

Gethin stills, his eyes dim and unfocused. I press my forefinger – the one unsullied by his head wound – into the soft flesh of his throat. His pulse should rise up to meet me, but it doesn't. I hold the pads of my fingers there for five seconds, ten, twenty. No matter how hard I press, how intently I feel, there's nothing there.

'Dead,' I say numbly. 'They're both dead.'

'I didn't mean to *kill* them,' Ffion hisses, casting a panicked look around.

Cat scoffs. 'What did you think would happen when you pushed them down two hundred stairs?'

'There are only one hundred and thirty-three in total,' I say quietly. 'It was probably closer to seventy.'

Cat glares at me, the steel of her gaze enough to force me to my feet.

'Maybe they're just unconscious.' The lack of conviction in my voice should tell everyone that this suggestion is mainly for Lili's benefit. 'I'm no doctor.'

Ffion leaves Lili clinging to the wall and picks her way around the rapidly growing pool of blood. She places two fingers at Arthur's throat and waits, eyes turned to the ceiling. Satisfied, she repeats the exercise on Gethin.

After a few torturous seconds, she declares, 'Dead. Wholly, irreversibly dead.'

'What are we going to do?' Lili cries. 'Ffion committed *murder!*'

'Pack it in, Liliwen,' Ffion snaps. 'I think you'll find I saved you all from being shot.'

Silence stretches between us. We study the men, watching as blood runs in rivulets between the flagstones. I don't know what the others are thinking, but all I can focus on now is how utterly, completely *fucked* we are. Ynys Halen already hates us. Now, we've killed not one, but *two* of their treasured wardens. The cooling corpses are a blade that will be used to fell us all, and not one islander will protest. Suddenly, as if coming to a collective realisation of what we must do, chatter erupts between us.

'We'll tie weights to them,' I suggest. 'Throw them out into the cove.'

'Or we could bury them,' Lili adds. 'Beneath the vegetable patch, so the freshly turned soil doesn't attract any attention.'

Cat murmurs, 'We could cook them.'

'Yes, we could burn them. Pretend we're having a bonfire . . .' Ffion pauses, her eyes narrowing as what Cat said sinks in – '*What?*'

Cat screws up her nose. 'It was just an idea.'

Ffion shakes her head, dispelling Cat's suggestion. 'You're sick, you know that?'

Cat flashes a devilish smile. 'Thank you.'

'Let's get them into the cellar,' I resolve, before I change my mind. 'Cat, you help me with Gethin. Ffion, take Arthur. Liliwen, help us with the door.'

Liliwen frowns. 'The cellar?'

'We can't leave them here,' I say. 'They'll . . . they'll *rot*. It's freezing down there, so they won't smell. It's where Rhian used to store . . .' *Meat*, I want to say. But it's too macabre, even for me. I shake my head. 'It'll attract less attention than a fire, and there's no chance of them washing up on the shore.' A tidewraith's appetite doesn't stretch to carcasses, so if the relatively intact bodies lolled up onto shore, everyone would know they were dead before they hit the water.

'The tidewardens know Arthur and Gethin were coming here,' Cat says, picking at the skin around her nails. 'When their men don't come back, where do you think they'll look?'

I ask, 'Do you have a better suggestion?'

It sounds like a rhetorical question, but I'm naively hopeful she'll smile and say *of course*, and we'll land upon the perfect solution to permanently erase our guilt. Instead, she shrugs, adopting a sullen expression.

In the absence of an alternative, I bundle Gethin into the woven rug that usually sits beneath our kitchen table. Catrin wraps Arthur in an old sheet Rhian used to lay down whenever she painted. Unfortunately, the last colour she spilt on it was scarlet. It matches the weeping wound on Arthur's head, which is at once more violent and less damning than Gethin's.

I heave open the trapdoor. Stairs disappear into the darkness. I've rarely gone down to the cellar alone. Rhian would always be a few steps behind, insisting that I'd need help carrying supplies back up the stairs. She never had such qualms about my physical capabilities when I was dragging sailors from the swell. I think she worried that I'd stray into the back room, and my juvenile lungs would wither with the stench of kerosene. I'm not sure where her concern for my health stemmed from: love, or my utility.

'We'll roll them down the stairs.' Once the kerosene up in the watch room runs out, I'll need to descend into the basement to fetch more. That's a bridge I'll cross when I come to it. 'It's cold as anything down there. It should stop them from . . .'

*Smelling* is what I was going to say. Fretting over bad smells seems unjust given that Ffion just committed manslaughter.

Ffion helps me drag Gethin over to the trapdoor. The carpet unfurls as we roll him down the stairs, his flesh thudding on each step. He comes to a rest in the darkness, chased by the second man. The silence that follows is a tangible force – a huge, shadowed entity that settles its bones inside the lighthouse.

Until something breaks it.

A low, howling moan. Rattling breaths.

Cat stares at me, eyes wide and mouth open like a baby bird.

'He's still fucking *alive*,' Ffion hisses.

Ffion begins praying desperately. Usually, she's the most even-keeled of us, but it seems her double murder – sorry, *single* murder – has driven her into the arms of fervent prayer.

'You're praying to the God who wants my blood?' Catrin scoffs. '*Un*-believable.'

'Well, it's not as if there are any other Gods on this island for me to pray to,' Ffion snaps.

Liliwen darts into the kitchen, emerging with a rolling pin clutched between her fingers.

'What are you gonna do with that?' I ask incredulously.

Liliwen looks at the rolling pin in her hand, as if she's only just realised why she grabbed it. 'I thought we could . . .' She shrugs her shoulders. 'You know, whack him with it.'

'*Whack* him with it?' I disarm Lili, snatching up the rolling pin. She looks quite thankful to be relieved of her murder weapon.

'Ffion, can you stop praying so damn loudly?' Cat hisses. 'I can't think with you doing all that.'

Ffion glares daggers at Cat, and does not stop praying. I seem to be the only one focused on the very imminent threat of the half-dead man. I'm not even sure which one of them it is, what with the inhuman sound they're making, and the sepulchral dark of the cellar. But then one of them extricates themself from the impromptu grave, and despite my internal plea of *let it be Arthur*, the silhouette is far too tall.

Gethin claws his way up the stairs towards us. With each laboured step, he casts a wild-eyed glance across his shoulders, almost as if he's being chased.

'Girls,' I murmur. 'What are we going to do about this?'

'Lili's gonna "whack" him with the pin, aren't you, Lil?' Cat grouses. 'A newly minted murderer at the age of sixteen!' Ffion's prayers grow louder. '*Please* keep it down, Ffion.'

Ffion screws her eyes shut tighter. 'And to our father Llyr, God of Sea and Storms, please keep us safe . . .'

'Llyr doesn't give a toss about us!' Cat snaps, and there's so much venom in her voice it makes me flinch without even being its target.

'Girls,' I say, watching Gethin stagger back. He's almost about to fall back down the stairs, and I think it'll be a mercy if that finishes the job – but then he rights himself. Blood leaks from a hairline crack in his skull, congealing down the side of his face like over-set jam. The sisters bicker between themselves, completely unaware.

*'Girls!'* My voice cracks.

Gethin, maybe sensing my urgency, lunges up the stairs. We stand there, looking down into the grim maw of the cellar, none of us knowing quite what to do. I brandish the rolling pin, but memories of our time together forbid me from bringing it down; Lili almost looks set to slam the trapdoor closed, but hesitates at the last second; Ffion screws her eyes shut, opting out of the situation entirely; Cat draws in a breath as if she's about to be plunged underwater.

He's close enough that I can see the bloody spittle dripping from his mouth. Can smell the rust tang of blood wafting from him in waves. His hands are curled into claws, and all I can think of is his daughters at home, his heavy weight on top of me, Cat tied to the pole out in the bay, the crack of the rifle, the shape of his lips, and the pool of blood . . .

The trapdoor snaps shut.

Without guidance or provocation, it *snaps shut* – a pair of sharp teeth meeting. Lili screams. We listen, breath held in a collective gasp, as Gethin falls back down the stairs. This time, he does not stir.

'Did anyone . . .' Ffion swallows around her dry mouth. 'Did anyone touch the door?'

Cat and Lili shake their heads with that strange harmony. I shake mine too.

Ffion lets out a shaky laugh, one hand pressed against her breastbone. 'My praying worked.'

Cat fixes her with a look that might be disbelief or reverence – I can't tell.

'It was the lighthouse,' I say quietly. 'The lighthouse did it. Not Llyr.'

Ffion offers me a soft smile, as if my devotion is ludicrous and hers is gospel.

'Is he actually dead this time?' Cat whispers.

'Should be, after that fall,' Ffion says.

I stand on the trapdoor, letting my weight click the mechanism shut. It can only be opened from the outside. Rhian got stuck down there once, and by the time I realised, she was mad as a bag full of gulls.

'If he's not dead yet,' I whisper, 'he will be soon.'

Lili stifles a panicked sound. I ought to work on my sensitivity.

Ffion clears her throat. 'Let's get this mess cleaned, then.'

# CHAPTER 12

*Catrin Morgan will be extracted before the solstice. Llyr does not wish for blood to be spilled in her capture. Have faith; hunger will drive her from Point Beacon before long. And when she emerges, we'll be waiting.*

—Notice hammered to the board
in Ynys Halen's town square

Fion cooks dinner, utilising the sad dregs of the pantry. Sardine fillets preserved in oil, dried mushrooms, a jar of tomatoes, and past-their-best potatoes. We eat in silence until the thudding starts.

It's laboured. Inconsistent. *Thud.* A pause. *Thud, thud, thud* – frenzied, rapid. Then everything goes quiet. My appetite returns, until the moaning starts. It's hardly human, like a gale blown through a cracked windowpane. Lili's cutlery clatters noisily to her plate.

'He's still alive?' she whispers, eyes drawn wide.

Cat saws at her potatoes, the knife screeching across porcelain as she cuts clean through. Lili pushes her plate away, one hand pressed to her stomach as if to quell nausea.

'Here, look. I'll sing for us,' Ffion says, her voice merrier than I think it ought to be.

She starts belting out some folk song about mermaids, missing more notes than she hits. Cat is the songbird of the family, but she remains silent. Still, Ffion's crooning does a good job of drowning out Gethin's groans. By the time the final note falls from the rafters, his moans have quieted.

'This is wrong,' Cat mutters.

I swallow a bullet-hard potato. 'Which part, precisely?'

She gestures with her knife towards the hallway. 'He's suffering.'

'I'd say he lost a third of his blood,' Ffion says absently. 'He shouldn't last much longer. I read that a human—'

'I don't care what you've read,' Cat says. 'I care that there's a man dying a slow death in the cellar, and we're the only ones who can do something about it.'

Lili chokes on her mouthful of food.

'What do you mean,' I say, '"do something about it"?'

Cat sits up straight in her chair and shrugs her shoulders as if she's suggesting we go for a nice walk along the coast. 'You know.' She stabs the air with her knife. 'Put him out of his misery.'

'And you're gonna do that, are you?' Ffion scoffs. 'Do you even know where the carotid artery is?'

Cat draws her lower lip between her teeth. 'I'm sure if I stab him enough times, I'll find it.'

That's dark, even for her. I shove my plate into the centre of the table, stomach roiling.

We finish supper quietly, and the sisters go off to bed while I set Point Beacon swinging. Cat's made it clear she'd rather be woken by my coming and going than have me absent entirely, so I retreat down the stairs when I'm finished and push into Rhian's bedroom.

She's laid beneath the cover, facing away from me. I whisper a greeting and get nothing in return. I know she's awake, though; I can just about make out the whites of her eyes in the mirror on Rhian's nightstand. Back when we used to have sleepovers, we'd lay awake for hours dissecting *everything* – but tonight, there's not so much as a word between us.

I clamber into bed beside her, leaving a gulf just to see if she'll close it. She doesn't. I roll onto my side, facing the door. The cellar's just metres away, out in the hall. Gethin's down there, dead or dying, and I'm lying in bed as if nothing's happened.

Part of me wants to throw open the trapdoor and command him to run. I realise the idiocy immediately: even if I did set him free, like a hound with its cage unlocked, it's not like he'd make it far.

Perhaps the kindest thing would be to do as Cat said. To put him out of his misery. Rhian had to do that once, and I still remember it. She used to have an old gelding – Eirlys. One winter morning, I went down to drag a hay bale into his and Mack's field. I found Eirlys on his side, stomach heaving, one of his legs snapped at the hock. He must've caught it in a rabbit hole. Rhian came out with her rifle, had me feed him an apple, then shot him through the temple. It was so methodical. So clean, yet so violent.

The immediacy of it stuck with me for weeks. He was this huffing, vital force of life, and then he was nothing at all. My stomach turns at the memory. I imagine Gethin looking up at me with those blue eyes, his nostrils flaring, his chest heaving. Any delusions of putting him down vanish.

The first half of the night passes in fitful bursts, punctuated by the blinding white of the lighthouse beam, the cold desolation of the watch room, and the dark comfort of curling up beside Cat's body in between. I wake suddenly, heart clenched tight as a fist in my chest. I feel like I've slept longer than I ought to, but the beam shines strongly. Still, I'm agitated enough that I'll not find sleep again easily, so I resolve to spend some time up in the tower.

Only when I stand do I realise Cat's no longer in bed. There's a recess where her body lay – a crescent moon beside my own imprint. I almost want to fold myself into it. To mould my body in her image.

Instead, I force myself out of bed. When I push out into the hallway, the trapdoor is ajar. My heart tightens anew.

I retrieve the lantern we keep hooked on the wall beside the cellar entrance. It sputters into flames of its own accord. I hold it above the lip of the staircase, casting dancing shadows into the pit below.

Cat's eyes meet mine. She's knelt on the stairs, straddling Gethin. A pang of something hot and caustic chases through me. There is something terribly grim about the way he's moving, or the way he's *attempting* to move. His hands flail clumsily, finding only loose purchase against Cat's nightgown, his bloodstained fingertips leaving burgundy streaks on the fabric.

I felt the caving in of his skull, the soft vulnerability of what lay beneath. The fact that he persists could be called a miracle, under other circumstances. If there's any part of Gethin left, I'm sure he wishes he was dead.

'You should be asleep,' Cat hisses.

I swallow around the lump in my throat. Gethin looses a low groan. He raises his arm as if to fend off Catrin. It falls back to his side with a *thunk*.

'What on earth are you doing, Catrin?'

'What does it look like?' She holds up the knife clenched between her pale fingers.

'That's a butter knife,' I say, as if that's the biggest problem with what's currently happening.

'Go back to bed,' she insists.

'What – and leave you here to kill him?'

'I'm hardly killing him.' Gethin gives another low groan, but I'm not sure whether he's agreeing or protesting. 'He's never going to recover, Guin. I'm doing him a kindness.'

'I don't think I'd call someone driving a blunt knife between my ribs a "kindness".'

Her nostrils flare. She tightens her grip on the knife, aligning it with his heart. There's a part of me that thinks she's doing this just to get a reaction out of me. That if I respond the way I want to – with abject terror – she'll laugh and let the knife clatter down the stairs, and I'll be embarrassed and she'll be triumphant.

But then she looks up at me with this unfaltering, dispassionate conviction. My gut twists.

'You don't have to watch this,' she whispers, and I can't understand how lips so perfect could say something so detached, so sick.

Gethin twitches beneath her. Is he afraid? If there's even a *chance* he's still in there – prisoner to a body that no longer obeys him – I can't let her do this.

Urgency ignites within me. 'Please don't, Cat.'

Too late, I realise my misstep. Her eyes narrow, knuckles tightening around the knife handle.

'What – do you love him?' She tilts her head. 'I always thought it was Osian who had your heart.'

'Don't be so stupid!' I snap. 'Forgive me for wanting to keep your hands clean.'

She arches one brow and extends the knife towards me. 'Well, if you're offering . . .'

I stand there, fists clenching and unclenching at my sides, chest moving as if I've just done ten laps up the tower staircase. Gethin's chest is inert, in comparison – only trembling every now and then as he attempts to shift beneath Catrin.

'Please,' she says, her voice quiet. Her hand trembles, the knife almost slipping from her grip. 'I don't want to do this.'

'There's no need,' I protest. 'Just leave him . . .'

'It's *cruel*,' Cat snaps.

'Come on, Cat,' I plead, trying not to let my desperation show in my voice or on my face. 'You'll have blood on your hands. You don't know how it'll change you.'

'Then do it for me,' she pleads again.

My eyes flit between the blunt edge of the knife, Gethin's shuddering chest, Cat's desperate eyes.

Quietly, I admit, 'I can't.'

She smiles sadly. 'Then *I'll* do it for *you*, Guin.'

Catrin guides the knife in. That makes it sound like a smooth motion, which it isn't. The muscles in her forearms stand stark as she attempts to drive the blade home. Her wrists tremble. There's this terrible crack, like an eggshell breaking but played out on a much larger instrument. And Gethin – his head lolls back against the step, blue eyes widening, pupils dilating. He gives a whispered exhale, and the blade sinks quicker.

By the time Cat stops pushing, she's almost finger-deep in

Gethin's chest cavity. He looks down at her hands around the blade, the blade in his chest, the pooling blood. His head lolls back. Despite knowing there's no way he could've lived, despite the fact there'd been no love lost between us, this howling grief tears through me. Bile stings my throat.

'I can't believe you just did that.' The words skim my papery lips.

'Don't get sentimental on me,' she mutters, wiping the blade on Gethin's shirt.

I realise, then, that it's the same white shirt he wore when he took me to the tavern, armed with a handful of coins and the confidence of a boy who thought he was a man. I remember asking about the thistle on the breast pocket, which he said his grandmother embroidered. Cat continues to buff the knife, smearing scarlet across the white, the thistle. Her casual manner makes my stomach turn.

My voice quivers. 'I don't recognise you sometimes.'

It's a lie. I know this side of Cat just as well as the other. *This* is the cold ghost I met that night on the beach, the one that rears its head every now and then – sometimes at a lustful boy, sometimes at a girl deemed cruel, rarely at me. But I don't like to recognise it. I'd prefer to think of her with whiskey-hot lips, a peeling laugh, a mischievous smile.

There's not so much as a whisper of that girl as she stands, climbing the few stairs between us. She shrugs past me, leaving Gethin where he lays. I stagger back as she lowers the trapdoor shut.

Catrin looks me in the eye and says, 'Me neither.'

When morning arrives, it's glorious. Gethin's spectral presence recedes with the sun. In the light, I realise that what Cat did *was* a mercy – no matter how terrible. I can't imagine the pain he was in, and God knows I couldn't have done what she did. If I'd gone down this morning and heard him groaning in the cellar, I'm not sure I could've taken it. Cat's always been willing to get her hands dirty. That doesn't stop a chill from racing through me as I recall the way she cracked his sternum, unfazed.

I hurry down to Sawtooth, praying the wind will air out the memory of last night. The millpond sea laps delicately at the sand. I love the ocean like this – all meek and mild. I kick off my shoes and clamber over the rocks, searching the rockpools for anything we can eat. A seven-armed starfish waves back at me from one; a green shore crab raises its pincers in another. I take the crab and dispatch it quickly. It'll give us a tablespoon of meat, but it's better than nothing.

I continue round the headland, one eye on the tide. A cluster of whorled periwinkles find a new home in my pocket, along with a fistful of cockles. I'm so preoccupied with foraging that I don't notice the man in front of me until I'm mere feet away.

All of my muscle fibres pull taut. I stagger backwards, my hand finding the comforting shape of my penknife in my pocket. Halenprophet Taliesin is hardly recognisable in his plainclothes – a beige shirt and slacks, worn like camouflage.

'*You*,' I snarl.

The Halenprophet holds up his open palms. 'I'm here to talk.' His eyes dart to the bunching of my hand inside my pocket. 'I came alone.'

I withdraw the knife, letting it catch the sun. 'Well, that was your first mistake.'

He nods towards the blade. 'You ever used that on another person?'

His question makes me falter. 'Why?'

'Arthur Vaughan and Gethin Thomas have gone missing.' Taliesin pauses, as if to elicit a response. When I remain silent, he says, 'You wouldn't happen to know where they are, would you?'

Waves burble against the sand. A flock of terns trill out at sea, their orange beaks held open. I consider my escape routes: either bolting past Taliesin, or back the way I came. I'm not sure how well I'll fare scrambling across the rocks at speed.

'You've only just brought the tidewardens under thumb, and you're already losing track of them?'

'Listen very carefully, Guinevere,' the Halenprohet says, his voice barely louder than the wave lapping at the beach. 'If you've seen either of them, you need to tell me about it.'

'Oh, I bet you're beside yourself with worry!' I jut out my lower lip. 'Poor little mites. All alone in the big wide world . . .'

'It's not about them.' He falters, rubbing a hand across his face. When he continues, it's in an even lower voice. 'Are they still alive?'

'Forgive me if I'm not in the talkative mood,' I say, taking careful steps backwards. 'It's just that when you sentenced my friend to death, it extinguished any desire I might have to help you.'

I take a step back, my heel sinking into the sand. Water bubbles around my ankle. I twist my body, ready to spring across the rocks – but Taliesin lunges forwards and catches me by the sleeve. I pull against his grip to no avail.

'Who killed them?' he urges, eyes wild.

'Worry less about them, and more about yourself.'

He's so preoccupied with his grip on me that he hasn't realised my penknife is sat flush against his abdomen. The Halenprophet looks down at the blade, then back up at me.

'I need you to do something for me,' he whispers. 'Dispose of the bodies. Completely. There can't be anything left of them. Not so much as a shred of flesh.'

My skin crawls. In the glaring sunlight, Halenprophet Taliesin looks completely sincere.

'Throw them from the cliffs tonight,' he suggests. 'Let the ocean drag them out on the receding tide.'

My grip on the penknife loosens. 'Why?'

'Just do it,' he snaps. His gaze flicks up to where Point Beacon looms on the headland. 'And fast.'

Taliesin lets go of my sleeve. I watch him clamber across the rocks, rounding the coast until he's out of view. Bewilderment keeps me pinned in place. I could understand the Halenprophet taking issue with us killing his men – but their deaths seemed inconsequential to him. It was the fate of their bodies that concerned Taliesin. What possible cause could he have for convincing me to get rid of their bodies?

Perhaps he's hoping it'll draw tidewraiths here, echoing the threat of Llyr's departure, and that we'll finally see sense. Whatever his reasoning, I've no intention of going in that cellar until I absolutely have to.

I only remember to move when the encroaching tide washes across my toes. I pick my way back around the shore. The rocks seem more slippery now, as if they're intent on tripping me up.

My foot catches on a serrated protrusion in the sand, almost sending me arse over tit. It's strange enough that I pause. My hands close around one of the prongs, pulling the curio free. It looks like the biggest set of spiked fish bones I've ever seen, until I realise this didn't come from a fish.

It's a ribcage. A *human* ribcage.

As if burnt, I drop the bones back onto the shore. I inspect my hand, thinking it will be slick with blood – but it's not. The bones are polished, pearly-white. Almost like they've been sucked clean. My mind revolts at that thought, but I can't shake it.

Another wave rolls in, bringing with it scraps of fabric and another bone – a femur, maybe. I'm sure Ffion would know; I'm less sure that it matters. I stagger backwards, something acidic cresting inside my throat. My skirts snag on the stone steps to the beach as I fling myself up them.

My heart is a wild thing in my chest, and I'm brutally cognisant of the way it thrusts against my ribs – ribs just like those out in the bay. In the hallway, the trapdoor is as much a glaring light as Point Beacon's beam; unignorable. Beckoning.

My nails chip as I scrabble for purchase. The mechanism clicks with a *thunk* that sounds like a bullet sliding into place. I heave open the door, hit by a wall of stench which is almost physical in its intensity – bitter kerosene and rusted blood.

I find the first body, slumped at the bottom of the stairs. I can't tell whose it is; men all look the same once they're bloodied and prone. My breaths come thick and fast as I scan for the second. It should be *there*, at the bottom of the staircase. But it isn't.

It can't be a coincidence, can it? A ribcage out on the shoreline; a body missing from the cellar. But a dead body can't have escaped by itself. If the body is down on the beach, it means someone took it there.

I think I know who.

# CHAPTER 13

*The origin of the first tidewraith is unclear. Some sources suggest contamination of the ocean – perhaps resulting from an oil spill – caused the rapid mutation and crossbreeding of multiple species, with the tidewraith as the end result. Sectarian sources suggest that the tidewraiths are a physical manifestation of human sin.*

—Excerpt from 'Classifying the Range and Behaviour of Tidewraiths', from the *Journal of Coastal Ecology*

'What did you do with him?'

Cat startles as I burst into the kitchen, heart bucking in my chest. She looks at me with wide eyes, the picture of innocence. The same eyes that betrayed *nothing* as she straddled Gethin's chest and sunk a butter knife through his sternum.

She cocks her head to the side, pin-straight hair flooding down her shoulder. 'What are you talking about?'

'I'm talking about the fact I just found a *ribcage* down on the beach.'

Cat stiffens, and suddenly becomes very interested with the state of the countertop. 'Must've been a sailor.'

'Oh, sure. And the fact there's only one body in the cellar is a total coincidence.'

She sucks in a breath. *Got you,* I want to say, but I don't. I stand there, stock still, lungs ballooning inside my chest.

During the course of our friendship, I've rarely confronted Cat about anything. The worst time, it was because she'd kissed the boy who was courting me. She didn't even like him – not that I really did, either, but she did it just to show that she could. My scant experiences have left me with the understanding that if I move too fast, speak too loudly, she'll disengage entirely.

Cat pours herself a glass of water from the jug on the counter. She drinks it languorously. I watch her throat bobbing. Trace the path of the droplets that escape her lips, dripping down her jaw, landing in the hollow space at the base of her neck. I want to drink the water like nectar from a flower – my lips on her skin, her pulse on my mouth.

'Well,' she says, and it's only when she speaks that I realise she's been watching me this whole time. 'We couldn't keep them in there for ever.'

I mean, she's technically correct, as she often is. Keeping two corpses in the cellar isn't sustainable. But it's the fact that she lied to me. The fact that she probably would've *kept* lying to me, had I not caught her out. It makes me feel sick, as if the room is tilting on its axis.

'Who was it? Arthur or Gethin?'

'What does it matter?' She laughs, a high, tittering sound. At my severe expression, she says, 'Gethin.'

It makes sense that it'd be him. Geth is the closest thing I've ever had to a boyfriend. Trust Cat to evict him from the lighthouse, even when he's dead.

'What the hell did you do with him, Catrin? There was nothing left but bones.'

Cat swallows. I watch her throat as it dips and swells, the light catching so I can see the purple spiderweb of her veins beneath the surface. 'Threw him off the cliffs. I would've done them both, if I'd had time. Lili was crying all night, you know. Clearly she can't stand sharing a house with corpses.'

'Oh, sure. It'll be much better for Lili when she goes down onto the beach and stumbles on his ribcage.'

Catrin pales. 'You didn't leave it there?'

A joyless laugh bursts out of me. 'Sorry – am I supposed to clean up your crime scenes now?'

She makes this small, strangled sound. Wraps her arms around her chest. Tears flood down her cheeks, and her chest seizes with gasping sobs.

Well, now I feel like an arse. I swallow down my pride and throw my arms around her. She untangles her own and loops them around my neck. Holds me so tight that her nails bite into the top of my spine.

'I'm sorry,' I whisper, even though I'm not totally sure what I'm apologising for. It's often that way with Cat. 'Don't cry.'

'They came in here and tried to take me, Guin. Came into *your* home. They weren't good men. They don't deserve to share our roof. I just – I just want to protect you all. That's why I had to put Gethin down. If he'd gotten out and hurt you, I never would've forgiven myself.'

The pedant in me wants to say that I doubt he could've done much of anything, even if he *did* get out. 'I know.' There's more I'd like to say – why didn't she tell me how she felt? Why did she do it in the dead of night? Why not talk about it? – but I don't want her to cry anymore. Especially not when it's my fault.

But with her arms around my shoulders, all I can think about is Taliesin's plea. He wanted me to do exactly as Cat claims she did – throw the bodies over the cliff. If anything, she's saved me a job. Why, then, do I feel as if she's still hiding things? If it was so important to her to get them out of the house, why not ask for help?

I don't know the answer. All I *do* know is that I can't tell her I spoke with Taliesin.

For an entire week, I wake with dread thrashing like a fish out of water in my belly. Calling it 'waking' probably does a disservice to the fact that I'm barely sleeping at all. My state of constant exhaustion since Rhian's death usually guarantees that I fall straight back asleep after going up to the watch room, but the nerves that writhe inside me keep my tiredness at bay.

The girls start to look at me strangely, and Cat repeatedly asks if I'm okay, which . . . no, I'm obviously not, but how do I say that to *her*? She's been sentenced to death. She felt compelled to kill a man, for God's sake. I'm sure I can withstand being a bit tired for a while. Truthfully, though, I jump when I see myself in the mirror. This haggard creature with blue half-moons beneath her eyes. I regret Cat seeing me in this state.

Each night, I debate dragging Arthur from the cellar and rolling him into the sea, just as Taliesin begged me to do. But unlike Cat, the guilt stops me. I can't bear to sneak around at night, she and the sisters oblivious to what I'm doing. If they knew I'd spoken to Taliesin at all, I'm not sure how they'd react.

Ffion starts following me up to the watchtower when I light Point Beacon in the evening. The third time she does it, I'm about to set to work when she asks me to pause. With practised precision, she fills the reservoir, buffs clean the lens, trims the wicks – repeating the steps it took me *years* to learn. She picks up the matches and glances to me for approval.

I wish I could adjust the wicks. Clean the lens better than she has. But the movements she just carried out were preternaturally precise. I give her a numb nod; she strikes the match, touches it to the burner. Point Beacon rears and the beam flares.

'Let me take half the night shift,' she says. 'The same way you and Rhian used to share it.'

My mouth opens and closes, searching for an excuse. This is *my* burden – a stone around my neck I have no choice but to carry. I inherited it from Rhian, as she did from her mother, and her mother, and her mother. I find the speed with which Ffion's tuned herself to Point Beacon's hissing, and her aptitude for gauging pressure from a touch, galling.

'How did you do that?' I whisper.

She grins. 'I've read a lot of books. I ordered some from the mainland after Rhian died: *A Keeper's Guide to Kerosene Lighthouses*, *Life on the Edge: a Lighthouse Keeper's Tale*. You know, all the classics.'

I nod, feigning understanding. I've never read books on lighthouses: my training was a baptism of fire conducted by Rhian. She'd get me to light up Point Beacon during the day and keep it running. If the flame sputtered out, she'd make me do it over and over until I cracked it.

'I thought you might need the help, so I did my research.' She lifts her chin, triumphant. 'The kerosene behaves a bit differently than I thought it would, based on my reading, but everything's a learning curve – even for me!'

I'm almost about to ask *how* the kerosene behaves differently, but decide to spare myself the hour-long lecture. 'That's really impressive,' I say, trying to fill my voice with as much enthusiasm as I can muster.

Ffion shrugs, sweeping a lock of dark hair behind her ear. 'So you'll let me help?'

Defeated, I nod my head. 'You can take the first watch. I'll take the second.'

Ffion falters, brow dipping. I think she expected more gratitude. I *should* be grateful. I should be throwing myself at her feet, thanking her for liberating me from Point Beacon – even if it is just half the night. But there's a sense of loss. Of something which was *mine*, as terrible as it was, being stripped from me. Fragmented and shared around.

# CHAPTER 14

*BUY LOCAL! We may not be able to grow all the fancy new varieties of fruit and vegetable found on the mainland, but crops grown on Ynys Halen will make you as hardy as they are! Don't waste your hard-earned coin on imported goods. Our shelves are full. Come on in!*

—Noticeboard outside the Meyrick greengrocer in Ynys Halen

If you've ever been hungry for a day, you'll understand it comes and goes in waves. You wake up ravenous, but there's no time to eat, so you set to work with this growling twist in your stomach. Eventually, it simmers down. Fades to background noise. Suddenly, dusk falls and you realise you've not yet lined your stomach. By that point, the thought of eating isn't really enticing anymore; your mind has spent so long suppressing the thought of food, and your body takes a while to warm back up to the idea. But then when you're stood over the pot, the hunger comes back with a vengeance – intense as a punch in the gut.

Now, with the pantry nearly bare, we've been hungry for a week. The sea buckthorn has started to make us sick; the currents that bring edible seaweed to our shore have shifted, leaving the beach barren; we've eaten most of the cockles and whelks and sea snails. Lasting two months until the solstice felt achievable, but with our resources dwindling and a fortnight left to go, I've started to panic. This is what the Halenprophet wanted: for us to become so mad with hunger that we leave Point Beacon of our own free will.

The hunger pangs come and go, but they're of a scale I've never suffered. And the *pain*. It's not just the protests of my stomach, acid sloshing around in an empty vessel – it's the aching of each joint, the torturous sensitivity of my skin, the clumsiness of my movements.

We eat, sure. But savouring the scraps we can afford to spare is somehow worse than not eating at all. It's like waving a big shoulder of lamb at a dog, then only letting it sniff the licked-clean bone. An animalism ignites inside us all, driving us to find food wherever we can. I have to put a lock on the pantry to stop us from picking it dry.

Sometimes, without even registering the journey, I find myself down on the beach ripping cockles from the rocks with my bare hands. I suck them raw from the shell, then lick my bloodied fingers clean. It only makes me hungrier.

Our vigils on the widow's walk are all but abandoned – traded for a guard duty taken sat on the front stoop, protecting our vegetable beds from greedy crows. There's little sense worrying about the tidewardens when we might well starve inside Point Beacon before they ever come to get us. The threat of the islanders fades to insignificance compared to the war being waged inside our own bodies. Fat deposits melting away, nails chipping, muscles withering.

I stare at the leaves of our potato plants, imagining the bounty of golden nuggets below. We pulled up one plant last fortnight, and the potatoes were like bullets. Hard and bitter on the tongue. Lili thinks they should be ready by the end of this week. I spend an entire hour daydreaming about what we might do with them: slice them thin and fry them in butter till the edges turn amber, mash them and turn them into a topping for shepherd's pie, bake them and stuff them with cheese.

But there is no butter, no lamb, no cheese. My fantasies will remain just that. Still, at least there'll be something to eat.

The morning of the Dig arrives, and without meaning to do so, we all wear our best outfits – as if we're attending the unveiling of a grand new statue, or one of the island's fancier weddings. We do not take breakfast these days, preferring to condense all our scraps into one singular meal – if you can call it that – at midday. We head straight for the garden once we're decent.

We stand in a line beside the vegetable bed while Lili fastens her hands around the first of the potato plants. She pauses, grinning up at us with a zeal I've not seen in weeks. The leaves shudder as they come heaving out of the ground, trailing long, fibrous roots and – and these small, misshapen tumours. They're gangrenous. Lili snatches one between her fingers. It turns to sludge at the slightest provocation, dripping back into the bed like pus from a wound.

'Try another one,' I urge. 'Maybe it's an outlier.'

She does, and it isn't. One by one, she pulls up the potatoes. My stomach squeezes like a cloth being wrung out. Ffion storms back into the lighthouse after the fourth decaying plant. I don't dare look to gauge Cat's reaction, because I'm trying my best to maintain some semblance of strength, and I worry her expression might break mine.

Liliwen finds the ability to stand and comes staggering over to Cat. She lodges against her chest, bleating like a newborn lamb. I can't believe we let her get swept up in all this. She's soft as a dandelion. It's simultaneously the best and worst thing about her. It makes her kind, empathetic. It also makes her an absolute liability, no more able to tolerate hardship than butter at the hands of a hot knife.

'We shouldn't have brought you here,' I whisper, almost to myself.

'Where would you have me go, then?' She looks out from the net of Cat's arms, eyebrows slanted down. 'To the village that condemned Cat to death?'

It would be better than the fate we all stand to face here. I don't tell her that, though. My body is too weary to argue, and from the look of Lili's collarbones, she's *definitely* not got the energy to spare. I thought she might fare better than the rest of us, what with her being so small, but she's shrunken even further. Her collarbones are jagged peaks, and you can see the etchings of her ribs beneath near-translucent skin. One strong gust could push her clean over.

I leave Cat and Lili to their mutterings. The lighthouse door swings open just as I reach for it. Today, the assistance doesn't much make me smile. If Point Beacon can sense my need for a hot bath, or open doors at will, why can't it conjure us some edible food? Why would it let sustenance planted on its ground turn to fetid mush?

We congregate in the kitchen. Ffion and Cat bicker over the division of our last provisions. There's a smear of laverbread, a handful of salted fish, and half a jar of strawberry jam Rhian made last summer. The strawberry crop was so bountiful that we couldn't eat them quicker than they grew. She made ten pots of jam, of which we've devoured nine and a half. The thought of such absurd abundance makes violent urges bud behind my eyes.

Percy sits on the counter beside the sink, tail swishing gently. Despite our slow starvation, he still looks princely. His fur is clean and soft, and his belly is rotund as ever. He must be finding food somewhere. I tried following him once, but he's surprisingly quick on his feet for such a spoiled cat. I stare at him until my eyes lose focus, and all I can see is the shape of his body. The *meat* on his bones. I wonder how many meals he'd provide . . .

'Why are you staring at Percy like that?' Cat interrupts.

I clear my throat, ashamed. 'Nothing.'

'We can't eat it all today,' Ffion continues, gesturing at our meagre provisions. 'There'll be nothing left for tomorrow.'

'There's no sense eating a teaspoon of food each. At least if we eat it all today, our stomachs mightn't protest so bad tonight.'

I clear my throat. 'And what of tomorrow?'

Cat looks back at me, pensive. Her hands are so cold they're turning blue, pale fingers clutching the jam like it's a lifeline.

'Let me hand myself in.' She slams the jam down onto the counter, and I wince at the thought of it shattering. I think I'd still eat it, glass shards slicing my lips as I gobbled it down. 'I've had enough of this. I won't let you all die in my name.'

I brace my head against my hands. 'This isn't even about *you*, Cat.'

'In what sense is it not about me?'

'You think if we toss you to the sea, it'll end there?' I ask.

Ffion places her hands on her hips. 'They'll never stop, Catrin. It'll go back to the way it was centuries ago.'

A charged silence falls across us, like the moments of deathly quiet before a storm breaks.

Liliwen stares down at her plate. She holds her fork loosely, fingers trembling. 'I might as well throw myself from the cliff and cut out all the suffering in the middle.'

Cat lurches into action. She leans across the table, shunting her own plate to one side. Lili yelps as Cat takes her chin in her hand. 'Don't you *dare* say that.'

Lili's eyes widen to the size of saucers. 'You're hurting me,' she squeaks.

Cat holds her for a second longer, eyes burning with something fierce, then lets go. She sits back down, plunges the tines of her fork into the strawberry jam and sucks each one clean individually.

'You're going to hate me for saying this,' Ffion says, looking down at her licked-clean plate, 'but there *is* something we can eat, Guin.'

My heart bucks in my chest. 'What?'

'The mare.' Ffion doesn't meet my eye, head bent as if in confession. 'She's doing well enough off the grass. We'd get a whole month of meals out of her . . .'

'No,' I snap. 'She's not food.'

'I get it,' Ffion says. 'Really, I do. But we're *starving*, Guin. We'll make it quick. She won't suffer . . .'

'If you touch so much as a hair from her mane, I will lock you from this lighthouse and watch you freeze to death.'

Ffion lets out a nervous laugh, but when she realises I'm serious, the smile melts from her face. Catrin worries her bottom lip.

Ffion jabs her finger towards Mackerel's paddock. 'You're really going to choose that creature's life over ours? She's just a horse, Guinevere.'

'She's not *just* a horse. She was a gift from Rhian . . .'

'Rhian is dead,' Ffion snaps. 'We will be, too, if you can't get your head out of your own—'

'*Ffion.*' Catrin's voice is sharp, whip-like. 'Leave it alone.'

'Oh, I'll leave it alone, shall I? We can all watch the horse prance about its paddock while we starve to death.'

'She has a name,' Liliwen murmurs. 'I don't want to eat Mackerel.'

Ffion screws up her face. 'This isn't about mackerel; it's about the horse . . .'

'The horse's name is Mackerel,' Cat says.

The growing tension snaps. Ffion exhales noisily through her nose. 'Who calls a horse Mackerel?'

I shrug my shoulders, a subdued smile at my lips. 'A ten-year-old with a bad imagination.'

Wearily, Ffion rubs her eyes with her fists. Her hands then drift to her scalp, which she massages. It doesn't seem to do much for her stress levels; her shoulders remain tight, her brow slightly furrowed.

'Just for the avoidance of doubt,' I mutter guiltily, 'the cat is off limits, too.'

Lili glances at Ffion. 'You wouldn't eat Percy, would you?'

Percy startles. He bolts from the room with his tail held up like a feather duster.

'Honestly?' Ffion laughs, a sound touched by hysteria. 'If I could catch him, I would.'

Silence falls over us again. It's an unnatural feeling. I want to go back to the afternoons we spent on the widow's walk, sun baking our skin, watercolours smeared across our fingertips, braids in our hair. When we were quiet, it was comforting, natural as the hush before a wave breaks. Now, we only talk if it's purposeful. Talking *has* to be purposeful, to be worth the energy.

'There's something else we could eat,' Cat murmurs.

We all glance up at her, but she's staring above all our heads at a spot on the wall.

'Don't be coy with it,' I reply.

'Apparently it tastes like pork.' She chews on the inside of her lip; I wonder what it feels like. 'That's what it said in the book about castaways you gave me, Fi.'

Lili folds her arms on top of the table. '*What* tastes like pork?'

'You know.' Cat rolls her eyes as if we're being obtuse. 'The meat we have . . . in the cellar.'

'You mean Guin's old boy?' Ffion leans forwards in her seat, alarm pinching her voice. 'You're suggesting we eat *him?*'

Cat fixes Ffion with a pointed stare. 'Not Gethin. Arthur. And besides, if it's good enough for Llyr . . .'

My blood simmers, fingers curling around the edge of the table. 'You could at least look us in the eyes when you tell me you want to *eat* Arthur.'

Cat's gaze drifts languorously towards me, her lids half-lowered. Enunciating each syllable, she says, 'I want to eat Arthur.'

I thrust back from the table. My chair makes a dreadful wail as it scrapes the flagstones. 'Sometimes, I think you say things just to rile me.'

The left corner of her lips hitches up. 'The hunger's making you awfully glum, Guinny.'

Night descends across Ynys Halen, and Ffion leaves to take first shift up in the watch room. Lili retreats to her makeshift bedroom, teasing Percy with a length of twine. Cat sits at the kitchen table looking contemplative. I think she's trying to coax me into apologising, or else dispel the tension that hangs over us – but I don't.

Quietly, so as not to alert the others, I slip outside. A flock of geese pass noisily overhead, bound for warmer climes. The gate to Mackerel's paddock whines as I open it. She trots over, hoof beats causing the ground beneath my feet to vibrate. I fling the gate open and step aside, letting her see that she is free. I think it's going to be terribly dramatic – that Mackerel will kick up her heels and leave me in a cloud of dust. Instead, she just stands and stares at me with kind, brown eyes.

'Go,' I tell her. 'They'll eat you if you stay here. I don't know if I'll be able to stop them.'

My deeper worries stay stuffed up inside me: that if I grow hungry enough, even *I* will want to eat her. She blinks long eyelashes back at me.

'*Go.*' I cluck my tongue. 'Join the ponies out on the heath. I'll come and see you one day, if I can.'

Mackerel noses at my pockets, warm breath huffing across my skin. I stroke her velvet nose with the back of my hands.

'I'll miss you too.' My throat tightens. I force the words out quickly, before tears rob me of them. 'I love you, Mack. Be good.'

I drive her out of the paddock, pushing her hindquarters until she edges out onto the trail. She doesn't understand why I'm being cruel. Her nostrils flare, the whites of her eyes flashing.

Eventually, painfully, she gets the message. The last I see of her is her silvery tail as she vanishes into the night.

# CHAPTER 15

*We are no longer procuring goods from the mainland. All tidewardens are focused on the upcoming Crowning of Catrin Morgan.*

—Notice hammered to the docks

Days later, I stand catatonic in the pantry. I feel like if I stare for long enough, I can will food into existence. A shadowed corner will illuminate, and there'll be a whole bag of potatoes we missed. I drag my finger along the shelves, searching for even the *suggestion* of food. Furtive, I lick the dust from my finger. It makes me cough.

Tending Point Beacon overnight has become an all-consuming affair. I drag myself up the steps, stringy muscles bunching. I've never seen the flame gutter as many times as it has in the past week.

The solstice will be here soon. It felt like the end point of our journey; if we could protect Cat that long, we could snatch her from death's jaws. The truth is I'm not sure we'll make it that far. Not because the tidewardens will drive us out, but because we're wasting away. Our bodies are shutting down.

'Enough,' I whisper into the dark. 'That's enough.'

I shoulder one of Rhian's canvas shopping bags. Shrug on one of her huge coats and pull the hood up over my head. No one in the village will know who I am. All I have to do is get in and out without being spotted. Sure, the fact that I'm skulking around with my hood up will draw eyes, but I'm too starving to care.

I emerge into the kitchen, staggering slightly with the weight of my decision. 'I'm going into the village.'

The sisters look up at me with blank eyes.

'You've been keeping them from the sacrifice they think will save the island,' Cat says. 'I can't imagine they'll welcome you with open arms.'

'We'll die if we don't find something to eat.'

'No.' Cat shoves her chair backwards. I think she intends to stand, but can't find the strength. 'You're not risking it.'

'Guin's right,' Ffion says. I think it's the first time she's ever said that. 'Going into the village presents a risk of death. Not going presents *certain* death.'

'I think it's too dangerous,' Lili whispers, glancing at Cat for approval.

I dig my nails into the flesh of my palm – God, that feels good, the sensation of meat beneath my fingertips – and stride out of the room. We're not going to reach an agreement, and each wasted word is energy we cannot afford to expend.

Just as I'm pulling the door open, Cat reaches across my shoulder to slam it shut.

'You're not going,' she snaps. 'It's ridiculous.'

'Do you want to die?' I ask. 'Because staying here is how we die.'

Cat stares back at me, nostrils flared, heavy breaths inflating her chest. I peel her fingers off the door and heave it open once more. She tries to wrench it shut, but can't find the strength. I push out into the brisk air before she can stop me.

'Wait,' Liliwen pushes past her, trembling. 'You don't have to go all the way into the village.'

I wait while she catches her breath.

'Osian only lives up the coast, doesn't he?'

My eyes snap to Catrin, whose mouth has set into a tight line. I think she'd rather starve than accept Osian's help. Even *I'm* unsure about going to see him, what with his attitude the last time we met.

'Maybe he'd help us,' Lili suggests.

I look at Catrin as I nod. 'You're right.'

'He's a tidewarden,' Cat snaps.

'He's not like the others.'

Cat gives a harsh laugh. 'Do you realise how daft you sound?'

She's right. 'It's our best chance,' I say quietly. 'And I'm not going to let us all wither away.'

Before Cat can dissuade me any further, I stagger down the path. She calls after me – initially pleading, then souring to anger once she realises I'm not turning back.

The distance from the front door to the garden gate seems to have grown exponentially in the past week. I'm sweating by the time I reach it. Suddenly, the trek to the Vaughan homestead seems insurmountable. I scan the purple haze of heather, estimating the distance in a measurement of door-to-garden-gates.

The Vaughans' land is surrounded by crooked drystone walls.

They look like the spine of a monster, buried deep underground, all the vertebrae protruding. I cling to them, rounding the headland at a glacial pace. A flock of windblown sheep scatter inside their confines, eyes flashing wildly in my direction, reacting to my presence the same way they would a dog's.

The Vaughan farmhouse is little more than a speck in the distance when someone barrels into me from the side. Under normal circumstances, I'd put up a fight – but in my weakened state, it's all I can do to brace myself for the fall. I collapse to the dirt, my elbow cracking painfully.

'Oh, God,' Osian mutters. 'Sorry, Guin. I didn't mean to come at you so strong.'

He pulls me to my feet as if I weigh nothing. I've always known he's stronger than me, but today, his physicality is an unignorable fact against my weakness.

I rub my elbow. 'Were you waiting for me?'

I'd intended it to be teasing, but my voice is too worn to convey anything other than fatigue. Either way, Osian tenses at the accusation.

'I've just been keeping an eye on things,' he says quietly. Before I have the chance to respond, he continues, 'You don't look well.'

'Thanks, Os.' I mutter. 'Starvation will do that to you.'

His eyes dart across my face, pupils focusing on my gaunt cheeks, my hollow eyes.

'Come on over. I'll make you some lunch.'

Osian starts off towards his farmhouse, beckoning for me to follow as if I'm one of his sheep. The offer of lunch – roast lamb, honeyed vegetables, maybe even a jug of gravy – is nearly enough to make me cry. But I can't feed myself while the girls go hungry.

'I can't come over,' I tell him. Out on the heath, I feel

rodent-like, liable to be picked off by an owl at any moment. 'But do you have any food you can spare? Enough for the sisters, too?'

Osian stops. He turns back to me, his jaw twitching. 'I can't do that, Guin.'

My voice cracks as I ask, 'Why?'

'The Halenprophet says we're not to feed you,' he admits, unable to look me in the eye.

'And since when you do listen to the Halenprophet?'

Osian rubs the back of his head, a flush of scarlet creeping up from his chest. As it spreads across his cheeks, I see an echo of Arthur in him.

'I'll feed you as much as you want if you come with me,' he murmurs. 'But if you're planning on staying at the lighthouse, I can't help you.'

His disloyalty feels like a hot needle through my heart. 'You'll betray me for *him?*'

'This isn't about the Halenprophet.'

'What's it about, then?' I advance towards him, and he doesn't so much as flinch. 'What could possibly compel you to leave four girls to starve? You've sacrificed your conscience, and for *what?*'

'The Halenprophet said that once she's gone . . .'

'Once she's *dead!*' I correct, my teeth snapping. 'It's not a dirty word unless you believe it's wrong, Osian.'

Osian gulps. 'Once she's . . . dead, the Halenprophet will arrange for us both to live on the mainland. There'll be a house, and new jobs, and we can leave all this behind.'

My heart fractures. This is the boy I knew from a child, who I cherished for his gentleness – how *unlike* other boys he was. And now, he stands before me and bleats that he's been promised me by another man. A reward for his good behaviour. I am no more worthy of involvement in the decision than a sheep when it's sent to slaughter.

Hot, angry tears bead along my lashes. I blink them clear, and when they drop onto my face, Osian's face shifts. His brows pinch together.

'I just want to keep you safe.'

'And I'm telling you I don't need your help,' I snap.

I pull back from him; he tightens his grip. My vulnerability crystallises in blinding clarity. I'm utterly outmatched, and we both know it.

'Let me go,' I say quietly.

His muscled arms stay locked around me, pincer-like. I go still and quiet, because at least that way I can pretend I could get away if I wanted to. It's better to think myself compliant than powerless.

Almost to myself, I say, 'I thought you were a good man.'

'I *am* a good man,' he insists.

Osian looks down at me where I'm pinned between his arms – my wide eyes, his biceps flexed with effort, the reality of our bodies.

'Let her go.'

Cat's voice is unmistakeable. Unerring in its command. Osian's eyes flick to where she must stand behind me. I imagine her face, haggard but beautiful as ever.

Without a word, Osian releases me. I stagger back, colliding with Cat's frail body. She wraps her hands around my shoulders and tells me to get back to the lighthouse. Usually, I'd not dare leave her alone with Osian – but today, I don't feel much like protecting him.

*

Cat returns a minute after I do. As the seconds wore on, I started to worry that Osian had got the upper hand and wrangled her all the way to the Halenprophet – but I should've known Cat's not the sort to be manhandled.

'What happened?' I ask.

'Nothing.' Cat doesn't meet my eyes; I have no choice but to disbelieve her. 'You need to rest.'

She steers me to bed as if I'm an overtired child, and I let it happen. Cat says she always knew Osian was a bad egg, and she's glad I can finally see it. She leaves me alone, Whaley clutched against my chest.

My breaths are shallow, unproductive. There's a quietness to my bodily processes: a feeble heartbeat, a dormant stomach, a sluggish brain. *This is how I die,* I think. Not at the hands of a colossal wave, nor a tidewraith. A slow, aching demise. How embarrassing. It should bother me more than it does. My eyes flutter like a butterfly coming to rest. I slip into a deep, suffocating sleep.

The next time I open my eyes, the molten glow of sunset bleeds through the window. The thudding persists. In unconsciousness, I somehow found the strength to throw the covers off myself. It's like a terrible oil painting: this gorgeous, tangerine light cast over the troughs of my body. A concave stomach, ribs like piano keys, collarbones sticking up like the reef from beneath the waves.

*If you don't get up, you're going to die here.* The voice in my head belongs more to Rhian than it does me. I think that's what gives me the determination to stand – slowly, painfully. I follow the thudding to the kitchen. Cat stands beside the kitchen sink, silhouetted against the pinkening horizon beyond the window. She brings a cleaver down. *Thud.* Brings it down again. *Thud.*

I clear my throat, not wanting to startle her when she's wielding a blade the size of my thigh. 'Cat?'

She jumps anyway. 'Bloody hell, Guin,' Cat mutters, glancing at me across her freckled shoulders. 'You move like my sisters.'

I walk to stand beside the fire smouldering in the range. 'What are you doing?'

'Brushing my hair,' she mutters. 'What does it look like I'm doing?'

'I mean – what are you chopping?'

'Supper.' She brings the cleaver down again. 'Should be ready by the time it's dark.'

With nausea rolling through my stomach, I pad over to where she stands. The sun paints the scene in a delicate rose-pink: the glint of the cleaver, the pale web of Cat's fingers, the meat flayed open on the chopping board.

My body reacts urgently and instantly, stomach lurching so fierce that I'd vomit if I had anything in me. 'Where did you get the meat from?'

'I found a wandering sheep.'

She doesn't offer anything more. It's a lie. I *know* it's a lie.

'So if I go down into the cellar, Arthur's body will still be there?'

*Thud* goes the cleaver. It lodges in the chopping board, the blade vibrating. Cat stares me dead in the eye and whispers, 'Don't ask questions you don't want the answers to.'

There's a darkness in her I've never seen before. A macabre commitment. It sends me staggering back until the small of my back meets the kitchen table. Cat drags in a breath and pulls the cleaver clean.

'We'll all feel better once we've got some food in us,' she says, voice light as a breeze.

'Some *food?*' My voice trembles, and I don't know whether it's with anger or horror.

'It's meat,' she snaps. 'It's survival.'

My empty stomach growls, twisting in on itself. I watch her work, stripping away fat and sinew.

'Do the others know about this?'

The line of her shoulders stiffens. She speaks through gritted teeth. 'Someone had to do it. Lili's just a child and Ffion's away with the fairies.' *Thud, thud.* 'If someone else had taken the initiative, I wouldn't have needed to . . .'

'"Someone else" meaning me?'

'"Someone else" meaning someone else,' she snaps. 'Look at us, bickering like old maids. This'll all be forgotten once we've got full bellies. There's more left in the cellar. It should see us through the month. We can make broth from the bones . . .'

Catrin pauses, pulling away from the chopping board. She presses one hand to her stomach as if she's about to vomit. She gags delicately, spits into the sink, then carries on chopping.

'There's some nettles growing 'round the headland,' she says. 'Go and fetch some, will you?'

When Rhian and I were feeling fancy, we'd have these grand three-course dinners on a Sunday. The main event was always a big, need-a-rest-after roast. A huge joint of meat, gravy thick as honey, roast potatoes and carrots and whatever else was in season. Dessert would usually be something Rhian bought from the bakery – baking requires a precision neither she nor I could muster – and the first course would often be nettle soup.

Usually, I'd wear gloves to pick the nettles from their stalks, but today I don't much see the point. They nip at my fingers, leaving them scattered with risen white welts. I'm so lethargic, my body so resistant to any sort of movement, that my gathering trip lasts until the sun falls entirely behind the mainland. Persnickety comes to see what I'm doing at one point, and even lets me stroke him. We're both quite startled by it, and he goes cavorting off through the tall grass shortly after.

I trudge back to Point Beacon having picked the entire headland clean of nettles. It's still a relatively pitiful harvest – if they grew in any abundance, we would've stripped them bare days ago. The lighthouse yawns open for me. I'm hit by a wall of aroma so potent that my stomach rumbles.

I set the bushel of nettles down onto the counter. Cat opens the oven and pokes at its contents. I don't dare look into it.

'Thanks, Guin.' Cat flashes a smile. She's changed into a clean dress – one of my own. It's the colour of periwinkles, and far too nice for what we might be about to do. She shrugs her shoulders. 'We always used to dress up for Sunday dinner. I thought we ought to carry on the tradition.'

I fetch one of Rhian's knitted sweaters from where it hangs beside the door, and throw it towards Cat. She catches it deftly, her reflexes lightning fast.

'We can't afford to lose any body heat,' I say.

Somewhat begrudgingly, she pulls the sweater over her head. When Lili and Ffion emerge from their rooms, I instruct them to fetch layers from Rhian's drawers – partially to ensure their warmth, and partially because I can't bear the sight of their sickly bodies. We've all shed weight without really noticing it – a decomposition that happened so slowly I didn't register the changes.

But even the largest of Rhian's jumpers can't mask Lili's decline. Her wrists are so small I could encircle them with my pointer and thumb. I wonder how many days she has left. The thought makes a terrible, aching pit open deep inside me. Reminds me that what we're about to do is objectively necessary.

Ffion flashes me a tight smile as she sweeps up the nettles and washes them in the sink. Unwilling to linger, I retreat to the bathroom and stand in front of the mirror, staring and staring until I don't recognise the person looking back. Her cheekbones cut like knives, her eyes are dead, her hair dull and stringy. She's a corpse of a thing. A foul, hungry creature who'd look more at home beside tidewraiths than other humans.

I press the pad of my finger up against the glass, almost expecting the girl in the reflection to stand still in defiance. She doesn't. Just raises her arm with a grim determination. Condensation blooms around my fingertip. I curse the lost heat.

'Guin,' Cat calls, her voice echoing all the way down the hall. 'Supper's almost ready.'

# CHAPTER 16

*'Please keep faith that the ocean's bounties will return upon fulfilment of Llyr's request. Until then, Vaughan lamb will be rationed, and the Bennion's will slaughter their pigs early to ensure everyone is fed. Please take only what you need. Think of your neighbours.'*

—Notice hammered to the board
in Ynys Halen's town square

The walk to the kitchen feels like marching to my own funeral. Percy lies beside the front door, tail flicking erratically. The girls are sat at the table, which has been laid with Rhian's best crockery. A glass of whiskey marks each place. Cat hums as she lays a bed of boiled nettles onto a serving platter.

Liliwen's chair screeches across the flagstones. She quietly excuses herself, slinking out into the corridor.

'Liliwen,' Cat barks. 'Come on. The food's almost ready.'

Lili's faint reply drifts down the hallway. 'Not hungry.'

A nerve in Ffion's jaw ticks, but I lay a gentle hand on her forearm. 'Leave her be.'

We sip politely at our glasses of liquor. It reminds me of all the times I sat waiting for Gethin to pick me up to take me into the village. I had to use the alcohol to settle my nerves. Sometimes I'd pretend it was Catrin I was waiting for – that she'd turn up in a dress, and we'd take a picnic on the cliffs.

Catrin opens the oven door, checking on its contents. The smell. God, the *smell.* My stomach growls, unashamed in its hunger.

'Ten minutes, I'd say.' Catrin slams the oven door shut, her hair mussed by the heat.

I down my glass. Then another. The imminence of our descent sparks a desperation in me. I cannot be sober for this. Cannot be even *close* to thinking, to feeling. The liquor muddles in my belly. I go to pour myself another glass and find the bottle empty. Ffion sways slightly in her seat, clutching her glass with white knuckles.

'I'll serve up, now,' Catrin says.

'Don't you think we should wait another minute?' My voice rattles around the room. 'Maybe ten, even. Make sure it's cooked through. There's no rush, is there?'

Catrin smiles sadly at me, pulling up a chair. 'We can wait another minute.'

But the minute passes too quickly. She's scraping her chair across the flagstones, padding over to the oven, stuffing her hand into threadbare mitts. She's got her back to us, dealing the hunks of meat – of *flesh* – onto platters. She's placing them gingerly on the table and sitting back down, one hand hovering just above her fork.

'Does anyone want to say anything?'

We look across at Ffion, who has a dreamy expression on her face.

'It feels like we should . . . give thanks, or something.'

Cat affects Ffion's voice, a lilting, dazed melody. 'Thank you for dying of a massive haemorrhage after we pushed you down a hundred stairs. We'll enjoy the spoils of your untimely death.'

Delirium bids me to open my mouth and say, 'Closer to seventy.'

The nerve in Ffion's jaw twitches, accompanied by the grinding of her teeth. 'Well. Sorry that it had to end this way.' She glances nervously at the steaming plates on the table. 'Your death wasn't for nothing.'

I think that must be it. The precipice. I wait for everyone to launch their forks at the meat – but it doesn't happen. Because they're waiting. Waiting for me.

It's me. It *has* to be me. This is my house. I am their host. If I don't eat, they won't. If I don't eat, I'll die. If I don't eat, we *all* die.

The sisters look to me expectantly. Swallowing around the lump in my throat, I spear a hunk of meat with my fork. It's too big. It lands on my plate with a wet sound. My hands shake as I slice off a sliver of flesh. It falls apart easily.

'It's beautifully cooked,' I say, before I can think better of it.

I bring the fork to my mouth. *It's just lamb,* I tell myself. My churning stomach doesn't believe me. I breathe in through my nostrils and hold the air in my lungs. With the meat suspended between my teeth, I am acutely aware that I'm on the brink of a precipice I will never return from. I suck it into my mouth. I chew. It slips down my gullet, into my belly.

'It's . . .' I pause, fumbling for words and trying to form them with a tongue that suddenly feels like a lead weight in my mouth. 'It's delicious.'

Cat and Ffion's eyes track my every move as I slice another piece of meat and slip it past my lips.

'Go on,' I say. 'Dig in.'

Catrin smiles weakly and adds a single sliver of meat to her plate. Ffion follows suit, taking tiny segments as far away from the bones as possible, as if that somehow dilutes what we're doing. I nod encouragingly at Catrin; she lets out a deep breath and chews thoughtfully on the meat.

'Wow,' she murmurs, her eyes glassy. 'It's really good.'

'God,' Ffion says, halfway through her own mouthful. 'You're right.'

Cat eats the meat on her plate and goes back for seconds. I mirror her, selecting a tender slice. I don't bother to cut it smaller before stuffing it into my mouth.

Everything accelerates. We cannot bring the forks to our mouths fast enough, cannot chew through the sinew and stringy flesh soon enough to please our aching stomachs. The platters begin to look bare, and suddenly we're all spearing meat and shovelling it onto our plates faster than we can eat it.

Catrin is the first to abandon her cutlery. She claws at the slab of meat, tearing fistfuls of flesh and stuffing them into her mouth. We mirror her, unwilling to lose out, crows squabbling over a washed-up carcass on the beach. The silence is punctuated by the snapping of teeth, the grinding of jaws.

For the first time in a very long time, my stomach is full and I feel *hopeful*. A smile leaps to my lips before I can stop it. Catrin grins back at me with bloody teeth, sinew clenched between her molars. It's only then that I realise the foul fucking nature of what we're doing – and it's too late. *Too late*, now that my belly is heavy with the flesh of a man who once hoped and dreamed and feared. *Too late*, now that my teeth know the sensation of tearing flesh from a man's femur. *Too late*, now that I know human flesh tastes like pork. Now that I know I *like* it.

I take another hunk of flesh, and stuff it into my mouth.

We eat until all that's left is bloody smears. Ffion takes the last piece of meat, and I hate her for it. I wish I could reach across the table and stuff my hand down her throat to take it back.

My fingers are wet and slick with blood. I lick them one by one. Ffion swirls her finger around her plate lackadaisically. Catrin catches me watching her, and busies herself with tidying the table as if she is a normal housewife and we are a normal family who eats lamb on Sundays.

'Oh my God.'

The shuddered exhale of a curse pulls our attention to the doorway. Liliwen stands there, silhouetted against the candlelight flickering in the hall. She stares at us, her mouth hanging slightly open. It's as if she's seen a ghost.

'What is *wrong* with you?' She exhales unsteadily, fists clenching and unclenching at her sides. 'You look like wolves.'

I cast a sideways glance at the mirror which hangs on the kitchen wall. It reveals the macabre truth of my appearance: bloody lips, scarlet smears framing my mouth, strings of flesh still lodged between my teeth. Embarrassed, I drag a sleeve across my face. It comes away stained red.

'What's wrong with *you?*' Cat asks, though the shame shows through her anger. 'You're going to starve if you don't eat something, Liliwen.'

'I'd rather starve than eat another human being,' Liliwen snaps. The disgust on her face is uncharacteristic. A wrinkled brow and snarling lip look out of place on her face. 'You all ought to be ashamed of yourselves.'

'We shouldn't be ashamed of surviving,' Ffion says quietly.

'There was nothing human left of him,' I murmur. 'It's not any different to eating lamb from the butchers. Not really.'

Liliwen's frail shoulders shake. She levels a bony finger out the window, towards the village. 'Maybe they're all right about you. Maybe you *are* bad.'

'If we're such monsters, maybe you should leave,' Cat snarls.

Liliwen's mouth drops open. Ffion grabs Cat's wrist and pulls firmly, a silent reprimand.

'She doesn't mean that,' I say. 'She just ... Liliwen, *wait!*'

Before any of us can stop her, Liliwen pulls open the front door. She has to wrestle with it – her muscles are wasting, and her joints have started to ache – but she manages. We watch as she staggers down the path, arms hanging limply at her sides. She doesn't make it to the gate before she collapses.

I rinse my mouth with water and go outside to retrieve her. Liliwen hisses at me, a weakened animal who no longer has the claws to defend itself. I scoop her up. She was always small, but she barely weighs a jot anymore. She fights me all the way back to her storage cupboard bedroom. I deposit her on the bed and shut the door. Her judgement smarts less when I cannot see her.

I go to check on Lili a couple of hours later. She does not rouse when I open the door. Light spills across her small frame, illuminating the sharp ridge of her collarbones, the wings of her ribs beneath her chest. My heart clenches, giving one anguished beat before it seems to halt entirely. We're too late. It's my fault ...

'What is it?' Lili's voice is little more than a breathy whisper, but it hits me like a gale.

'You're awake,' I reply, trying to repel the tears threatening to spill over. 'I brought you food.'

Liliwen props herself up onto needle-sharp elbows.

'Beef stew,' I lie, letting the liquid flood into the curved recess of the spoon. Cat used the bones to make a broth, and added a few hunks of meat for good measure. I blow on it three times, then lift it to her lips.

'Really?'

I let out a deep breath. 'You'll die if you don't eat, Lil.'

She clamps her lips shut, only opening them once I set the spoon back in the bowl. 'Then let me die.'

'Please, Lili. Just a couple of spoonfuls.'

She shakes her head emphatically, arms crossed on her chest.

'Cat wants to force you to eat. Let's do it nice and quietly, instead. Just you and me.'

'I'm not eating it, Guinevere.'

Locked in a stalemate, we stare each other down. My heart aches. Her lips are chapped, bleeding at the seams; her skin and hair is dull; her eyes are slightly glassy, as if she's here but not really *here*.

'Okay.' I blow out a breath, setting down the bowl of stew beside her. 'I'm sorry, Lili.'

'Sorry for what?' she calls after me.

I slink out of the door and do not look back. Not as Cat and Ffion rush to take my place. Not as she shuts the door behind her. Not as I hear Liliwen ask, 'What are you doing?' her voice growing in volume and terror. Not as I hear Cat tell Ffion to hold Lili down. Not as Lili screams, the sound cut short by her choking down the stew she'd rather die than eat.

# CHAPTER 17

*'There are some hungers you survive,*
*and some hungers that survive you.'*

—Etched into the beams of
Ynys Halen's church.

In the quiet bubble of the watch room, I feel irrevocably changed. It's the same as when I lost my virginity. Gave it up to some boy from the village whose name I can't even remember, long before Gethin. Two minutes of wondering, 'is this it?' – the feeling there was an itch he couldn't quite scratch, tucked up in some warm hayloft with cows lowing beneath. I went home to Rhian, and I thought she'd be able to see the guilt on my skin. A glaring warning suspended above my head: This Girl Lost Her Virtue!

If I went out into the village, they'd have me locked up, I'm sure – but not for the sin I committed last night. No one else can see it, but I can *feel* it. I have to keep checking my appearance in reflective surfaces, expecting to see smears of blood around my lips or gristle in my teeth.

Someone pads up the stairs. I expect to see Ffion, ready to take over, but it's Cat. There's a pink tinge to her cheeks, and her eyes are livelier than I've seen them in weeks.

When I felt halved by the loss of my chastity, it was her who made me realise I'd not given anything up. That a man's 'appendage' was not nearly powerful enough to change me in any significant way. But what about a man's *flesh?* Can that change me?

'We got her to eat,' Cat says.

I expect her to elaborate, but she doesn't. Instead, she comes and nestles herself into the space beside me, burrowing amidst the mass of blankets.

'I told Ffion I'd help you tonight,' she says.

I exhale loudly. 'Don't you need your beauty sleep?' Cat's notorious for going to bed early and sleeping late. Anything that comes between her and sleep must have a damn good reason to do so.

She looks me dead in the eye, blue irises glistening. 'Do *you* think I need it?'

I swallow hard. 'No.'

The corner of her lip drags up. I study her in the surge and fade of Point Beacon's light. Her dark eyelashes cast long, finger-like shadows across her cheeks.

She burrows her face in the side of my neck, nose pressed against my throat. I freeze at the sharp, bright heat of her mouth against my skin.

'We did something terrible,' she says, and each word spoken across my flesh makes me ache. 'Something *terrible*, Guin.'

She was so casual about it earlier, preparing the meat in the blinding light of the kitchen as if it was utterly normal. I'm not sure if her sudden shift in tone is reassuring or infuriating.

'Cannibalism,' she muses, the word heavy on her tongue. 'I never thought I'd be a cannibal.'

I'm reminded of the first time we met, down on the beach. My life was moulded by the ocean and its monsters, yet she was the most haunting thing I'd ever seen. I can still hear her asking, *'Do you really think Llyr did that? That he ate people?'*

'Just like Llyr,' I say grimly.

Catrin pulls back to study me. Moonlight washes through the window, illuminating her from one side. Her eyes are redder than usual, but also sharper than I remember them. The beam swings around beyond the window, washing out the room. Cat's irises flash, tiny moons of their own. I'm briefly struck by the thought that human eyes shouldn't shine like that.

'I can't imagine what it's like,' she murmurs, 'to eat someone that you loved.'

The hairs on my arms rise. Heat creeps up my chest. 'What?'

'Gethin,' she says. 'You loved him, didn't you?'

'We ate Arthur, not Gethin.' My stomach clenches. 'You threw Gethin into the sea, remember?'

A smile spreads slowly across her face, lighting up her features. 'Yes. Of course.'

'Catrin,' I say, my voice trembling. 'We ate Arthur, didn't we? Not Gethin?'

'Does it really make a difference?'

'Of course it makes a difference!'

My anger rings around the watch room; Cat doesn't flinch. She braces her weight on her forearms, leaning over me.

'If I made you eat him,' she purrs, 'would you still love me?'

'What kind of a question is that?' I spit, turning my head so she cannot see to the core of my being. 'Why would you do that, Catrin? If you . . .'

Her lips silence me. Cat's body pools over mine as if she is a wave, and I am the recess she's spent centuries craving. A shudder runs the length of my battered body. Her lips are soft, *divine*, but they are also ravenous. She kisses me as if her life depends on it, one hand resting against my throat while the other grips the front of my dress.

'You probably don't want this anymore, do you?' she pants, breath fogging against my skin. 'Not if you think I butchered Gethin.'

I shouldn't. I *shouldn't* want this. She's just taunting me. We ate *Arthur*, not Gethin, because Geth's body has long since been consumed by the tidewraiths. But even if it is just a taunt, that should be enough to shut down my body's response. How can I lust over someone who goads me for fun? Someone who I believe *could* feed me my ex-lover, without an ounce of guilt?

Cat hovers above me, wearing the same ghost of a smile she wore the first day I met her. Quietly, I ask, 'Do *you* want this?'

'Oh, Guin.' A soft laugh ripples across her chest. 'Let me show you.'

She kisses me again. Deeper, this time. Her teeth graze my lower lip, and I yield to her, shivering at the heat of her tongue against my own. This time, there is no misinterpreting what's happening. This is not friendship, or a drunken mistake, or a dare. This is lust. This is *hunger.*

Cat straddles my midriff. I wind my hands around her waist,

ignoring the protests of my body. She pauses for air, panting and feral, strands of loose hair clinging to the sweat on her forehead. And then she moves down – trailing kisses along my collar bones, between the peaks of my breasts, across the expanse of my stomach beneath my skirts.

Skirts which she pulls up singlehandedly. Cat smiles, teeth glinting in the moonlight, and then she devours me.

If it weren't for the sharp sting beneath my skirts – nail marks gouged into my hips, the skin pink and puckered – I might convince myself last night never happened. The vital heat of Catrin's body, her blackberry-sweet breath. She went down to bed halfway through the night, leaving me to replay each movement of her mouth.

My first encounter with a man left me feeling sullied. Today, I am resplendent. Clean and whole and *alive* – but I can't stop her taunt about Gethin from eating at me. One way or another, I need the truth.

I take the stairs two at a time and stand just short of the cellar door. If I open it, my fears will either be vindicated or dispelled. I'll find the remains of Gethin, or the remains of Arthur. I'll know for certain whether I ate the boy I once kissed. Whether Catrin is cruel enough to do that to me.

My heart hums beneath my ribs. I place a hand on the trapdoor, its cold radiating through me.

'Open it,' I tell myself.

My fingers curl around the handle. I suck in a breath, bracing myself for what comes next. I rock my weight back, pulling until the mechanism clicks . . .

I slam the door shut. It rings through the hallway, trembling the same as my heart. Some secrets are best left buried. We ate a man last night. It hardly matters who.

The door to mine and Cat's room is slightly ajar. I nudge it open, stopping just before the point it starts to whine. Cat's nestled deep beneath the covers. The bed creaks as I settle my weight beside her.

'Cat,' I murmur.

She doesn't shift, or respond, or give any indication she heard me. I place my hand on her shoulder, and still, she does not rouse. Panic lances through me. I take the quilt and peel it back, revealing a heap of pillows arranged to look like a sleeping body.

And that's when I see the note.

I stare at it for three breaths, unwilling to take it in my hands. Eventually, I peel it from the bed. The paper flutters like a moth between my fingers.

*'My darling Guin,*

*I'm sorry for giving you less of a goodbye than you deserve. Look after my sisters. One day, I hope you can find it in yourself to forgive me. When you do, I'll be waiting.*

*Love always,*

*Your Catrin.'*

'No,' I murmur, my hands trembling even fiercer. The parchment crumples between my fingers, fault lines cracking across its surface. '*No.*'

My vision chars around the edges. I can hardly keep myself upright. My insides calcify, rock hard and unmoving. I realise, with a sick tilt of my stomach, that we've made it to the week before the solstice. We've *made it*, and she's given herself in. Turned herself over to the greedy wolves who bay for her blood. Maybe if we hadn't done what we did last night, she'd still be here. Maybe if I'd talked to her more, or kept her safer, or, or, *or* . . .

I come screeching into the kitchen, breaths pounding against my chest. Ffion looks up from her cup of water, eyes bleary. Liliwen is barely alive, propped up in a chair like a haunted porcelain doll. The force-feeding might've saved her life, but it's broken her spirit.

I hold the note up to them, my entire body shaking so badly I can hardly form words. 'She's gone,' I pant. 'She's handed herself in.'

'Cat?' Ffion's brows pinch together in the middle of her forehead.

'*Yes,* Cat,' I snap. 'They might've already . . .'

My voice splinters. I stagger over to the kitchen window, fingers curling around the sink to keep me upright. The pole to which Catrin will be strapped protrudes from beneath the waves. Relief swells and crashes inside me: she's not dead yet. There's still time.

The lighthouse door flings open before I have the chance to push it. My boots struggle for purchase on the slick grass. I look for Mackerel in her paddock and curse when I remember I set her free. The journey to the village barely registers, smears of purple heather and blue skies racing past on either side.

Ynys Halen hums with activity. Everyone's standing in the square. There's bunting strung up from the shop fronts. *Bunting,* as if this is some quaint folk festival, and not the day of my best friend's sacrifice. A trio of men play fiddles; Mrs Llywelyn carries a basket of currant-studded griddle cakes, handing them out to hungry hands; children play clapping games beside their parents; Mr Meyrick wears a cravat of blushing pink, watching the festivities unfold with genteel amusement. A stage has been erected, set against the backdrop of the heath and distant cliffs.

And at the centre of it all, there she is.

Cat is sat in a chair on the stage, propped up like some sort of pallid marionette. The islanders stand with their heads tilted up to watch her. Her hair shines like black silk in the morning sun. A girl I don't recognise is brushing it, while another braids in wildflowers. A third girl presses a pink stain onto Cat's lips with the pad of her finger. Disgust and envy and grief swirl inside me.

Amidst the crowd, I find the white blot of Halenprophet Taliesin's robes. I barrel towards him, my head filled with nothing but rage. Whatever strength last night's meal gave me is filed down, directed squarely at Taliesin.

I knot my fist in the front of his robes and pull him in close. Osian surges forwards to stop me, but the intensity of my gaze is enough to make him falter.

'If you kill her,' I whisper, my teeth gritted, 'there'll be nowhere you can hide to escape my fury. Nowhere on this island where you'll be safe.'

The Halenprophet affects a laugh. 'Oh, Guinevere.'

He steers us out of the crowd without me even really understanding what he's doing. We stand beside the brick wall of the apothecary, its shadow cast across his face. The islanders watch us, their gentle whispers stirring like a breeze.

'You got rid of the bodies, didn't you?' he whispers.

I pause, just for a second. The Halenprophet homes in on my hesitation. He takes me by the shoulders, and drops his voice even further.

'Tell me you got rid of them, Guinevere.' His voice is fractured, pleading. 'Tell me you didn't do what I think you did.'

I whisper, 'What do you think we did?'

Taliesin tucks a lock of hair behind my ear, his fingers skimming my neck in the process. He looks at the newly exposed skin, pupils narrowing until they're barely visible against the brown of his eyes. I glance down, finding a burgundy smear on my throat I failed to wash clean.

'That's blood,' he whispers. 'Isn't it?'

I swallow hard enough that my ears pop. Taliesin inhales shakily. He staggers away, almost drunk in his lack of coordination. The crowd parts as he lurches through their ranks, finally coming to a stop at its heart.

Taliesin doubles over in pain, clutching at his head. Tidewardens rush forwards to aid him, but he bats them away.

'It's Llyr,' he utters, the words ground out between gritted teeth. 'He has spoken. He does not want Catrin Morgan. Not anymore.'

His words are like salt on an open wound – raw, biting. After all we've suffered through – everything we did to protect Cat . . . how can a God's mind be so easily changed? How can a prophet turn the tide so suddenly?

Up on the stage, Catrin's mouth drops open. I beg her to look at me – to understand that this is a *gift*, no matter how absurd. Instead, she furrows her brow and shakes her head.

For a moment, there is silence – a rift torn by the Halenprophet's words. After a beat, noise erupts. Gasping lungs, muttering lips, shuffling feet as people consult their neighbours for how to feel. A hungry wind worms between us, pulling at the bunting where it hangs.

'He doesn't want her?' someone blurts, incredulous.

'Then *who?*' Mr Meyrick snaps, his voice distorted with panic.

'But I brought her here,' Osian protests. 'I did as you asked.'

Revulsion coils in my gut as I look at him. I wonder – was that what Cat spoke to him about the other day? That she planned to hand herself in, and he could be the one to do it?

But Cat *hated* Osian. Why would she do anything to benefit him?

'No,' a gravelly voice says. 'This is *nonsense*.'

Aledd shoves his way through the crowd, face twisted up in a snarl.

'We could've had this whole affair sorted a month ago – but no. You insisted we wait. That we starve them out, rather than *pulling* them out.' Aledd spits on the floor. 'No more waiting, I say. We resolve this *now*. And if you won't take action to keep our island safe, we will.'

The crowd appears split; half murmur their agreements, while the other half jeer.

'Who's with me?' Aledd demands, one hand in the air.

Hands rise tentatively. No matter the reason for Llyr's sudden change of heart, I realise this is it. This is my chance to save her.

'And what is your voice worth?' I spit. 'Have you Blythin blood? Are you a conduit for Llyr's voice?'

My father's face distorts into a terrible grin. 'I don't need to be his conduit to understand his appetite.'

I turn my wild eyes to the crowd, picking out people I know – people whose guilt might be enough to make them stand behind me. 'Surely you see the absurdity of this.' Mr Meyrick avoids my attempt at eye contact. 'If Llyr does not want Catrin, we ought to listen …'

'And then what?' Mrs Llywelyn asks, her face blotchy. 'When he picks one of our daughters, or sisters, or nieces – will you sequester *her* at Point Beacon? Or does your morality only extend as far as Catrin Morgan?'

My mouth drops open, heart ricocheting behind my ribs.

'I do not mean to be unkind.' Mrs Llywelyn's voice softens. 'But Llyr must be sated. I think it's better to do it quickly. We can't keep prolonging this suffering.'

'You know nothing of suffering,' I snarl. 'Catrin is . . .'

'Guinny.'

Catrin looks down on me from the stage, her blue eyes like pools of warm water. The entire crowd snaps to attention, their gazes suddenly focused back on the girl they wish to sacrifice.

'It's okay.' Cat smiles. It's not one of her normal smiles – sardonic, or mischievous, or hungry. It's the smile of someone with shallow thoughts, the absence of a monstrous streak. 'You don't have to worry about me anymore.'

It's as if someone has taken Catrin and sucked out everything that makes her *her*, leaving behind this limp, feeble creature who plans to go quietly to her death. I stare back at her, incredulous. Behind me, a chorus of whispers rolls across the crowd. It feels like one of the unsettling dreams I have whenever I'm feverish. Everything's wrong, and I'm the only one who sees it. The only one who can stop it.

'You are not his Salt Queen,' the Halenprophet protests, straightening. 'You will not sate him!'

'I love this island enough to give it a chance,' she says.

The girls on stage nod their heads in unison. Aledd charges through the crowd towards Catrin. At his behest, a group of tidewardens make a beeline for the Halenprophet. He's the one who damned Cat in the first place, but now, he might be my only ally.

'This is heresy!' I shout, speaking the only language this flock know. 'If you have any faith in Llyr, protect your Halenprophet and heed his words!'

But it's futile. The crowd is too frenzied – too fixated on the stage, where Catrin's being pulled to her feet and marched away. Aledd and his goons manoeuvre her through the crowd. Women press kisses onto Cat's cheek; children tug at the hem of her dress; men hold her dainty fingers in their great, violent paws.

Halenprophet Taliesin puts up an almighty fight, mobbed by his own tidewardens. He knocks one man out, and sends another running with a bloody nose. I'm torn between helping him, or following Cat as she's led to slaughter.

One of the tidewardens wrestles Taliesin's arms behind his back. He thrashes against them so violently I think his shoulders might pull from the sockets.

'You're damning yourselves,' he growls. '*Listen* to me . . .'

A tidewarden, no older than seventeen, punches the Halenprophet in the face. How easily their piety transfers. I search for Osian, planning to invoke whatever loyalty still remains – but he's following the procession, bound for Sawtooth beach.

'Guinevere,' Taliesin pants, spitting blood onto the floor. 'Don't let them hurt her!'

*Don't let them hurt her.* I'm transported back to Sawtooth beach, the night of Rhian's death. She uttered the exact same words. I'd forgotten them, until now. It can't be a coincidence – but how could Rhian know what would happen to Cat?

'Stop them,' he urges. 'Go *now*.'

I spare him one last look before I turn and sprint after the procession. It's like trying to move through molasses. The crowd sucks me under, intentionally or not. Tidewardens try desperately to restrain me, panicked islanders' bodies a wall I cannot permeate. I'm dragged along with the tide. A guttural wail inches between my lips.

'Catrin!' I shout, straining to glimpse her head above all the others.

Hands close around my forearms, pinning them behind my back. I look up at my captor, teeth bared. *Osian.*

'It's going to happen,' he says softly. 'You don't have to watch.'

'I want *you* to watch,' I snarl, rabid. 'If she's to die, I want you to meet her eye as it happens. To know you could've stopped it, and chose not to.'

Osian swallows. His eyes dart to the front of the procession. Ahead, the crowd engulfs Liliwen and Ffion as they pelt towards the village. They find Cat first – radiant in her white gown – and then, in their horror, they find me. Dragged behind like a dead lamb found in the field.

Their mouths are open, and I'm not sure if they're shouting aimlessly like I am, or trying to ask me something. My ears are droning too loudly to tell. They attempt to plead with Aledd. Lili drops to her knees in front of the procession, and it comes staggering to a halt. The pitch of her mewling makes my back teeth ache.

Cat crouches down and takes Lili's face in her hands. They exchange a few fraught whispers. Ffion joins the conversation, gesticulating wildly. I strain against my captor, but they hold fast. Whatever Cat says next makes Ffion's face drop. She shakes her head, staggers back. Asks another question.

Whatever answer Cat gives, it's enough to make Ffion take Lili's hand and drag her back to the lighthouse. Lili screams all the way, her face pink with grief, this ungodly howl somehow caught by the wind and amplified till the crowd all shrink against it.

Still pinned by Osian's hands, I'm dragged down the stairs onto Sawtooth beach. The same stretch of sand Rhian died on months ago. The same stretch of sand that will soon be slick with Cat's blood. A flock of kittiwakes go screeching overhead, as if they, too, understand the monstrosity of what will happen today.

The crowd parts around me. When I look up, tears coursing from my eyes to the edge of my jaw and to the sand, Cat stands in front of me. She glances at Osian; he releases my hand. It's the first time I've seen them not in conflict. I think my suspicions were correct: Cat *asked* Osian to turn her in. I just don't understand why.

Cat throws her arms around me. I'm almost driven to push her away – to ask her how she could give up so easily. How she could abandon me this way after everything we did to survive. Her sins will be scrubbed clean while mine will persist, and I'll be forced to endure them alongside the gut-wrenching grief of losing her.

'You're damning every woman on this island,' I whisper. 'If you go meekly to your death, they'll expect it of the other girls, too. We'll be made expendable.'

She twirls a strand of my hair around her finger. 'Oh, Guin. We already are.'

I think of my ancestors, all women, each giving their life to Point Beacon; of the girls shipped over to the mainland for the sin a man put inside them; of my mother's butterfly bruises.

Cat whispers, 'If I asked you to die to save my life, you would, wouldn't you?'

I don't answer, because I don't need to. We both know.

'I wish it didn't have to be like this,' she murmurs, 'but it's the nature of Ynys Halen, Guin. The nature of Llyr. It's his price. And if it keeps you safe, I think it's worth paying.'

I lean in closer. 'If you knew you were going to do this, why didn't you do it last night? Before ...'

'Last night went too far.' Her voice is blunt as an axe thudding down. She swallows, softens her expression. 'I wish I'd seen it sooner, but this is the only way out.' Her lips brush my ear. 'Do you trust me?'

'Of course I trust you,' I cry. 'I trust you with my whole life.'

'Then let me go.'

'That's not what trust means.' I pull back, and the weight of her gaze almost knocks the breath from my lungs.

She makes a frustrated little sound. 'Guinevere Wyn. I have never lied to you. I need you to trust me when I say this is not the end.'

Hope burgeons inside my chest. It feels as if my organs are swelling, growing too large to be restrained by the feeble lines of my ribcage. Heat presses against my eyelids. I drop my voice to a whisper. 'You swear you'll come back to me?'

'There's my girl.' Catrin uses her thumb to wipe the tears from my cheeks. 'Make it look believable.'

'*Please*, Cat,' I whimper. 'Don't do this. There must be another . . .'

'Hush.' She tucks a strand of hair behind my ear. 'I want you to know that I love you, Guin.'

We've said those words to each other a million times: *I love you*. But still, after all these years, I don't really know what they mean. Does she love me the way she'd love a sister? The way she'd love a friend? Or does she love me *more* than that? Does what we shared the other night mean anything, or was it the desperate act of a girl who already knew the only way out was death?

'Love me how?'

Catrin tenses. 'Love you the way I always have, Guin.'

Someone rips her away. I reach after her, fingers fastening around the space where her body used to be. The crowd contracts again, and Cat is led away. She goes willingly, meekly, a lamb gambolling down the path to slaughter. Osian retakes his grip on my arms, pulling me against his firm chest. I used to imagine this – how it would feel, pressed up against the hard plane of his torso. I never could've imagined how sick with rage it would make me.

Cat's bare feet meet the lapping tongue of the ocean. The tide is out, and they wade all the way to the pole. By the time they reach it, the water licks at Cat's thighs. It turns her dress see-through, highlighting the contour of her knees, the gooseflesh on her skin. I thought they might strap her up facing the ocean, so she could watch the horizon as the water overwhelmed her, but no. She'll be made to face us. Forced to die in front of an audience.

The men throw a coil of rope around her middle and tie it so tightly behind her back that she bends in the middle. She flashes me a smile as if to say, 'this isn't so bad'. But then they take her wrists and bind them behind her, followed by her ankles, and she could smile the brightest, most luminous smile in the world and I wouldn't believe it. How can I see anything other than her suffering?

Finally, Aledd reaches up and places something on her head. A crown made from salt, sculpted into three sharp points. Her neck bows under its weight.

The sun beats down; my tongue swells inside my mouth. My scalp begins to burn. The tide is coming in. Slowly, surely, it's coming in. It laps at her hips, then her waist, then her chest. There remain a handful of books documenting the crowning process, complete with illustrations. In them, the Salt Queen affected a dazed smile, her pert breasts protruding from the surf. She was grateful to be sacrificed, and she looked beautiful doing it.

Cat – my beautiful Cat – looks nothing like the illustrations. Her eyes are panicked, teeth clenched behind blue lips.

*She's got a plan*, I tell myself. My voice is weak even within the confines of my brain. *Any minute now.*

A huge wave crashes up against her back. Only her arm breaks the surface. She thrashes so violently that for a second, I think she might make it. She'll slip her bonds and reveal herself as an adept swimmer, cresting the waves like she was born in them. We'll watch as she swims and swims until she's just a tiny speck on the horizon, bound for the mainland.

But then she's slipping beneath the waves. Each time she strains to keep her head above water, a wave breaks across her head, snatching the breath she intended to take. She retches, saltwater and bile fleeing her body.

'She's dying,' I choke. 'She's *dying*.' She told me this wasn't the end – but how can it be anything else when the ocean is climbing down her throat? How could she lie to me so easily?

Osian has gone very still. 'I know,' he says, voice tight with genuine emotion.

'Let me go to her,' I plead. 'If she's going to die, let me die with her!'

'I can't.' He wipes a sleeve across his face. 'It'll be over soon.'

Out in the bay, Cat lets out a panicked scream. The water is sucking hungrily at her now. Each time a wave breaks, it leaves her gasping.

'I love you, Cat,' I howl. 'I love you!'

The water rises above Cat's head, so all that's visible is the crown. She does not resurface.

# CHAPTER 18

*Creating the Salt Queen's crown was the staple of the Salt House calendar. Artisans still make one each year, in homage to the outlawed tradition.*

—Excerpt from 'The Sanctity of Salt'

I drop to my knees and wail until I taste blood in the back of my throat.

Osian tells me he's so sorry. That he didn't realise how terrible it would be until it was already too late. I spit straight into his face. He wipes it clean, his expression like a dog who doesn't understand what it's done wrong.

As the crowd thins, some of them try to offer consolations. Mr Meyrick kneels beside me and bleats out how sorry he is. I take him by his pink cravat, drop my voice to a whisper, and tell him Cat's blood is on his hands.

You'd think my manner with Mr Meyrick would dissuade Mrs Llywelyn from risking her hide, but it doesn't. She potters over to me, rests a hand on my shoulder, and murmurs empty platitudes.

'It'll be your granddaughters next,' I snarl. 'And when the Halenprophet reads out their names, I'll laugh.'

She leaves, after that.

I'm so still for so long that gulls swoop down and perch beside me. Ffion and Liliwen don't reappear, but I occasionally hear their wails from up in the lighthouse. I dig my nails into the sand, convinced that if I let go of the earth, I might crumble entirely.

The tide continues to roll in. It bites at my toes, then my thighs, before pooling underneath me. For a moment, I think it might consume me altogether, the way it did Cat. It hangs suspended there for a moment, absorbing the reds of the setting sun, and then pulls back out.

Someone approaches me from behind. I'm briefly struck by the thought that they might be here to do me harm, but I can't bring myself to care very much.

'Can I sit with you?'

The familiar voice makes my fists knot in the sand. 'Stay away from me, you fucking ghoul.'

There's a pause, and he sits down anyway. He smells slightly sour, like whiskey but without any of the warmth.

'Isn't it a relief?' he asks. 'It's over now.'

I turn, looking my father in his hateful eyes.

'Don't be down on yourself, Guinevere. At the end of the day, Catrin wanted what happened to her.' Aledd lets out a deep sigh, as if this day weighs on his conscience. As if he has a conscience at all. 'Just like your mother did.'

Rage pulls my spine tight. It would take so little to unleash it – hot, caustic wrath spilling over. My fingers tremble where they're lodged in the sand.

'Say it again.' My voice is level, each word clipped. '*Say it again.* I dare you.'

He grins, showing crooked teeth. 'Your mother *wanted* what I did to her.'

Aledd doesn't even have time to breathe before I'm upon him. I fasten my hands around his throat and *squeeze.* He scrabbles at my fingers, but I drive him back until his skull meets the sand. It takes so much strength, all my weight bearing down on that singular point. His face turns red, then blue. Aledd's eyes – *my* eyes, embedded in his face – bulge from his skull.

'Beg for your life,' I snarl.

Aledd convulses, chest jerking. A guttural sound scrapes up from his throat. It takes me a second to realise that he's laughing. Incensed, I press down harder, feeling his windpipe fold like paper beneath my fingers.

'Do it,' he grates out. 'Like father, like daughter.'

All the anger flees me. My grip loosens. I stare down at my repugnant father. He's pitiful – eyes bloodshot, drool slick across his mouth, age and hatred written in every fold of his skin. He huffs out another laugh, but it sounds like a child trying to prove they are not scared.

It's taken me this long to realise revenge won't make anything better. If I kill my father now, it doesn't clear my mother's name. If anything, it multiplies her infamy: a deviant mother and her murderess daughter.

But more than that, it won't bring Cat back – and she's the only thing that ever really mattered. Not revenge, or justice. Catrin Morgan.

Aledd struggles to his feet and scuttles across the sand like a crab fleeing the tide. I watch him go, and there's not a single stitch of me that wants to give chase. He casts a wild-eyed glance across his shoulder as he trips up the steps.

I lay back on the sand.

By the time I sit up, it's almost dark. There's a lingering warmth, a residual light, but it won't be long before it's sucked away. The pole peeks out from beneath the waves, a coyly beckoning finger. It doesn't take long for the crown to emerge from the surf, though it's all but melted – broken down, returned to the place it came from. The top of Cat's head follows, limp and lolling forwards. Her black hair pools like oil in the water.

Tidewraiths snake across the reef, drawn in by the scent of blood and suffering. The leviathan wails out at sea. My head snaps back to the lighthouse behind me. The tower is dark and still. Point Beacon looks naked without its beam. I wonder if I'll ever light it again. If our sacrifice worked, Llyr himself will stop the wraiths from making land. He'll command storms whose lightning will chase them back to the deep. Me and my lighthouse will become defunct.

But it doesn't matter, because they're not aiming for me, nor the shore. They're aiming for Cat.

Unthinking, I blunder into the water. Do not stop even when the current tangles around my calves, almost pulling me clean off my feet. Blood blooms in the water around the pole. Mottled tails break the surface. Talons and teeth clash beneath the waves.

'Leave her alone!' I wade faster, staggering forwards until I'm almost face down in the water. I won't let them desecrate Catrin further. She deserves a quiet resting place – somewhere still and verdant. 'Get off of her!'

One of the wraiths pokes its head above the water. Pale green eyes glint back at me, slitted pupils widening and narrowing as they gain focus. It swims towards me with three beats of its powerful tail. Puckered lips draw back over sharp teeth. It hisses, low and guttural.

The wraith plunges towards me, diverting at the last second. I think it expects me to scream, or flinch, or lose my footing; when I stand there, stock still, it circles back around and stares at me.

'I don't care,' I whisper.

The tidewraith hisses, its maw releasing the scent of death and decay. I hold out my arms in defeat, wrists exposed. If it latches onto them, the blood will leave me so violently I doubt I'll even know what's happening. I'll fall asleep cradled by the ocean. Point Beacon will watch as I reunite with Catrin.

Lightning fast, the creature fastens its jaws around my forearm. It jerks its head the way a terrier shakes a rat to dispatch it. Serrated teeth saw through my flesh. I *see* it happening, and logically I know it should hurt – but the cold has numbed every part of me. All I feel is pressure, and what little warmth remains fleeing my body in a plume of scarlet.

We writhe through the water, a tangle of skin and scales. The creature knows I need air to survive. It uses its body weight to push me beneath the surface. My lungs ache. Bubbles slip past my lips.

There is a moment of peace. The water cradles me. Seaweed caresses my ankles, lulling me into a stupor. Moonlight filters through the water, drawing patterns that dance across my skin.

If I cared for my mortality, I might pause to curse Llyr. It's *his* job to drive the tidewraiths back now. We gave him what he wanted, and in return, he was supposed to keep us safe. Where is his lightning? Why did he take Cat if he had no intention of meeting his end of the bargain?

A wave buffets against us. I tumble head over heels, losing all sense of which way is up. I'm spat out onto the sand. I heave onto all fours, saltwater streaming from my mouth, my nostrils. The tidewraith slithers up onto land after me. It lashes out with one of its taloned arms. Pain bursts across my ribs.

Knocked onto my side, I writhe in the sand. This isn't the serene death I had planned. It fucking *hurts.* I can hear Rhian shouting, *Get up! Get up, you fool!* After all, if spirits exist, hers is riding the currents in this bay, and she's having to watch her only granddaughter succumb to the creatures she spent her whole life fighting. Her only granddaughter who will not fight to save her own life. Who does not see anything worth saving.

Cat is dead. *Dead,* and I still love her. Damned to love her for evermore.

The tidewraith looms over me. When it lunges for my jugular, I welcome it.

Something orange flies past my face, latching onto the creature. The tidewraith snarls, falling backwards as it attempts to extricate whatever has latched onto its head. Only as I gain context – a tail, furiously swiping paws, orange eyes – do I realise what I'm staring at.

Persnickety.

Persnickety *saved* me.

He yowls, digging his fangs into the tidewraith's skin. Little pinpricks of inky blood spring up around his teeth. The distraction is enough for me to right myself, heaving to my quaking knees. I sift through the sand for something solid. My fingers are so numb I might not even know if I brush against it.

Percy caterwauls. It's a haunting sound, enough to break my concentration.

The tidewraith holds Persnickety by the scruff. Blood blooms around each of its talons, staining Percy's ginger fur red. Even now, he vibrates with fury.

My voice breaks as I shriek, 'Percy, no!'

But it's too late.

The tidewraith grasps Persnickety by the neck and throws him. He collides with the rocks. A sickening crack splits the sound of the tide. Percy slides limply onto the sand.

'What did you do?' Grief scratches across each syllable. 'What did you do to him?!'

Bloodthirsty, I throw myself at the wraith. It falls backwards onto the sand; I fall with it. Trembling with rage, I take fistfuls of sand and stuff them into the monster's gills.

'You killed him!' I pant. 'He was my cat. He was a *good* cat. And you *killed him!*'

The tidewraith flails beneath me, suddenly cognisant of the fact it cannot breathe. Its slitted pupils narrow, no more than strands of thread in its eyes. I cannot bear to see the panic there. It's an insult.

I take my thumbs and drive them into its eyes, bearing down with all my weight until I hit bone or cartilage. It's not enough. I'm so fucking *angry* and I have nowhere to put it. The monster becomes my vessel. I tear at its skin with jagged nails and deliver clumsy blows to its face until my knuckles are bloodied.

'It's not fair!' I sob, my punches weakening as the strength flees my body.

The wraith is no longer moving. Its body is cold beneath me. I collapse onto my side, sand gathering in the seams of my mouth. Above, the sky is brilliantly clear, pinpricks of light cast by the stars.

'It doesn't matter,' I whisper. 'None of it matters.'

I expect the universe to refute me. To show me that there is still a reason to live. To give me a *fucking sign*. A shooting star, or a wave so tall it drags me all the way out to sea.

My sobs reach a crescendo, and then they recede. Somehow, the quiet is scarier. I would throw myself into the sea just to spark something – but when I try to rise, there is a leaden weight on my chest which does not abate.

The cold will take me soon enough. I can no longer move my toes, nor my fingers – but my chest is stubbornly warm. Something inside me hums, gentle vibrations shuddering their way across my skin.

The weight on my chest meows.

I peel my eyes open. Another howl rolls across my chest. '*Percy*.'

He is bedraggled and sodden, but he is *alive*. Percy purrs gently, attempting to knead life into my stuttering heart. I throw my arms around him, holding so tightly and for so long that my elbows freeze into place.

# CHAPTER 19

*Rejoice! Llyr took readily to the sacrifice of Catrin Morgan. In the coming weeks, we will see the fruits of her sacrifice. Let us lower our heads and give thanks for her selflessness. We will remember her always.*

—Speech given by Aledd on the night of the Crowning

A wagon arrives the next day. It's laden with wheels of cheese, pots of clotted cream, fresh berries, salted fish, joints of meat. Mr Meyrick must've arranged it – the same man who bayed for Cat's blood. He didn't deign to deliver the goods himself. The rosy-cheeked boy driving the cart offers to bring it down into the cellar. I tell him no, we've got half a body down there. He laughs nervously, even when I tell him I'm not joking.

The sin I committed was not enough to make any substantial difference to my emaciation. I'm starving. Withering. I gather an armful of provisions – more than I can possibly eat – and spread them all across the kitchen table like a banquet. Persnickety purrs as I load his dish with slices of lamb, a hunk of artisan cheese and an entire mackerel. Only in retrospect do I realise this is an outrageous amount of food for a pint-sized cat, but I don't want to sour our fragile armistice by taking it away from him.

His purrs form the backdrop for my feast. I devour an entire punnet of blackberries, their juice smeared across my lips; half a loaf of drizzle cake made with wild strawberries; three slices of bread with cheese that tastes like a goat shed. Wash it all down with a glass of milk, its surface thick with fat which clings to my lips.

Lili and Ffion come dragging their heels into the room and look at me, sickened. Their faces are swollen, cheeks streaked with tears.

'How can you stand to eat?' Ffion asks, nose wrinkled.

I'm grieving Cat and I hate her for giving up. It's resulted in a strange state of apathy which probably isn't healthy, but I'm loath to look too far into it.

I shrug, stuffing a hotcake into my mouth. 'Hungry.'

Lili murmurs, 'I can't muster an appetite.'

'You'll not feel any better grieving on an empty stomach.'

Something about my logic convinces the sisters to pull up seats at the kitchen table. Lili tentatively loads a plate with berries, crackers and cheese, though she spends more time pushing them around the porcelain than she does actually *eating* them. Ffion seems to remember that she quite likes eating, and devours the remaining half of the drizzle cake.

'Can we light the beam tonight?' Lili asks quietly. 'I prefer it to the dark.'

I stiffen. For the first time since Rhian trusted me with Point Beacon, I failed to light it. If I hadn't been going hand to hand with a tidewraith, perhaps I would've paused to consider it.

'We don't need it anymore,' Ffion replies. 'Llyr wanted Cat, and he got her. He'll drive them back with his lightning.'

I didn't see any sign of his lightning last night when there was a tidewraith at my throat. They might not have overrun the island, but that could just as easily be attributed to strong currents preventing them from reaching the beaches. I've no faith in his desire to protect us – not when Cat's gristle still clings to his intangible teeth.

My eyes are drawn out to sea. The pole has been picked clean. Nothing remains of Catrin. It's as if she never existed.

I exhale loudly through my nostrils. 'The tidewraiths were hungry.' Hungry, though I've never known tidewraiths to consume dead flesh.

Lili sniffles loudly.

'Guinevere,' Ffion snaps. 'That's sick.'

My eyes glaze over as I stare out the window. 'She *wanted* to be sacrificed.' I laugh bitterly. 'Everything we went through, all while she knew she was going to give up.'

Cutlery clatters onto the table. Ffion asks, 'What do you mean?'

'I think she spoke to Osian and asked him to turn her in.'

Ffion and Lili look at each other, their mouths downturned.

'But that was before . . . before we . . .'

'I know.'

They sit quietly, and though I can't see their faces, I can feel their horror spreading through the atmosphere – this huge, tendrilled beast. Good. I hope it shakes them as much as it shook me. If I have to live with the sullied memory of Cat, let them endure it too.

If we're to believe that Llyr has been sated by Cat's sacrifice, there's no need to light the beacon now. He'll protect us, just as he did in the days before Point Beacon. The beam will fall dark, and his lightning will stave the tidewraiths off.

Muscle memory forces me up the tower regardless. There are kerosene canisters slung about the place. *Slovenly*, Rhian would spit. The thought of her chastisement is enough to force me into action. I'll take the empties down to the cellar. Leave the watch room pristine.

I crack my heel against each container, searching for a full one so as to discard the others. All but one ring out with a hollow echo. I clutch as many beneath my arms as I can and begin my precarious descent to the cellar, muttering beneath my breath about the bastard, stupid things. My anger is fanned further when I ease open the trapdoor and remember what else awaits down below. Half a man's body, strung up like a leg of lamb.

I retrieve a huge canvas bag Rhian used to take to Sunday markets, tiptoe down into the dark, and feel around until something cold and fleshy hit my hand. Into the bag it goes. I don't dare find out which of the men I ate. I throw the whole thing into the sea. In the scorched sunset, it crashes up against the cliffs over and over until it finally sinks.

'Sorry,' I say in a fractured voice. 'This needn't have happened.'

No amount of apologising will cleanse this particular sin. Guilt coils around me like seaweed as I stalk back to the house.

Back to the matter at hand. I cross the cellar, canisters clutched at my sides, and throw my shoulder against the door to our kerosene storeroom. I can practically hear Rhian yelling, *Your lungs, child!* so I put down the canisters, pull my sleeve over my hand and use it to cover my mouth as I enter the room.

It's a bigger space than I'd thought – somehow larger than the lighthouse on top of us. There's a huge wall of canisters – full, I hope – built up in the centre of the room, with a small gap to the left-hand side, almost as if someone got halfway through building a house with them and couldn't figure out how to install the door. The canisters rattle with each of my footsteps. I'm half afraid the whole wall will come crashing down on top of me.

I'm about to stack my empties against the wall when I feel it.

There's a humming beneath the floorboards. A warmth. Thumping, fluttering – as if there's a fire raging under the lighthouse's foundations. I afford myself a single unobstructed breath, kerosene stinging all the way down my throat. I follow the sensation, passing through the gap in the canisters.

My tongue dries inside my mouth. Disturbance rattling my bones, I press my hands against the floorboards, feeling for an explanation. An unexplained water pipe. A forgotten furnace. *Something.*

My eyes snag on a loose floorboard in the centre of the room. The splintered edges catch painfully against my nails, drawing pricks of blood. I squeeze the tips of my fingers between the gaps, scrabbling for purchase. The boards whine and protest as I shimmy them loose, working against decades of spilled kerosene, of wear and tear. The first comes loose with a guttural snarl. Beneath, a dark, slick material pulses. It looks like . . . like *flesh.*

From that point, I barely breathe. My nails chip as I tear up more floorboards. My progress grows swifter, more forceful. They shake and whine beneath my grip, but I do not relent. Not until I've opened a huge wound in the foundation of my lighthouse – a gaping hollow stretching wide as a rowboat.

The humming, thumping *thing* stares back at me. It's a mounded, burgundy slab of . . . I don't know what. With shaking fingers, I reach out a hand. Place it flat on the surface. It's warm and slick. Ridged, peaking and troughing beneath my fingertips like the shell of a leatherback tortoise. There's a pipe attached to it which disappears beneath the untorn floorboards, but from my brief assessment, it must connect to the copper spigot on the wall.

I'm suddenly reminded of Rhian's insistence that I never come down here. She said it was out of concern for my health – that the acrid fumes would make my lungs sting, my head spin.

'What the fuck were you hiding, Rhian?' I whisper into the gloom.

My knees shake as I right myself. I cross the room and curl my fingers around the spigot. It's inexplicably warm. I grit my teeth and turn the tap. It sighs. Shudders. A stream of hot, acerbic liquid spatters onto the floorboards. I'd recognise that smell in a coma: it's kerosene. I shut the tap off quick as I turned it on.

Two things happen in quick succession. First: the thumping intensifies, and when I turn around, I notice that the viscera beneath the floorboards has begun to pulse harder. Second: the lighthouse groans, old mortar settling. Except – except it's not 'the lighthouse' in a general sense. The noise comes from *here*. The cellar.

I turn the tap again, only for a split second – long enough for a dribble of kerosene to hiss onto the floorboards. That moaning sound rushes through the cellar again, reverberating against the cans of kerosene. This time, I'm attuned enough to track it to the far wall. I place my palms flat against the stone.

I narrow my eyes, heart beating out of time against my ribs. Whorls in the aged rock and plaster suddenly start to make sense, the same way a cloud can look like a cloud in one breath, then a dog or a man or a whale in the next. I pick out eyes like sapphires embedded in the brick, a strong nose, a gaping mouth which reminds me of an empty wasp's nest. And then, once I've seen those things, I realise they're all embedded in one strange-looking patch of the wall. Sort of pinkish – like skin flayed from the body then stretched out, like the way they do in the tannery.

It's a face. A *face*, staring out at me from the walls of Point Beacon's cellar.

My body revolts – stomach clenching, heart pounding, fingers trembling like leaves on the breeze. It's then that my eyes track to the thumping, oozing *thing* beneath the floorboards. The way it contracts in time with the pounding in my ears ...

It's a heart. A heart and a face, here in Point Beacon's basement.

Blind terror bids me to lunge for the doorway, desperate for escape. My movements are so clumsy that I clip the wall of canisters with my elbow, sending it crashing down. An almighty racket explodes as I slam the door shut behind me, throwing my back against it to stop – well, I'm not entirely sure what.

In a frenzy, I pull old crates across the cellar and stack them in front of the door. I'm not even sure why I'm doing it – only that my body feels whatever the fuck I just saw in that room is *dangerous*.

I stand stock still, staring at the door and daring it to move. Eventually, the sound of Ffion and Lili discussing something upstairs forces me to wrench myself out of my abject horror. I ascend the stairs, lungs stinging.

I go straight into the room and sit numbly on the bed. The

more I stew, the more questions form in my mind. Why didn't Rhian tell me we had a kerosene tap in the cellar? She said she got it in bulk shipments from the mainland. And more to the point, why was the tap connected to a *heart?*

'The tap hardly matters when there was a face in the bloody walls,' I mutter to myself.

Rhian must've known about it. Why does everyone in my life die and leave me with unanswered questions?

Cat is dead. Things are supposed to be going back to normal. Why, then, does it feel as if her death was simply the patching up of a surface-level wound? As if to really purge the rot, I'll need to go much deeper?

I'm in two minds. One half of me wants to go back down to the cellar and show the sisters what I've found. At least then, it won't be my curse to bear alone. The other half wants to board up the basement altogether. Condemn it.

'Guin?'

My entire body jolts. Liliwen stands in the doorway, head cocked. Why do they all move so quietly?!

'Bloody hell, Lil,' I mutter. 'You scared me.'

'Sorry.' She gives me one of her beaten-dog looks. 'I wanted to check you were okay. I heard lots of banging in the cellar, but when I went down to check, you weren't there.'

'Don't go down there again,' I say, too quickly.

Lili studies me intently and eventually resolves to sit at the small desk in the corner of the room. 'Your arm will get infected if you're not careful. Can I bandage it?'

I glance down at my forearm, where the jagged edges of the tidewraith's bite have begun to weep.

'Yes, please,' I respond.

Lili cleans my arm with a jug of water, then foul-smelling disinfectant which makes it feel like my bones are on fire. She bandages the wound methodically, humming beneath her breath.

'How are you holding up?'

For all her infantilism, Liliwen has these rare flashes of maturity beyond her age that make me want to tell her, 'You're just a kid. Don't you worry about that.' Still, I suppose there are few things that'll age a child quicker than watching her sister die.

'I'm all right.' I wave her off, busying myself with a thorough inspection of my hands, the quilt, the state of my shoes. 'You lost her too.'

'Come on,' she chides. 'Don't bottle it up.'

'I'm excellent at bottling things up,' I say absentmindedly. 'I should open a bottling factory.'

She groans. 'I've got Ffion to speak to. *You* need to speak to someone. I know usually that person would've been Cat, but . . .'

'I've not yet perfected the art of séance.'

'You're so like her sometimes, you know.'

I'm insulted and flattered at once. Cat's defensiveness and refusal to address anything serious was one of my least favourite things about her. Maybe that's because it reminded me of myself.

'You don't need to suffer alone, Guin.' She turns in her chair, facing toward the wall. 'Suffering makes monsters.'

The hairs on the back of my neck stand to attention. 'I've heard that phrase before.'

'Cat, probably.'

She's right. I can see it now, clear as day. A dark night punctuated by a bright blot of a moon. Girls down on the beach. Stone steps biting at my feet. The roar of the ocean, the curve of Cat's smile. I had no idea, then, what she'd become to me.

'It's one of Mother's favourite phrases,' she continues.

'I didn't think you remembered anything of your mother.'

Liliwen's brow twitches. 'Hmm. I suppose I don't.'

# CHAPTER 20

*Over the years, our fear of the tidewraiths has driven Ynys Halen to conjure up myriad folkloric beasts, few of which are substantially evidenced. There was the Heathland Hound, a black dog said to haunt the heath; the Obsidian Lady, a ghost thought to possess those drinking to excess in the tavern; and, of course, the Leviathan – a colossal tidewraith.*

—Excerpt from 'Ynys Halen's Folklore'

Lili makes a handful more futile attempts to break through my shell. I think she's convinced that if she pushes a little harder, digs a little deeper, I'll crack, and all of the rot will come spilling out. The truth is that I've been hardened by the sea and wind since long before Cat's death.

I take to my bed but can't find rest. My entire life has been underscored by Point Beacon – the routine of cranking the tank, the flash of its light, the gentle comfort of the watch room. The island may not need it anymore, but *I* do.

I drag a handful more blankets up the tower, adding them to the makeshift bed in the watch room. My brain barely has to engage with the practised choreography of lighting Point Beacon. It hums to life, casting its gaze across the ocean.

Comforted by the hiss of kerosene, I arrange myself beneath the covers. Wind howls across the windows. The leviathan hums somewhere out at sea.

Unsurprisingly, the monotone drone doesn't make for the most relaxing lullaby. Rather than chasing sleep, I take one of the novels Ffion brought up here and begin to read. It's not something that comes naturally to me – the idea of sitting still for so long *intentionally*. My eyes beg to skip over words.

I make it halfway through the book before I have to crank the tank again. One of the characters reminds me so much of Cat that it's almost eerie. I'll tell her about it in the morning.

My heart seizes.

I won't tell her about it in the morning, nor the afternoon, nor the next day. For the first time, I'm struck by the permanence of what has happened to her. She has gone to a place I cannot follow. Never again will we lie in bed together and laugh. Never again will I feel her embrace. And I'll be reminded of that aching loss every single day, because she is the first person I think of, *always*. Bad day? Cat will make it better. Good day? Cat will want to hear about it.

She'd know what to do about the heart in the cellar.

The watch room is suddenly too hot. I feel the walls bowing in around me, pincers snapping shut. I sling one of the blankets around my shoulders and shove open the door to the widow's walk. The wind is so strong that it wrenches the door away from me, flinging back against the watch room's external walls.

With wind whipping against my cheeks till they're raw, I brace my hands against my knees, doubled over at the waist. Part of me believes that if I vomit up my guts, it'll make me feel better – as if Cat's death is a nasty bout of stomach flu I can overcome.

Sweat beads along my hairline and pools against the small of my back. I tighten my hands around the railings, using them to contort myself upright. As soon as I do, my nausea returns with a vengeance. A thick, suffocating fog rolls in from the ocean. Something prickles at me – hairs rising across my nape, heart stuttering through its rhythm. It's a sensation I'm familiar with. An inbuilt survival mechanism – the ability to feel when something is watching me. It's usually a tidewraith coiling out in the bay, its fury growing with each pass of the beam.

My eyes move in a practised arc from Sawtooth's steps, across the sand which is all but obscured by a shroud of fog, all the way out to the murk of the ocean. I repeat the motion twice, but it's only on the third pass that I focus my eyes closer to Point Beacon. Fierce, white light swings around, illuminating the scene before me.

Mere steps from where I'm standing, there's something hanging from the railings.

I hold my breath as the beam swings back around. My heart pounds incessantly, the sound beating against my eardrums fierce enough to rival the ocean's roar. The beam glances off its form. The creature peers back at me from between the railings, bathed in bright white. Eyes reflect the light – twin moons staring back at me.

My brain struggles to untangle what I'm seeing. Could it be Percy? No. The eyes are too far apart, and he wouldn't lower himself to leave the house during a windy night. It's too large to be a gull, but if it's not either of those things, I don't know what it could be.

Each of my shuddered exhales are lost to the gale as soon as they pass my lips. Goosebumps rise in sequence across my arms, my breasts, my throat. I relinquish my grip on the railings, staggering away until my back meets the cool surface of the watch room's exterior.

The creature scrabbles against the railings, hoisting itself up to perch on top of them. When the beam swings around again, it illuminates my observer in terrible detail.

She crouches with the balls of her feet on the railings. It's not a pose a human could comfortably hold. It's too precarious. Fog curls languorously around her body. Her dark hair falls in a shroud, soft as it was on the last day I saw her.

Darkness falls again. I hear her moving, iron creaking beneath her weight. The balcony sags as she drops down onto it. Her cold breath smells like spun sugar as it caresses my face. My body is torn between warring urges: something primal screaming *run*, something human wanting to pitch forwards into her arms.

Point Beacon lights up. She stands mere inches from me, every muscle in her face pulled tight. Her rosebud lips pull back, exposing sharp teeth. The wind plays with her hair, whisking it over her back. Feathered slits line the column of her throat, as if someone's taken a paring knife to the flesh without spilling any blood. She doesn't blink, even as the wind howls between us.

'Catrin,' I whisper, the word at once a prayer and a plea.

She lets out a short, sharp hiss and vaults off the widow's walk. The last thing I see is the gust of her dark hair flying upwards as she falls.

I fling myself against the railings, reaching out for her

hand – but it's too late. She hits the ground with a thud. Breaths shudder out of me, curling into the night air as I stare at her crumpled form. Her body twitches.

A sob tears free of my lungs. I fly down Point Beacon's stairs and out the front door. My entire body quakes as I round the corner, prepared to see her broken form.

But she's not there.

I rub my fists into my eye sockets until stars explode across my vision. It changes nothing. The space she occupied is empty. I'm struck by the fleeting thought that perhaps it was all a sick hallucination – that maybe *all* of this, the heart, the face, the girl, was a kerosene-driven hallucination . . . but I can see the imprint where she fell. The displacement of earth and flattening of grass.

Nobody could survive a fall from that height.

She had gills. That's what I saw on her throat. Not cuts, but *gills*. The realisation only properly settles over me when I'm stood there, staring at the space where she fell. Catrin – my *dead* friend, the friend I watched die with my own eyes – was alive, clinging to the balcony, and she had *gills*. That's not to speak of her haunting, animalistic eyes.

Something shifts behind me. I spin around and come face to face with her. Cat's lips are slightly parted, showing the pointed tip of her teeth. It's her, but at the same time, it's not her at all. It's the shape of her, the size, the weight – but the eyes staring back at me do not belong to Cat. Not with their slitted pupils and inhumanly light irises.

She reaches out, resting one hand on the side of my throat. I expect her heat to bloom through me, but her skin is cold, like something dragged from the sea. I swallow thickly as she brings the other hand to mirror the first. Can she feel my heart hammering there?

Her grip on my neck tightens. A shaky breath flutters between her lips. I go totally still, totally defenceless, the same way a rabbit gives up when it knows the hounds have it cornered.

'Catrin,' I whisper. 'Cat, it's *me.* It's Guin.'

She pauses. Cocks her head. Cat parts her lips and attempts to speak, but all that comes out is a scraping hiss. She coughs deep in her chest.

'Guin,' she says, her voice deeper than I remember it. 'Guinevere.'

'Yes.' Relief rushes through me in a torrent. 'That's me. We're friends, remember? Best friends.'

She smiles, and it's all teeth. I flinch. Her mouth deepens into a pout. 'Do you . . .' Cat pauses. Clears her throat. 'Do you still think I'm b-beautiful?'

'Yes,' I murmur, without thinking. 'You will always be beautiful.'

The corners of her lips twitch. Her hand drifts to rest on my cheek. Before I can say anything else, she turns and sprints away at breakneck speed. I watch as she vanishes into the fog, bound for the sea.

# CHAPTER 21

*A lighthouse keeper is a lonely woman. It is imperative that she surrounds herself with friends and family to stave off the madness that comes with isolation. Trouble is, I've never been one for company.*

—Excerpt from 'The History of Point Beacon', an unpublished novel penned by Rhian Wyn

Cat is alive. She's *alive.*

But I watched her die. Stood and quivered as she slipped beneath the waves. Saw the pole picked clear of her remnants. There is no conceivable way she could be alive.

That doesn't change the fact that the creature I just saw wears her face, speaks with her voice, employs her mannerisms.

After a moment's hesitation, I sprinted after her. Ran until the muscles in my calves threatened to snap, until my lungs were choked with fog. I felt the bite of seawater on my bare toes.

Tidewraiths called from beyond the reef, the leviathan's hum a chorus to their song. But Catrin was gone. Nowhere to be seen.

My entire body seizes up with the cold as I retreat to Point Beacon. The door swings open of its own accord as I make my approach. When I step across the threshold, it snaps shut behind me, over-cautious.

My still-wet feet slap across the flagstones, leaving behind sodden silhouettes. I can't face ascending the tower, so I make my way to the kitchen. Embers flicker in the range, their residual heat failing to chase the cold from my bones. I take a candle from one of the sconces on the wall and use the guttering flames to light it.

As the candle sputters to life, it sheds dancing light across the kitchen table. Lili and Ffion are sat there, knees drawn up to their chins. Steaming mugs of tea spit herbal vapour into the air. It's still dark, and I almost open my mouth to ask what they're doing awake, before I realise the answer doesn't precisely need spelling out. As far as they know, their sister is dead.

Ffion looks up at me with dull eyes. 'Who were you talking to?'

The memory of what I just saw pounds against my skull. My eyes dart between Lili and Ffion, assessing precisely how mad they'll think I am if I tell them I've just seen their dead sister – ah, except she's got gills and slitted pupils. The grief etched on their faces leads me to think they'll probably have me committed.

'Percy,' I lie.

As if corroborating my story, Percy trots into the kitchen. He meows pleasantly and leaps up onto one of the kitchen chairs. Good cat.

'Very convincing,' Ffion mutters. 'It only took you a whole ten seconds to come up with that.'

My facial muscles twitch. 'Why would I lie?'

She shoves to her feet. 'I saw Halenprophet Taliesin outside two minutes before you went out.'

The last time I saw Taliesin, he was being forcibly restrained by the tidewardens. I wonder how he managed to worm his way out of the gaol. Maybe the islanders finally saw through Aledd's attempted usurpation. What good's a Halenprophet who can't divine spilled salt?

'You think I'm conspiring with the man who condemned Cat in the first place?'

Taliesin's sudden change of heart niggles at me, but it's not enough to forget what he did.

'What was he doing?' I ask.

'Even *I* can tell you're lying,' Lili says quietly.

An accusation from her is as good as a guilty verdict. My protestations will only make things worse. I shake my head.

'I knew it,' Ffion snaps. 'What – so you're having a tryst with the man who had the bright idea of sacrificing Cat in the first place?'

My blood immediately boils at the implication that I've been unfaithful to Cat. 'We weren't betrothed, Ffion.' We weren't even lovers, not really. I'm not sure *what* we were, and now I'll never know.

Ffion screws up her face. 'I didn't mean it like that.'

Suddenly, I'm aware I've said far too much, given too much away. The sisters eye me strangely.

'I just don't understand why you're lying,' Ffion says.

'I told you: I was talking to Percy. I didn't know Taliesin was out there. I didn't even see him.'

'We heard someone talking back,' Lili murmurs, a gentle

expression on her face, as if she's helping me come to terms with my failure to confront the truth.

Incensed, I mutter, 'Well, it wasn't Taliesin.'

Ffion flashes me a sardonic smile. 'Who was it, then?'

I exhale through my nostrils. 'No one.'

'Liar,' Ffion says.

'It was Cat!'

Lili's hand flies to clutch her chest; Ffion's mouth drops open. We sit there, the silence only broken by Persnickety's gentle purring, the dull hum of the ocean, the fire popping in the hearth.

'Are you happy now?' I mutter. 'It wasn't Taliesin, all right?'

I don't think they *are* happy. Lili's gaze drops to the table, while Ffion fixes me with a look that's caught somewhere between revulsion and intrigue.

'Guin,' Ffion says, her voice thick, 'we know you're having a hard time, but that's a bit fucking mad.'

The bluntness of her assertion almost forces me into laughter. 'Isn't it just.'

'You want to get yourself down to the apothecary,' Lili says. 'I had a friend who kept seeing this black dog everywhere she went. Now she takes a tincture I mixed every day, and she doesn't see the dog anymore. I mean, *sure*, it's made her a bit batty, but at least the dog's gone . . .'

'I don't need a tincture,' I snap. 'She was here. She was . . . different, but it was her. I wouldn't lie to you about this.'

With my feet planted firmly against the floor, I swear I can feel the thumping down in the cellar – the heat of organs and viscera radiating through the foundations, through the flagstones, humming against the soles of my feet.

'You were down in the basement before, weren't you?' Lili

doesn't look up from where she's tracing the whorls in the table. 'Didn't Rhian say the fumes could make your mind go a bit … loopy?'

'I'm not mad, or loopy, or any other word for it,' I argue.

There's a beat of silence before Ffion comes padding over to me, all slow and purposeful, as if I might flee at any minute. I jerk away as she lays a comforting hand on my shoulder.

'Here, listen. Go get some rest.'

'For the love of all that is holy,' I hiss. 'I'm not mad.'

But then Ffion gets up, takes me by the arm, and steers me towards my bedroom. She pushes me down onto the bed, crosses the room, and shuts the door. I lie there for the remainder of the night, Cat's eyes looming behind my eyelids.

Morning comes and sobers me up. Not that I was intoxicated, mind. It's just that when insipid light filters through my window, my world sort of … knits back together. What I think I saw is *impossible.* I watched Cat die. Shuddered as she slipped beneath the waves.

But I felt her hands on my neck, the cold of her touch. It felt so *real.*

My fingers find Whaley's familiar shape. I clutch him to my chest and burrow my face into his worn fabric. His scent wakes a violent nostalgia inside me, a vessel for those that I've lost. Cat's blackberry hum, Rhian's salt sting.

When I haul myself into the kitchen, Ffion and Lili are sat there as if they never left. In fact, I'm fairly certain they haven't. Their mugs are in the exact same place, and when they raise their heads, there are red imprints on their knees from where their chins have rested.

Ffion glances up at me. 'The sacrifice worked.'

'Every time the tidewraiths tried to cross over the reef, a wave pushed them back,' Lili says distantly.

'You let the light go out,' I accuse.

'The island doesn't *need* the lighthouse anymore,' Ffion says. 'Llyr's watching over us.'

'At least Cat's death was worth something,' I mutter.

Ffion stares at the table, a ghost of a smile on her lips. 'I thought you said she was still alive?'

It's almost like with Cat gone, her malevolence has leapt to inhabit Ffion. I spear them both with a withering look. 'If you think I'm mad, perhaps you ought to leave. There's no need for you to stay cooped up here anymore.'

Lili gives me the pitiful expression she wears so well.

'You're right,' Ffion says. 'No sense us all getting on each other's nerves.'

I didn't really mean it. I don't want to be out here alone, without so much as Point Beacon's relentless rhythm to keep me occupied. The fact that Ffion let go so easily makes my heart sink in my chest, as if it's about to drop through into my stomach.

'Fine,' I say, even though it's not. 'Gather your things.'

And with that, our family fractures. They collect their belongings, Lili sniffling all the while. I watch the sisters retreat across the heath. It's strange seeing just the two of them. They look off balance, like a poorly composed painting. Cat should be beside them.

The wind's blowing fiercer than an unfit cart-horse. It has the rhythm of a living thing: a quiet, still inhale; a furious huff of an exhale. I wonder if Llyr's hand stirred the brewing storm, his exultation shown through violent clouds. Rain falls sideways, skittering off Point Beacon's windows. The sisters have their heads low, their backs hunched. I should've offered for them to wait out the storm, but I didn't.

When it rained like this, Rhian used to flit about 'cosying up' the lighthouse. She'd stoke a fire in the kitchen, put a pot of tea on to boil, and light all the candles we have. I emulate her movements precisely, humming as I wait for the kettle to start whistling.

The tea burns my lips, my tongue. I probe at the blistering flesh and pretend I don't feel the pain. Light a few more candles, stoke the fire. Stroke the cat, look out the window. Sit at the table and wait.

It feels like trying to breathe life into something long since dead.

The day passes painfully slowly. My thoughts ricochet: Cat's head disappearing beneath the waves, gills at her throat, the cold of her skin, the face in the cellar, the heart that beats somewhere beneath us. Three times, I shove to my feet, intent on investigating the basement properly – but fear arrests me before I can swing the trapdoor open.

When evening falls, it's a mercy. Persnickety follows me to my bedroom. The absence of Ffion and Lili hits me harder than I thought it would. I retrieve Whaley from Rhian's room and settle myself beneath the covers.

My hand curls beneath the quilts, as if poised to hand-crank the tank. It's the first night in living memory I've not had my sleep stolen by this Godforsaken lighthouse. The storm grows fiercer, hungrier – determined not to let the night pass easily.

'You had your pound of flesh,' I mutter into the dark. 'The least you could do is be grateful.'

A form of sleep settles over me eventually. It's patchy,

indistinct, and I cannot tell the difference between sleeping and waking. Each time I listen for the gentle hiss of kerosene and cannot find it, my throat seizes up. My body rejects this new normal violently – stomach twisting, skin beading with sweat, heart hammering against my ribs as if it's looking for a way out.

*Thump, thump, thump.* I sit up in bed, ears trained to hear past the baying ocean outside, the various grumblings of Point Beacon. My heartbeat pulses through my ears, but there's something else behind it.

I throw myself out of bed and into the hallway. Someone's pounding on the front door. The metal shakes and groans. I push up onto tiptoes, glance through the porthole, and throw the door open.

'Oh, thank God,' Lili cries.

Her face is streaked with rain, her eyes bloodshot and swollen. When she raises her trembling hands, I notice they're streaked with something dark and slick. Blood.

My own blood runs cold. Ffion stands just behind Lili, her face pale and drawn. Both their chests are heaving, as if they've run all the way from the village. Ffion's in her nightclothes, and Lili's day dress is torn at the hem.

'What happened?' I demand, ushering them inside.

'They're here, Guin,' Lili bleats. 'The tidewraiths are in the village.'

# CHAPTER 22

The sisters shiver in the kitchen, their sodden clothes dripping onto the flagstones. Silver slants of moonlight filter through the window, making Lili and Ffion appear even ghostlier than usual.

Lili drops into a crouch, arms wrapped around her small body. 'There was so much blood . . .'

'You need to light Point Beacon,' Ffion says, her voice quivering. 'Drive them back out to sea.'

My chest heaves. 'If they're already in the village, it's too late. The light only touches the coast.'

Ffion runs a frantic hand through her hair. 'Light it anyway. Stop any more coming up onto land.'

Outside the kitchen window, the ocean swells. A dark, clotted mass of tidewraiths lingers just beyond the reef. The tide is rising, hungrily consuming the shore. In a few minutes' time, it'll be high enough for them to swim over the reef. If they make land, they'll swarm the lighthouse. Not only that, but the Vaughans' farm to the west, the Bennions' homestead to the east, the Williams' cottage just down the coast.

I owe these people *nothing* – but I can't help instinct taking over. It forces me to hurtle out into the hallway and up the stairs to the lantern room. The sisters' footsteps echo my own. There's no time to polish the lens, which is still smudged from its last use. I trim the wicks haphazardly and scrabble for a canister of kerosene to fill the fuel reserves.

'Guin,' Lili quavers. 'They're on the beach.'

Disbelieving, I let the canister clatter to the floor and throw myself out onto the widow's walk. The storm pulls me towards the edge. Down on the beach, tidewraiths are slumping free of the surf, making a beeline towards the headland.

'Are we fucked?' Ffion asks. 'Is this it?'

'Not if I have anything to do with it.' I glance between them, breaths pounding out of me. 'Ffion, get Point Beacon going. I'm going down to the beach.'

'No!' Lili cries. 'Please don't go down there.'

My heart clenches painfully. I'm reminded of another stormy night when the same plea came from my own mouth. Of Rhian's blood spilled across the sand.

'I have to,' I insist, fighting the lump in my throat. 'They'll overwhelm the island if I don't do something.'

Lili clamps her lower lip between her teeth and nods. I feel Rhian two steps ahead of me, repeating the same motions she made the night she died. With a lit lantern clenched in my hand, I take the steps down the watchtower two at a time. The caged flame shudders and bends as I move, almost flickering out entirely as I throw open Point Beacon's door and the gale rises up to meet me. My chest pounds as I round the headland, and I almost lose my footing on the way down the stone steps to the beach.

Throat stinging with the cold, I charge towards the point in the sand where our kerosene ley line hides. It's marked by a rock in the shape of a leatherback – a ridged hump Rhian and I chose for its recognisability. But as the rain sputters, offering a window of clear sight across the sand, I realise I'm too late.

A swarm of tidewraiths drag themselves up the beach. There must be a hundred of them. Maybe more. And the kerosene ley line that could buy me time, if not save me, lies metres behind them. It's useless.

I'm struck still, my plan extinguishing before my eyes. I glance up at the lantern room, desperate. There's a fleck of light suspended there – a tiny flame which will catch, and grow, and Ffion is going to save us . . .

The flame goes out.

My breaths shudder out into the air, curling between drops of rain. The tidewraiths hiss and snarl, jaws snapping. They drag themselves towards me, talons lodged in the sand to pull them forwards. I stagger backwards, brandishing my lantern at them. The creatures flinch, but do not stop.

If I turn and run now, I can probably make it back to the lighthouse. I could throw myself over the threshold. Slam shut the fortified door. Cower as the tidewraiths rattle against the metal, the mortar. Lili, and Ffion, and Persnickety – we'd survive, as long as they don't shatter the windows. All we'd have to do is wait it out. Wait for the sun to rise.

But I'm so fucking tired of this. Tired of waiting for the next terrible thing to rear its head. Tired of living at the ocean's mercy. Tired of living without Cat.

The wind howls, animalistic. Waves pound down onto the sand, spitting more tidewraiths onto the shore. I bend at the waist and set down my lantern. Smooth out my skirts. A wraith faster than the rest makes its way towards me. It has haunting green eyes and teeth like a shark – rows upon rows, tucked neatly behind each other.

'Okay,' I whisper. 'You win.'

As if understanding my admission of defeat, the tidewraith surges towards me. It opens its jaws. Extends one terrible forearm towards me, talons poised to rip out my throat.

Lightning flashes.

The tidewraiths hiss and cower. As the bleached edges of my vision fade, a shadow throws itself in front of me. It bows its head and lets out a guttural sound. Not a growl, but a series of glottal, deep vocalisations. The tidewraiths falter in their path up the beach. All their eyes go wide.

*Catrin.*

But not my version of Catrin. I realise that much when she glances across her shoulder at me. She's not the girl with the pink-plastered bedroom, the silken hair, the endless blue eyes. It's as if everything soft about Cat has been stripped away, everything *mean* about her amplified.

Her eyes are a paler blue, and her pupils have turned into little black slits. She's smiling – I *think* she's smiling – but all I can see are the sharp points of her teeth.

'You're real,' I whisper. 'I wasn't imagining things.'

Catrin wets her lips and rasps, '*Real*.'

The smile slips from her face. She turns back to the tidewraiths and lets out a low, rasping rumble. The tidewraiths falter, their talons digging into the sand the way mine knot in my skirts whenever I'm afraid. Cat stalks towards them, moving not with the fluid grace she used to, but a predatory intent.

All at once, the tidewraiths turn. They drag themselves back towards the water, their tails carving thick channels in the sand. One by one, they disappear into the surf.

Cat turns back to face me, and it's all I can do not to flinch. She's so familiar, and so monstrous at the same time. Her hair lies in tangled, sodden strands across her shoulders. I want to reach out and brush it, but then I see the sharp angle of her teeth, and I don't know who she is. *What* she is.

I stand utterly still, barely daring to breathe as she reaches out and cups my cheeks in her hands. Catrin presses her forehead against mine. Her skin is cold, her breath even colder as it huffs against my face. She smells not like blackberries, but like the clean, sharp tang of ice. Rivulets of rainwater carve a channel between us. They gather in the seam of her lips, and cling to the dark fringe of her lashes.

'I'm changing,' she says, her voice hoarse.

'You've already changed,' I whisper.

She shuts her eyes. '*Still* changing.'

Almost instinctively, I reach out and take her still hand between my trembling fingers. 'What do you mean?'

Catrin blinks back at me, mouth opening and closing as if she can't quite form the words.

'Guinevere!' Ffion's voice cuts through the ebbing storm. 'Are you down there?'

Cat's eyes flash. She pushes away from me, out of my grasp. She glances up at the headland, her lips pulled tight.

I step towards her, one hand outstretched. 'What are you, Cat?'

'Guin!' Lili's voice floats down towards us. 'Are you okay?'

Catrin's chest rises and falls heavily. I glance over my shoulder, waiting to see Lili and Ffion's silhouettes appear above the beach. By the time I turn back around, Cat is gone.

The sisters' footsteps echo down the stone steps. I hurry to pick up my lantern, and do my best to scrub the utter horror from my face. Lili barrels into me. She's so warm and vital and *alive.*

'I thought they'd got you,' she whispers, her voice cracking.

'You were nearly fish food for a second there,' Ffion says.

I glare at her across Lili's shoulder. 'No thanks to you.'

'Oh, pardon me for being a little nervous in the face of a tidewraith horde!' she grumbles. 'My hands were shaking, all right? Anyway – they all scarpered. No harm done.'

Lili pulls back, studying my face. 'Why *did* they scarper?'

'I lit the ley line,' I lie. 'The rain doused it, but it spooked them enough to send them back to sea.'

A divot appears between her brows. 'Ley line?'

I forget most people don't realise how thin the line between us and the tidewraiths is. Rhian and I let the islanders believe that all we need to do is keep Point Beacon chugging, and the wraiths give us a wide berth. If only it were that simple. I give Lili a brief explanation, which seems to satisfy her. Ffion, on the other hand, watches me with a furrowed brow.

We trudge back up to the lighthouse, slogging through wet sand and mud. The storm is just about dying out now, and the sun peeks over the sea. A flock of guillemots come crash-landing into the bay, their white bellies smacking the water. Purple tongues of heather whisper as we take the track to Point Beacon.

'That'll send the ones in the village packing,' Ffion says, nodding towards the rising sun.

In all the chaos, I'd almost forgotten what brought the sisters here in the first place. 'How many of them were there?'

'I didn't stop and count,' Ffion mutters, pushing open the front door.

Lili follows her inside, kicking off her sodden boots on the threshold. 'There must have been a hundred, at least.'

'They came up from the dunes. I saw it all happening from the library attic.' Ffion swallows hard, and her eyes go dull. 'There was a birthday party at the tavern last night. They were all stood in the street, drunk as anything. I tried to warn them . . .'

Lili rubs Ffion's shoulder. 'It was your hollering that saved me. I'd been on a house call for old lady Blayney, out by the bluffs. If I'd not heard your warning, I'd have met the same fate.'

'The sacrifice didn't work,' I say, my voice hollow.

Ffion meets my eye. 'No. It didn't.'

The island fared well enough the first night Ffion let Point Beacon go out. She and Lili said the waves pushed the tide-wraiths back each time they tried to cross the reef – but maybe our mistake was attributing that to Llyr. Maybe it was just the ocean exercising its mercuriality – protecting us in one breath, murdering us in the next.

'She's dead,' Lili whispers, 'and it was all for nothing.'

I don't dare to correct her.

I expected the islanders would come. I just didn't think it would be so soon.

The last time they darkened my door, it was in pursuit of Catrin. Now, it's me they're looking for – but their eyes aren't hardened with hatred. They're *broken*.

There must be a dozen of them, all piled into Point Beacon's front garden. Dawn has barely taken hold – a feeble, flushed rebellion against last night's storm. I've stoked the fire in the kitchen to frankly irresponsible heights. The islanders gaze in through the kitchen window, their faces bathed in warmth they cannot feel.

'You remember my boy, don't you, Guinevere?' Mr Meyrick presses his sweaty palms against the windowpane. His voice is muffled by the glass. 'He brought your supplies last week. He's gone now.' Mr Meyrick's voice fractures. 'A tidewraith ripped out his heart. I watched it happen.'

'And my eldest granddaughter.' I don't look up, but I recognise Mrs Llywelyn's voice. 'It was her birthday, and now . . .' A terrible sob tears free from her, so potent it almost forces me to meet her eye through the window. 'She's dead.'

'Please, Guin.' Osian must have shoved his way to the front of the crowd. 'Don't let anyone else die. We need you.'

A bitter laugh scrapes up from my throat. I shove to my feet, fists bunched at my sides.

'Don't go out there,' Ffion cautions from where she's sat at the kitchen table. 'You won't get anything from it.'

Lili nods in agreement, Percy purring on her lap. I ignore them both and stride into the hall. The door shudders as I unlock it, and whines when I shoulder it open.

'I'm so glad you're all here to tell me what it's like to lose someone you loved,' I spit. 'Not as if I have any experience in that area, is it?'

They blink back at me with wet eyes. I'm not sure if it's shame or disappointment that cows them into dipping their gazes. Mr Meyrick shifts his weight uncomfortably.

'I can't believe your nerve,' I continue, my jaw so tense I think it might crack. 'You killed my best friend, and now you've realised it was all for nothing – that she died for *fuck all* – you expect me to help you?'

'We were fools,' Mr Meyrick says.

I turn my ire towards him, hot and focused as Point Beacon's beam. '"Fools" drink too much at the tavern and have to be carted home. They don't condemn young women to death.'

'We believed the Halenprophet.' Mrs Llywelyn's grey hair dances with the wind.

I put my hands on my hips. 'And when the Halenprophet told you Cat wasn't the one Llyr wanted, your belief suddenly faltered?'

Mr Meyrick reaches towards me; I jerk back, as if he is a flame and I am likely to burn. 'If I could turn back time, I would.'

It took one moment to extinguish their dogged belief in the Halenprophet's authority; one night to make them question Llyr's benevolence. This island's faith is mercurial, liable to break at the slightest provocation.

'In a way,' Osian says, his brown eyes lowered, 'I know we deserved what happened last night. I'm sorry.'

And I believe him. In the dead of night, when the world was quiet and Osian shut his eyes, I believe he saw Catrin's terrified face. Heard her pleading. I hope they *all* do. But what use is an apology when she's dead? 'Sorry' can't bring her back to life. It can't change the fact that I've spent my life protecting this entire island, and they refused to protect Cat in return.

'We should've listened to you, Guinevere. It was a fatal mistake. One we won't make again.' Mr Meyrick clears his throat and adjusts his cravat. I always used to find it endearing when he did that – like a little boy in an old man's body. 'You always were our beacon.'

Llyr said it took suffering, cannibalism and martyrdom to become a God – but all it took was a swarm of tidewraiths to deify me. They look up at me like a flock of faithful sheep, as if they're awaiting my command. They're entirely at my mercy – the same way Cat was at theirs. Two opportunities hang before me, each one tantalising in its own right. In the first, I prove myself more benevolent, more human than them. I show mercy. In the second, I take their cruelty, amplify it, and reflect it back towards them.

A muscle in my eyelid twitches. It's all I can do not to throw myself at them. I'm desperate for something to take my anger out on, and they make a good enough target. It would be so easy to tell them all to fuck off – but I'm undecided, and I don't owe them any sort of certainty.

'Go back to your homes,' I mutter, tamping down the anger in my chest until it becomes something hard and smouldering.

'Please don't forsake us, Guinevere,' Osian says, eyes soft and sincere.

I meet his gaze, hold it for a span of seconds, then retreat inside Point Beacon.

# CHAPTER 23

Liliwen makes us lunch. It's a strange parallel. The last time she did this, we were picking over bare cupboards, looking down the barrel of a slow and painful death – but Cat was still alive. Still *human*.

I managed to explain away the first time I saw her. A hallucination brought on by hunger, fatigue, kerosene fumes. I've no rational explanation for her still being alive, nor for the ways she's changed. 'Still changing,' she said. Changing into *what?*

I can't ignore the fact that she looks something like a tidewraith. The same sharp teeth, the same fluted gills. She *communicated* with them. What kind of creature is she – something half-human, half not?

'Guin?'

Ffion's voice snaps me out of my thoughts. 'What?'

'I said maybe we ought to move back in,' she says slowly.

'Sure. Absolutely.' My agreement comes too quickly.

Ffion has always been the most observant of the sisters, studying people the same way she studies books. I catch her doing it to me now, eyes narrowing for a fraction of a second, lips pursing.

She knows something's troubling me – something beyond Cat's death, the island's losses.

I'm not willing to have the minutiae of my facial expressions diagnosed by Ffion. I excuse myself from the table, referencing a penknife forgotten on the beach. It's tucked inside my pocket, really, but they don't need to know that.

Rain hisses across the heath. It drums against the hood of my raincoat with a comforting hum. I round the headland, boots slopping through the mud. Through the misty rain, I can make out a lone figure stood on Sawtooth. Their breaths curl out into the air in smoky plumes. It's not uncommon for people to flock here in the summer, keen to picnic on its white sands – but on a day like today, the figure's presence is abnormal.

The steps down to the beach are even more precarious than usual, given the rain. As I near the figure, I discern their dark skin, their ebony hair which falls in dark waves.

'Taliesin,' I shout, voice distorted by the wind.

He glances sideways at me, barely moving his head. 'Guinevere.'

I stand beside him, eyes cast out to sea. It's calm despite the rain. 'You survived the massacre, then.'

'Barely.' He pulls down the collar of his shirt, showing a ring of teeth marks. 'Do you know what the tidewardens did while wraiths stormed the island?'

I shake my head.

'They fled to their ships.' He laughs bitterly. 'Most of them came back once the dawn broke. Some of them didn't. Aledd, for example.'

I stiffen. My father is gone. It feels like watching an adder slip away into the grass – out of my reach, free to spread its venom elsewhere.

I should've strangled him when I had the chance.

"How did it feel to watch your men abandon you?'

He exhales loudly. 'Do you think I ever considered them my men?"'

'I have no idea what your game is,' I hiss. 'Condemning a woman to death, only to change your mind at the last minute.'

He makes a low sound of agreement. 'It must feel very confusing.'

A flock of razorbills pass overhead, whistling as they go. It's all I can do not to throttle him the way I did Aledd.

'Have you seen her?'

My muscles contract all at once, overwhelmed by the same terror I'd feel if lightning struck out of the blue. Taliesin looks down at me, his dark eyes so intense that holding his gaze takes all of my effort.

'Seen who?' I whisper.

Taliesin stares back at me. Not just *at* me, but straight through me. His eyes narrow; a vein in his forehead ticks. He runs his tongue across his teeth. Tilts his head to the side, as if he needs a better angle to assess my truthfulness from.

'Hmm.' Taliesin turns back towards the ocean. 'Never mind.'

My heart kicks against my chest like Mackerel bucking on a spring morning. I swallow, and swallow, but the knot in my throat can't work itself out. It's *my* guilty heart that led me to believe he meant Cat. Maybe he was talking about Lili or Ffion.

'What will you do now?' he asks, without turning to look at me.

'How do you mean?'

Taliesin makes a sweeping gesture at Point Beacon. 'I can't imagine you're much inclined to protect the island after what they did to Catrin.'

'*They?*' A violent laugh pushes past my lips. 'You're the guiltiest of all, Halenprophet.'

I think of Osian, Mr Meyrick, Mrs Llywelyn. I imagine them twitching open their curtains, staring at Point Beacon's impassive silhouette, and praying that it will light up.

'I wish you'd never come here,' I mutter. 'I wish you'd stayed on the mainland where you belong.'

'Me too,' he replies.

I roll my eyes at the ocean. 'If you're so keen on it, go back.'

He scoffs. 'I wish I could.'

'You *can*. You know how to sail.' I cast an arm wide. 'No one's stopping you.'

'You're not the only one with a duty here, Guinevere.'

I stare at the side of his face, trying to imagine what sort of twisted duty could compel him to damn Cat, then attempt to save her when it was already too late. Before I can ask him anything else, he turns and makes his way back up the beach.

'I wouldn't take the boards off your windows just yet,' he calls back over his shoulder.

I watch him go, my heart in my throat.

Dusk comes to roost. All the seabirds quieten, save for the odd oystercatcher screaming across the bay. Pipistrelles zigzag through the air, wings fluttering as they dart past my head. Out at sea, the tidewraiths must be waking – surging up from the darkest reaches of the ocean, ready to make an attempt on Ynys Halen. If I'm to light Point Beacon, I'll need to do it now.

I've always been this island's protector. No matter what the tidewardens or the Halenprophet want people to believe, it was Rhian and I that kept Ynys Halen safe. I saw it as a sacred responsibility. Something owed to the island that had birthed me. Now, I feel I owe them nothing at all.

The trapdoor to the cellar crashes against the flagstones as I fling it open. I march down the stairs, into the kerosene store. The face in the wall – the *face in the damned wall* – groans. I drag kerosene canisters across the floor so violently that it drowns out the sound.

I take them up the stairs, one tucked under each arm, until the fuel room is almost bare. I do not look at the face in the wall, even as it mumbles for my attention. Ffion and Lili stand quietly in the hallway, supper plans forgotten. They do not move to stop me.

I take the garden wheelbarrow and load the kerosene into it. The rusted wheel whines as I push it over to the cliff edge. My hands shake as I unscrew one of the caps, and I don't know if it's rage, or cold, or grief which causes me to tremble.

'Damn this island,' I hiss, holding the one substance that can keep back the tidewraiths. 'And damn you, too.'

I stare down at the waves, and imagine them being pulled by Llyr's hands. His useless, lazy hands.

'You were meant to save us,' I hiss. 'That's why they gave her to you. Because you were meant to *save us*.'

The ocean lunges at the cliffs, rabid.

'But you took her – drank her blood, tore her flesh – and gave us *nothing* in return. But that's not how it works. You don't get something for nothing.'

Before I can change my mind, I upend the canister. Dark, viscous liquid glugs from its bowels. It pisses down over the cliff, splattering into the sea below. The waves turn briefly burgundy before it's sucked away, out to sea.

'I hope it chokes you,' I spit. 'I hope you taste kerosene for ever.'

When the first canister is empty, I discard it and lunge for the next. Over and over, I pour them out. Even when the wind switches course, blowing the acrid liquid back into my face, I don't stop. I just wipe my face with the back of my sleeve and unscrew another canister.

The waves turn red, the same way they did when Catrin died. I think of all the creatures below, collateral damage in my meagre revenge. The basking sharks that occasionally grace our coasts, their mouths cast open like fishing nets; leatherback turtles with their kind eyes and mottled skin; starfish that look like miniature suns, each of their limbs a ray of light; sleek dolphins that corkscrew out of the water, creating rainbows of light in their wake.

I think of them, but I don't stop pouring.

Eventually, all the canisters are spent. Night's falling now. The lantern room will cease to ignite. Tidewraiths will overrun the island. And me – I'll be safe, up in the tower. The people who watched as Catrin died will know what it means to be helpless. They begged for my mercy, the way I begged for theirs.

And if Llyr is still here – his presence bound to this ocean, this island – I hope he can never wash the taste of kerosene from his hateful mouth.

White light explodes – washing over the cliff, the ocean, the sand. Point Beacon lurches to life, casting light out as far as the eye can see. All the tidewraiths lingering by the reef recoil, chased back to the depths.

I stare accusingly up at the lantern room. After a few moments, Ffion comes out onto the widow's walk.

'Do you feel better now?' she shouts down, her voice hoarse.

'No,' I screech back.

Ffion grips the railings, the wind clawing at her hair. 'We're not like them, Guin. We can't be. It's not what Cat would've wanted.'

But she's wrong. Cat was never more alive than when she was exacting revenge.

The next day, a whale washes up on the beach. It happens often enough, but I'm astounded every time. It's one thing to understand that these huge, hulking creatures live in the water. Another entirely to see them *here*, on land, their carcasses baking in the sun.

Except this one's not yet dead. It looks like a humpback – white-bellied, its back the same colour as the waves. I have a particular affinity for humpbacks, due in part to Whaley. I pull on my boots and head down to Sawtooth, heart aching at the sight of the poor brute on its side.

It smells like seaweed and fish guts. As I approach, it looks back at me with human eyes. I place a hand on the side of its cheek. The whale huffs, moving hopelessly in the sand. It must've been down here a while, based on the crescent moon it's dug into the beach.

'How did you get here?' I whisper, eyes tracing the gouges along its side. It almost looks as if something dragged it over the reef.

Something twigs in my peripheral vision. I swivel to focus on it, but I'm not fast enough. It darts out of view, behind the whale. I follow it, my fingers trembling either on account of the cold or the horror of the whale.

Crouched behind the humpback, Cat blinks back at me with her pale eyes. I let out a soft gasp – something much smaller, less threatening, than the noise I'd really like to make. I don't want to startle her. Not when I have no idea what she's capable of.

Amidst my trepidation, there's vindication. I began to convince myself that maybe the past days were all the product of kerosene fumes. The face in the basement, the heart beneath the floorboards, Cat in all her terrible physicality. But she's *here,* and it's daylight, and my head is clear as the sky above us.

'Catrin,' I breathe.

She looks at the calf. Back at me. Blinks those haunting eyes.

'Did you do this?' I ask.

She nods – a fast, bobbing motion so unlike the way humans nod. 'W—' Cat falters, frustration etched in the wrinkles between her brows. 'W— Whale— y.'

I don't know whether to laugh or scream or cry. The girl I loved – *love?* – brought me a humpback whale to match the plush one that sits on my bed. It'd be awfully romantic if it wasn't horrifying on every level. The poor, dying calf gives a plaintive cry. Its mother must be somewhere out at sea.

'Whaley can't live out of water,' I say gently. 'Whaley needs to go back in the sea.'

Catrin's upper lip twitches, exposing the tips of her sharp teeth. She lunges towards me. I don't even have time to blink before her hard weight collides with my body, knocking me to the sand. It forces the wind from my lungs. I lie there, gasping down air. She straddles my chest, hands braced in the sand on either side of my head.

Catrin lowers her head. Burrows her face in the nook of my throat. Her hot breath moistens my skin. *My* breaths turn into these weak, fluttering whispers. I barely want to breathe at all, lest she take it as a threat and sink her fangs into my jugular.

'I love it, Cat.' My voice wavers. 'I'm so grateful.'

A low rumble comes from her chest. She doesn't remove her mouth from my neck.

'I'd just rather see him in the ocean.' I swallow, and it feels like a misstep. 'His mother is waiting for him.'

She pulls back, settling her full weight on my chest. Her eyes roam my face, darting from my eyes to my lips, then settling back on my throat where I'm sure my pulse is visible against the skin.

Before I can speak again, she leaps to her feet. I scramble to my own. The sudden release of pressure makes me flighty, and I retreat up the beach. I'm half-expecting her to bowl me over and end my life there and then on the sand, but she doesn't. I don't dare look over my shoulder, and only stop for breath once I've shut myself inside Point Beacon.

From the watch room, I see the humpback calf breach the water out in the bay.

By some small miracle – or whatever the *opposite* of a miracle is, given that I'd quite like them to believe me about Cat – neither Lili nor Ffion witnessed the humpback fiasco. I tell them about the whale over breakfast, leaving out the part about Cat because I don't particularly fancy being shut in my room again.

Cat always struggled with showing affection, ricocheting between sickly sweet and devastatingly aloof. Sick as it was, the whale stands among the most thoughtful gifts she's ever given me. It should horrify me, to know that she has the strength, the *conviction*, to drag a whale from the ocean without any regard for its welfare – but there is a part of me that cherishes the gesture. She remembers me. She *cares*.

Someone knocks at the door.

It's almost polite, at first – the knock given by an acquaintance or a respectful family member. Three knocks, evenly spaced. We all freeze in our seats, plates glistening with honey we dipped hotcakes into, the bloody smear of blackberries on our lips.

'You expecting anyone?' Ffion asks.

'No.' I swallow my mouthful of food; it lodges in my throat. I think of the face in the cellar, the glaring *wrongness* of this place which must surely be visible from the outside. Of Catrin wandering around Ynys Halen with sharp teeth and malice in her eyes.

But then – and we all react the same way, sitting up straight in our chairs, forks clenched like daggers in our fists – the knocking gets louder. More frantic. I'm not sure I'd even call it knocking, what with the lack of pause in between each beat. It's an assault on the front door.

Our eyes dart to the kitchen window that faces inland. Sometimes, when people don't get an answer to their knock, they appear there with an expectant look on their face. I wrenched some of the slats off the windows after Cat died. Now I'm starting to wonder if that was a bad idea.

Something flies past the window – a blur of white and black rounding the curve of the lighthouse. Percy hisses, arching his back. My fingers fasten around the edge of the table. I swivel around, this time fixing my eyes at the kitchen window. I'm waiting for it – for *her*, let's be honest – to spring up from a crouched position. When she drops down from above, I can't help but scream.

Catrin lands deftly, her fingers curling round the exterior windowsill, matching the way mine clench the sink. The glass embedded there – remnants of our paltry fortifications – slices the tips of her fingers, letting loose rivulets of silvery blood. She doesn't seem to register the pain. A cup, or maybe a plate, falls to the floor behind me. There's this huge intake of breath, each of us gasping simultaneously.

'That's Catrin,' Ffion says, her voice trembling. 'That's our *dead fucking sister.*'

'What was it you told me?' I affect Ffion's lilting voice. '"Guin, we know you're having a hard time, but that's a bit fucking mad?"'

'Yeah, well, apologies,' Ffion spits out.

'What does she want?' Lili asks. When we don't answer, she presses her palms up against the window and asks through the glass, 'What – do – you – want – Catrin?'

'I think she wants to come in,' Ffion says quietly.

'Oh, in that case, let's put a brew on!' I scoff.

'Maybe she's cold,' Lili suggests. 'She's barely got a stitch on her.'

Catrin's breath fogs against the glass, curling from her nostrils as if she's a bull contemplating charging. Her eyes flit to meet mine. The corner of her lip twitches up into a devilish smirk.

'She's just cut her fingers to hell and didn't even notice,' I say. 'I don't think the cold's bothering her.'

Cat presses her forehead against the window. 'In,' she demands.

'I'm not going to let you in while you're acting like this,' I tell her.

A divot appears between her brows. 'Let – me *in*.'

'What do you want from us?' I ask. 'You're just going to come in and sit at the kitchen table, is that it?'

She shakes her head. 'Want to – go below.'

'Go below? To the cellar?'

Catrin nods grimly.

'And what are you going to do down there, Cat?' A realisation forms in my head. 'If you're after the . . . meat, it's long gone. I threw it from the cliff.'

'Don't want meat,' she forces out, each word forming condensation between us. 'Want kill.'

'Want to kill *us?*' Ffion blurts out. 'We're your damn sisters, you silly cow . . .'

Catrin slams her fist against the windowpane. It fractures beneath her hand. We should've left our bloody defences up.

'Want. To. *Kill.*' She repeats, her words hampered by the fangs sliding slowly from her gums.

'She's going to get in,' Lili whimpers. 'We're going to die, aren't we?'

Cat cranks back her fist, aiming for the fragile spot in the glass. There's something I should do in this moment – I'm sure of it – but I can't compel my body to move. She's going to break through the glass, clamber through it and cut her skin into ribbons in the process. One by one, she'll hunt us down and kill us. But all I can think about is her fangs at my throat. Of my life draining into her mouth.

A crack of thunder splits the air. Cat whips around, pinpoints something in her vision, then sprints away. Another crack. Liliwen shrieks. I run through the house in the direction Cat fled, into my old bedroom. She leaps down the stairs onto Sawtooth beach, bleeding profusely from a wound on her calf.

When I realise who shot her, my heart leaps into my mouth. It's Halenprophet Taliesin. He stalks after her, smoke curling from the barrel of his rifle. He cocks it again. Fires. The bullet strikes the beach just short of where Catrin stands. Sand explodes outwards.

Cat flees, wading into the ocean until it rises to her hips, her chest, her neck, and all the while, I'm stood there with my heart in my stupid chest thinking *you can't bloody swim, Cat!* Chin-deep in the same water that stole her last breaths, Catrin turns and looks directly up at the window where I'm stood. She smiles, blinks, and vanishes beneath the waves.

# CHAPTER 24

Halenprophet Taliesin stands at the threshold to Point Beacon panting hard, sweat slick across his forehead. The image of the unruffled prophet dissipates. He clutches his rifle to his chest.

'Can you explain what the fuck is going on?' I snap.

'I'd love to,' he says breathlessly, 'but perhaps you'd like to invite me in first. I'd rather keep the door shut, given your recent visitor.'

I step to one side; Taliesin walks into the lighthouse. Ffion immediately barks at him to 'put the damn thing down', at which point he rests his rifle gingerly against the wall.

We retreat to the kitchen, where Liliwen is busy re-hammering the boards to the now fractured window – internally, given that none of us much fancy standing outside. She's doing a piss-poor job, but I'm just glad to see her engage with her surroundings.

Taliesin pulls up a chair at the kitchen table and settles himself into it. I take the seat facing him, elbows braced against the table.

'How much do you know?' he asks.

'I know I watched Cat die. I *also* know that she turned up alive a few nights ago.' My brow furrows. 'But more than that, I know that you set these wheels in motion.'

Taliesin cocks one eyebrow. 'And that's *all* you know? You don't understand what she is?'

How he adores having the upper hand. I cross my arms and wait for him to continue, not willing to give him the satisfaction of asking.

'Well, as I assume you've gathered, the creature I just shot in the leg isn't entirely Cat. It's not *not* Cat either.' His eyes dart to Ffion and Liliwen where they're stood. 'How's their emotional fortitude?'

'Fragile,' I respond, at the same time Ffion spits, 'None of your business.'

'Hmm.' Taliesin drums his fingers on the table. 'I'll save that for later, then. Do you know why Cat wants to get into the lighthouse so badly?'

'She said she wanted to kill us,' Liliwen murmurs. 'Is she coming back?'

Taliesin shakes his head. 'Not for some time, anyway. She'll be off to lick her wounds for a while.'

I clear my throat. 'She said "want kill", specifically. She spoke about wanting to go below. Down into the cellar.'

'And I presume Rhian never told you about the cellar, did she?'

'Only that I should never go in the back room,' I admit.

My own heart pulses in remembrance of the heart in the cellar. I don't want to share more with Taliesin than necessary, and I certainly don't want to tell the girls anything else that'll chip away at their mental state. Not if I can help it.

'Of course not.' Taliesin blows out a breath and pushes to his feet. The chair scrapes against the flagstones. 'That would make things far too fuckin' easy, wouldn't it? Come on, then. Down to the cellar.'

I let out an incredulous laugh. 'You think I'll just follow you into the cellar without even a clue as to what's going on?'

'It's easier to show you than it is to tell you,' he says.

If he has even an inkling of what's down there, and why, I need to know.

I exchange a look with Ffion and Lili – the former violently shakes her head, while the latter looks at me with a bone-deep sort of terror – and follow Taliesin into the hall. He opens the trapdoor, despite never having been shown how, and descends into the darkness. I grab the lantern and follow him.

Taliesin crosses the cellar, dodging meat hooks dangling legs of lamb and shelves housing huge wedges of cheese. I'm briefly grateful I had the sense to get rid of the corpse. My gratitude ebbs as he gets to the next door and sees it barricaded behind boxes and old furniture.

Taliesin gives me a knowing look. 'What have we here, then?'

I shrug, heat creeping up my chest. 'Thought I heard rats down here.'

He steps towards me, pushing a wave of dark hair behind his ear. 'You've seen it, haven't you?'

My head bobs without me really bidding it to. I can't meet his gaze as I respond, 'Yes.'

'Well,' he says, letting out a breath, 'at least that's one life-changing revelation out of the way.'

Taliesin sets to moving aside the crates. My eyes linger on the way his biceps tense as he lifts them, the veins on his forearms standing stark. It's been a long time since I've been in such close proximity with a man. He smells vaguely woody, with an undercurrent of . . . rosemary or something like it.

Taliesin catches me looking and flashes a lopsided grin across his shoulder. 'What? Never seen a man put in a bit of hard graft before?'

As his hand hovers over the doorknob, I'm compelled to say, 'It's bad for your lungs.' It's as if Rhian's ghost has reared up to speak through me.

He throws a scathing look at me and pushes through the doorway. I follow him, lingering on the threshold.

'What happened in here . . .' he mumbles. 'What a mess.'

I peer past him, seeing the result of my last visit: canisters strewn across the floor, the carefully constructed wall dismantled. Taliesin picks his way around them.

'Oh. You tore up the floorboards, too. Perfect,' he continues muttering, with the air of a mother observing her child's clutter.

I follow him into the room sheepishly. The pulsing organ still beats in its cradle, but the surface has begun to crack and desiccate. We stare down at it, nausea rolling through my stomach.

'Tell me what it is.'

Taliesin must see the dread and terror in my face, for he lets out a sigh so sincere it almost makes me detest him less. 'The fuel you feed the lighthouse – it's not kerosene. It comes from here.' He gestures at the thing beneath the floorboards.

'It's a heart, isn't it?'

Taliesin nods. 'The blood is what lights up Point Beacon. *His* blood, from *his* heart.'

'Whose blood?' I insist, my stomach coiling tighter.

Taliesin strides over to the face stretched across the mortar. Its blue eyes track his movements. Taliesin rips a rag from its mouth, balls it up in his fist.

'*Mine.*'

The word is spoken in a guttural snarl. It's followed by a heaving breath, like air sputtering from decrepit bellows. I study the face on the wall, and realise that the sound is coming from its yawning maw. It *blinks.*

'My blood,' the face drones. Dust sputters from the seams of its lips. 'Have you come to release me, girl? I have given you so much. It's time to give back.'

'No such luck, old boy,' Taliesin drawls.

I look between the two of them, horror creeping through me like a fatal infection. 'Tell me what's going on, Taliesin.'

He braces one shoulder against the wall, brushing cobwebs off the face. It shudders in response.

'Manon Wyn – your ancestor – was the first lighthouse keeper. Her daughter was crowned Salt Queen. She spent years researching methods to drive off the tidewraiths, to prevent other girls being sacrificed. Eventually, she found it. The only thing that scared them.'

'Blood?' I whisper.

Taliesin jerks his head towards the face. '*His* blood, specifically. When you burn it, what you're actually doing is channelling his power. Casting it out over the ocean as a threat.'

I meet the wall's blue-eyed gaze. Recognition thrashes inside me. 'Who is he?'

'The only one who was ever able to drive back the tidewraiths,' Taliesin says.

My heart tolls like a bell, inevitable and jarring. 'Llyr.'

# CHAPTER 25

*Even without a body, Llyr watches over us from afar.*
*You are never alone on Ynys Halen.*

—Excerpt from a Sunday service

'A God cannot be killed, unless by another God – but they can be broken down. Imprisoned. That's what Manon did. This is all that's left of Llyr.'

I stare and *stare* at the face embedded in the wall, trying to equate it with the God I've seen painted on the church walls since I was a child. My mind can't quite bend around it.

'How long has he been down here?'

'As long as Point Beacon has been used to stave off the tide-wraiths.' He rubs a hand across his face. 'There's a lot to explain, and I'd love to do this all slow and gentle, but we don't have the time. She should have told you this, but . . .' His chest rises and falls with the effort of a sigh. 'It was bad timing.'

*Bad timing?* God, I could slap him around his daft little face.

My gaze tracks back to the wall, where Llyr's eyes have begun to glaze over.

'Most Gods eventually lose their grip on corporeality. Llyr had his body torn from him.' The corner of Taliesin's lip quirks up, almost as if he's about to grin but thinks better of it. 'Manon poisoned his wine. Incapacitated him, cut him into pieces, and embedded the body parts she needed into the masonry. Manon kept his face. Stretched it across the wall so he could see what she had done to him, and his heart to power Point Beacon.'

'*Why?*' is the only word I can utter.

'The lighthouse has never run on kerosene, Guinevere. It's his blood. *He* is the only thing the tidewraiths ever feared. When you burn his blood, it emulates his lightning.'

'*Bitch*,' Llyr spits.

Taliesin elbows Llyr in the temple. 'Mind your manners. Without Llyr, Point Beacon would go out. Tidewraiths would overrun Ynys Halen.'

The horror of his existence – dismembered body parts confined in mortar – settles over me like a rolling fog. I imagine being dissected, my body parts forced to endure in stasis, conscious but unable to move. Nothing but mildew to smell, nothing but canisters and peeling brickwork to look at.

'Don't feel bad for him,' Taliesin says. 'He's a murderer. Slaughtered the woman he was supposed to love.'

'Bronwen?' My hand flies to cup my temple, a movement I've only ever seen written in books. In this moment, it feels vital if I'm to stop my mind imploding entirely. 'The *leviathan* killed Bronwen.'

Taliesin shakes his head. 'He drowned Bronwen out in the bay. Held her beneath the water until the bubbles stopped coming.'

'Why? He said he loved her.'

'Why did your father kill your mother?' Taliesin's jaw firms, muscles twitching beneath the skin. 'Because he *could*. Because she was disposable. But that wasn't all, was it?' He sneers at Llyr. 'You'd spent the year you were married making her life a misery. You beat her. She was terrified of you. Explain why you did it, beyond the fact you're an incomprehensible bastard.'

'I did it for her,' Llyr rasps, his voice like a gust blowing down a dry chimney. 'Did it to make her *better*.'

Taliesin directs his gaze back to me. 'See, the scripture says Bronwen's death drove Llyr to pursue Godhood, but that's not true. He'd always had his sights set on it. But he didn't know that it would work, and wasn't brave enough to test it himself. So, he tested it on *her*, against her will. She was simply a path trodden in his pursuit of Godhood. The wife he swore to love in sickness and health. He made her suffer. Made her eat *human flesh*. And then he killed her.'

Suffering, cannibalism, martyrdom. I meet Llyr's eyes where they're embedded in the stonework. 'You tried to make her a God.'

'Llyr was the one who popularised the idea that suffering, cannibalism and martyrdom were the pathway to Godhood – because that's what he wanted people to believe. He didn't want anyone else following in his footsteps, nor did he want them to discover what he'd actually done.

'Suffering is human. It unites us. But becoming a God is about *forsaking* your humanity. Sacrificing it.' Taliesin's fingers clench and relax, the beating of a heart. 'He murdered his wife. The woman he was supposed to love. *Murder*, cannibalism, martyrdom. He killed her, *ate* her, and was celebrated for it.'

'Tried to make her a God,' Llyr says. 'Made something else, instead.'

'Just as there are specific requirements to turn a human into a God, there are conditions which turn them into something worse. Bronwen didn't die. She changed. Became something equal parts woman and ocean. Something angry and vengeful and *sad*.'

'I hear her sometimes.' Llyr coughs violently, ejecting a spider from the divot of his mouth. 'Calling for me, out at sea.'

I'm dragged back to the night I first met Cat. My bare feet in the sand, sea spray lashing against my exposed calves. *Suffering makes monsters,* she told me. A realisation drums against my skull, an open door buffeted by the wind.

'The leviathan,' I breathe. The hideous, bloated creature that writhes out in the bay. That hums at night – *lums*, as Rhian and I called it, for the unmistakable 'l' sound at the beginning of each chorus. She was trying to speak. Trying to say his name.

Taliesin nods. 'She was the first tidewraith. And then this island just carried on making its own monsters.'

'I wanted the island to be s–scared,' Llyr snarls. 'Wanted it to need me.'

Something about my face must move Taliesin to pity; his eyes soften, and he ducks more than he needs to in the cramped cellar. He's trying to make himself look non-threatening. Empathetic.

His voice is uncharacteristically soft when he says, 'Do you understand what I'm saying, Guinevere?'

I shake my head, even though I think I do. It's too terrible for me to acknowledge.

'Bronwen was the first tidewraith, but not the last. Monsters are born from suffering, and no one on this island has suffered more than its women.' He swallows, waiting for something to twig in my mind. 'The tidewraiths are all the women crowned Salt Queen.'

My vision distorts. The bottom drops from my stomach – the same sensation as standing on a cliff edge. Llyr made Bronwen into a tidewraith – a *monster* – then demanded more women in payment for the plague he created. And when each Salt Queen suffered at his hands, she transformed.

'This island's only infestation was of its own making.' Taliesin barks out a humourless laugh. 'The women were so disposable to them that they never paused to think. Never paused to see that they were inflating their own problem with every death.'

Ynys Halen isn't cursed. It's complicit. This island slaughtered the women in the name of a God who had deceived them all along. My entire body quakes. I think of the tidewraith that killed Rhian. The glint of its teeth, its sickle talons. She was a woman, once. A daughter fed to the sea.

'They're angry,' Taliesin murmurs, 'and they want to come home.'

I imagine myself out at sea in a body I do not recognise. The mass of my homeland above the waves. A searing white light which I cannot pass, no matter how much courage I muster. The knowledge that everything I know lies just beyond it. The aching desperation with which I want to return, even knowing how badly that place hurt me.

The tears start to fall without me really noticing it. I feel my mind fragmenting, searching for an anchor – something to make all of this make sense.

'Your Rhian was one of the Keepers on this island. She knew Llyr was down here. Knew about Bronwen and the tidewraiths. She would've passed that knowledge on to you, one day.'

'"One" of the Keepers?'

Taliesin nods. 'For generations, there have been two Keepers. It's a task passed down through familial lines. The first is the lighthouse keeper; the second is who islanders know as the Halenprophet. My mother passed the knowledge down to me at my father's request. One family keeps the lighthouse; the other keeps the spawn.'

'The spawn?'

'Every couple of decades, Bronwen can … reproduce. She severs part of herself, and it grows into a babe – more of a clone than a child. They are not entirely human, but they're not tidewraiths, either. Part monster, part human. They share a direct line to Bronwen's consciousness, though they don't always know it. Usually, when they come of age, she tells them what they are. What they have to do.'

'Foul creatures,' Llyr snarls, spittle gathering at the seams of his lips.

'Bronwen's spawn are brought into existence with the sole goal of ascending to Godhood and killing Llyr, and exacting revenge for what he did to Bronwen. It's the spawn keeper's job – *my* job – to find them and prevent them from ascending. Because if they kill him, the lighthouse goes out, the tidewraiths overrun Ynys Halen, and the island falls.'

'Failure of a boy,' Llyr rattles.

Taliesin takes a rag from the floor and stuffs it into Llyr's mouth. I drive my knuckles into my temples. My mind is a swirling maelstrom, filled with Gods and murder and tidewraiths.

I've almost forgotten why we came down here in the first place: because of Cat. Because she was desperate to come down here. To come down here and *kill.*

My heart palpitates – the same sensation as missing a step when you're descending a set of stairs. It feels as if every certainty in my life has been stripped away. I'm left adrift, clutching hopelessly to the remnants of everything I knew – everything I *thought* I knew – about my closest friend.

Quietly, I say, 'Catrin is Bronwen's spawn.'

I want Taliesin to laugh and tell me I'm wrong. He doesn't.

'Bronwen's canny. She grew wise to our tactics. This time, when she severed part of herself to make a new spawn, she further divided that fragment into three pieces that matured at different rates. Three chances at ascension. Three bodies for me as the Halenprophet to track, never knowing which one would manage. They're essentially a colonial organism, sharing part of their minds, but not their bodies.'

Lili. Ffion. Catrin.

'Three sisters.'

'But they're *real*. And Cat was . . .' My mouth dries out, and I can't find a word that fits quite right. She was more than a friend. A lover, sometimes. A liar and a confidante and the spawn of a monster. A puppet for Bronwen's revenge. 'I *loved* her . . .'

Taliesin's eyes flicker, brows softening. He reaches out as if to take my hand, but drops his at the last second. 'What you felt for each other was real. There may have been times where Bronwen exerted her influence, but Cat existed, just as the sisters exist.'

I'm dragged back to the first conversation I ever had with Catrin, down on the beach. We spoke of it then, though at the time, we thought the first prerequisite was suffering. My heart lurches violently.

Murder. Cannibalism. Martyrdom.

I think of everything Cat orchestrated. Not only her ultimate sacrifice, but the events that preceded it. A butter knife shattering the eggshell of Gethin's sternum. *Murder.* The terrible act we committed to survive – gristle between our teeth, bones sucked clean. *Cannibalism.* The way she went meekly to her end, the perfect sacrificial lamb – the way people looked at her, worshipped her. *Martyrdom.*

'Catrin has grown beyond humanity,' Taliesin says, in the same voice Rhian would use to break the news of a sailor's death.

'She's a God,' I whisper.

I would give anything for Taliesin to bark out a laugh and tell me this is all a joke. For him to shake his head, furrow his brow, or launch into an explanation of what this all really adds up to. Instead, he gives a single nod of his head. A simple affirmation of something that cannot possibly be true.

'I believe she killed my father and half-sister,' Taliesin says.

I imagine Cat hunkered down by the harbour, waiting for the unsuspecting Halenprophet to pass. I wonder how she did it. Was it enough to toss them into the water, or did she kill them first?

'They must've been closing in on her,' he continues. 'When I came to Ynys Halen, it was with the intention of stopping the spawn. It didn't take long to pinpoint who it was. Cat taunted me from the day I arrived. I knew I had to stop her before she could ascend – but I could never get her alone. And so I had to think outside the box.'

'So you declared her sacrifice necessary for the greater good.'

He nods. 'When you fled to the lighthouse, I thought it would buy me some time. To become a God, she needed to commit both murder and cannibalism before martyring herself – and I knew she wouldn't hurt you or her sisters.'

'But Arthur and Gethin didn't know that,' I say quietly. 'That's why you told me to get rid of the bodies. To stop her from eating them.'

'Would've saved us a lot of pain if you'd done as I asked,' Taliesin mutters. 'When I realised she'd already fulfilled two of the three prerequisites, I tried to stop it – but the fervour I'd whipped up worked against me.'

Still, there's things that don't make sense. Feasibly, Cat could've quietly murdered someone, eaten them, and gone to her slaughter. But she didn't. She dragged me into it. Made me suffer alongside her. Made me eat *human flesh*.

'But why did she orchestrate all of this?' I ask, my voice breathy. 'Why did she involve *me?*'

'I think she was afraid,' Taliesin says. 'She didn't want to go alone.'

The implication makes my stomach churn. 'She wanted to make me a God too?'

Taliesin nods, and for some inconceivable, rotten reason, my heart twitches at the romance of it. Cat *knew* how to become a God. She could've done it quickly, surreptitiously – but she didn't, because she wanted to take me with her. I think of her insistence that I be the one to kill Gethin. It makes me hate her; it makes me love her even more.

I pause, thinking of Cat's newly slitted pupils, her sharp teeth, and suddenly realise I cannot imagine her without them. 'Is that why she looks the way she does? Because she's a *God?*'

Taliesin lets out an unsteady breath. 'Gods shouldn't look like that, no. But Cat isn't just a God. She's a monster, too.' At my perturbed expression, he continues. 'She's part tidewraith, part God.'

'So Ffion and Lili are part tidewraith, too.'

Taliesin nods. 'Bronwen favours Cat, I think. She can

communicate with the spawn – they have a sort of hive mind. But I'm not convinced Ffion nor Liliwen know what they truly are.' He chews on his lip. 'It's a shame Cat was the one to ascend. We might've fared better if one of the others had.'

'What do you mean?'

'When Bronwen divided them into three, she divided *herself* – her personality. As such, each of the spawn . . .' – he shakes his head at my obvious distaste for that word – 'each of the *sisters* embodies a part of who Bronwen was, as well as fulfilling a function of the colonial organism as a whole. I believe Liliwen is the heart: she represents Bronwen's empathy and innocence. Ffion is the brain: she represents Bronwen's intelligence and humour.'

I scarcely dare ask, 'And Cat?'

'Catrin is the teeth. The protector. She represents Bronwen's fierce loyalty, her keen sense of justice, and her appetite for revenge.' Taliesin swallows uncomfortably. 'And she will stop at *nothing* to get it.'

That sounds like the Cat I know. Her sense of justice was always a double-edged sword – simultaneously one of the things I most admired about her, and the aspect of her personality that scared me the most.

'That's why she wants to come inside,' I whisper. 'She wants to kill him.'

'If she kills Llyr, the lighthouse will stop working against the tidewraiths.' The pieces slot together in my mind, each one heightening my nausea. 'Much as I loathe him, Llyr is the only thing stopping them overrunning the island. She and the tidewraiths will claim the land, and they will kill us *all*.'

I stagger, dizzied, but there's nothing to grab onto except an unsteady wall of canisters I now know are filled with blood.

Taliesin lunges to stop me from falling. I cling onto his arm, breaths pounding against my chest.

'How am I going to tell Ffion and Lili about this?' I whisper, almost to myself.

'I'll help you,' he says.

We leave Llyr in the darkness. He makes a muffled cry through the rag still stuffed in his mouth.

Ffion stands at the maw of the stairs, silhouetted against the light. Liliwen cowers behind her like a beaten dog. I'm struck quite nauseous by the sight of them – two girls who do not know where they truly came from, or what they truly are. With enough time, I reckon Ffion could come around to it. But sweet, soft Liliwen, the embodiment of Bronwen's kindness and innocence . . . I'm not sure how she'll fare.

I've never been good at breaking bad news. It's part of being the lighthouse keeper; whenever a sailor is lost to the sea, there's a decent chance they'll wash up on Sawtooth, and we'll be the ones to find their mangled body. Rhian used to bear that burden for me, though I can't think of many people worse suited to delivering such devastating news, what with her general prickliness. Still, I wish she were here now. Wish she could help me tell the girls what I now know.

'Come and sit in the kitchen,' I tell them, hiking up my skirts as I ascend the stairs. 'We need to have a talk.'

'That we do,' Ffion says grimly.

Her tone is enough to coax my gaze upwards. I notice, now, that she's stood defensively – shoulders braced, knees a stride apart. It takes me several seconds to register that Ffion is holding Taliesin's gun. Less than a breath to understand once she cocks it.

'*Explain*,' Ffion demands. The barrel shakes as she jerks it towards us.

'Put the bloody gun down, Ffion!' My eyebrows nearly touch my hairline. 'What do you think you're doing?'

'Easy, now,' Taliesin says. 'Let's not do anything hasty.'

'We both heard it,' Ffion says between gritted teeth, eyes darting to Taliesin behind me. 'I'm not going to let you hurt her.'

'What are you talking about?' I ask. 'I'd feel much better having this conversation if I wasn't looking down the barrel of—'

'This isn't a fucking conversation, Guinevere! I'm not going down easy. And you sure as hell aren't touching a hair on Lili's head.'

Lili gives a stifled sob, peering around Ffion.

'She's talking to them,' Taliesin murmurs. 'Bronwen. She's opened the connection. She's in their minds.'

'*Bronwen?*' Ffion brandishes the rifle again; Lili yelps behind her. 'What are you on about?'

Taliesin says, 'Someone spoke to you, didn't they? A woman. Straight into your mind.'

Lili squeaks, 'How do you know that?'

I stare around Ffion's frame and tell her, 'Because the same thing happened to Cat, and now she's dead.'

'She's not dead.' Lili sniffs. 'I saw her out the window.'

I wipe a hand across my face. 'Oh, for the love of all that's holy, you know what I mean.' Addressing Ffion, I say, 'Please put the rifle down. I've not got so much as a spoon to defend myself with, and you're worried I'm gonna— what? Tickle you to death?'

The venom in Ffion's expression falters. 'She said you're going to hurt us. That that's been your plan all along.'

'Think about it, Fi.' I try to soften my voice, which isn't something that comes naturally. 'If I had designs to kill you, I'd have done it a long time ago. You've both been a pain in my backside ever since you moved in here.'

The corner of Ffion's mouth twitches. She lets the rifle drop to her side and stalks away from the staircase. Lili scurries dutifully behind her.

'I should've stayed on the mainland,' Taliesin mutters. 'Ynys Halen doesn't deserve saving.'

# CHAPTER 26

*When a piece of coral breaks loose and settles in a suitable location, this fragment can attach to the seabed and grow into a new, genetically identical colony.*

—Excerpt from 'An Introduction to Marine Biology'

'I'm *real!*' Liliwen wails, sinking her head onto the kitchen table. 'Not just a . . . a *protuberance* from a sea monster!'

I lean back against the wall in the kitchen, Percy winding around my calves. Ffion took the news surprisingly well, though I'm not confident she totally believes us. I suppose when you and your sister have experienced the same voice speaking into your mind, preceded by seeing your monstrous *dead* sister appear at the window, not much else can come as a surprise.

'Of course you're real, pet,' Ffion says, stroking her shoulder.

'Corals grow that way, you know,' I say absentmindedly. 'If

a branch snaps off, it can form its own distinct structure. It's no less real than the coral it came from.'

'Can you go longer than five minutes without referencing the ocean?' Ffion mutters.

I scoff. 'That's rich coming from the walking encyclopaedia.'

'No.' Liliwen sniffs, wiping the back of her sleeve across her cheeks. 'I like that. The coral thing. It makes me feel better.'

Ffion looks down at her younger sister with what might be maternal affection, or else abject hopelessness. Her eyes dart to Taliesin. 'If Cat's a God, why hasn't she killed Llyr already? Surely a little brick and mortar isn't enough to stop her.'

'A newborn God isn't too far off a newborn baby,' Taliesin explains. 'From what Llyr told my father, it takes them a while to find their feet. It varies between individuals, but based on what my father told Llyr about Catrin, he thinks she'll likely reach maturity by the end of the week. She'll become stronger. Less human.'

'Sorry.' Ffion rubs her fists into her eyes hard enough that she must be seeing stars. '*Llyr* told your father that? I know your family are Halenprophets, but I didn't think you had back-and-forth conversations with him.'

Taliesin rubs the back of his neck. 'Halenprophecy isn't real. Spilling salt is all smoke and mirrors. All of the religious ceremony is designed to gain the islanders' trust, so in instances where the spawn keeper succeeds in *killing* the spawn, no one suspects them.'

Ffion pulls a face. 'So how're you talking to Llyr, then?'

'Llyr's in the cellar,' I say distantly.

'He's in the fucking *what* now?'

Taliesin explains how Llyr was imprisoned in the cellar, his blood used to light the beam that keeps the tidewraiths at bay.

When ignited, it provides the same effect as his lightning – a deterrent to any wraiths intent on making land. Lili clamps a hand over her mouth and turns a pale green. As always, Ffion has a dozen intricately thought-out questions. Taliesin begins to answer them, then mutters that we don't have time.

'Once Catrin grows into her powers, we won't be able to stop her. Bronwen's desire for revenge will be all she knows. She'll breach the lighthouse, and she *will* kill Llyr. Bronwen has hungered after his death for centuries; the second she gets the opportunity, she'll take it.'

'And if Cat kills Llyr, Point Beacon will stop working, and tide-wraiths will overrun the island,' Lili says softly.

Taliesin nods. 'Unless we stop her.'

Ffion slumps over in her chair, wiping one hand aggressively across her face.

'But Cat's a *God*. How can we stop her?' My eyes dart between Ffion and Taliesin. 'Only a God can kill a God, and I don't think Llyr's up to fighting, what with the fact that he has no hands, or arms, or legs . . .'

'Then we need to *make* a God,' Ffion says grimly.

I fold my arms across my chest. 'And how, precisely, would we go about doing that?'

Taliesin tuts. 'Did you not listen to a single world I said in the cellar?'

'Oh, sorry. Must've been lost in translation somewhere between the fact that Catrin's a God-monster and Llyr being strung up on the wall like a painting.'

He huffs out a laugh, then nods towards Ffion. '*She* gets it. I told you: she's the intelligent one.'

'I'm quite clever, too,' Lili murmurs.

I throw up my hands. 'Well, it'd be awfully lovely if one of you would clue me in.'

'Now that Cat's a God, we'll need a God of our own to stop her. Fortunately, we know exactly how to *create* a God: murder, cannibalism, martyrdom.'

'What – so you think one of us should try to become a God? And all it'll require is a light spot of murder, a bit of cannibal—'

My voice falters. We're already cannibals. We've already stepped away from humanity.

Ffion clears her throat. 'There is one person in this room who has already fulfilled two of the requirements: cannibalism and murder.' She lets out a deep, shaking breath. 'What I mean to say is that they only need to fulfil the final requirement, and if my assumption is correct, they'll become a God. They'll be able to stop Cat from killing Llyr.'

I remember the way Arthur and Gethin crumpled as they fell down the stairs. Their deadly stillness at the bottom. It was Ffion who pushed them, shattering the thick shell of their skulls. She sat at the table and ate human flesh with us.

'Oh,' Liliwen says, her voice a trembling exhale.

The idea of Ffion becoming a God feels so absurd that it makes my head fill with fog. 'What would it take to make you a martyr?' I ask, my voice thick.

'A martyr is defined as someone who dies for a cause – typically religious, but not always.'

'Thanks for that, Ffion,' I mutter. Clearly, the threat of death hasn't rattled her enough to stop providing dictionary-accurate definitions. 'I mean more in the sense of what we're trying to achieve. What can we feasibly do to make you a martyr?'

'What we did to Cat worked,' Taliesin muses glibly.

'But Ffion would have to *die*,' Liliwen says, her pale brow contorted.

'If everything went to plan, it wouldn't be permanent,' Ffion says.

The half-hearted assurance does nothing to comfort Liliwen, whose eyes are growing glassier by the second.

'And you're all right with that, are you?' I ask. 'Dying.'

Ffion shrugs. 'Do I really have a choice? Either I die to stop her, or we *don't* stop her, and I die when the tidewraiths overrun the island.' At Lili's resulting whimper, Ffion plasters a grin onto her face. 'Besides, I've always had delusions of grandeur. I think I'd make a fine God.'

My gaze swings to Taliesin. 'You reckon you can stage another crowning?'

He grins. 'I'm nothing if not a visionary.'

The same islanders that led Cat to her death file into the pews, chatting carefully among themselves. It makes me sick. What sort of conviction allows a person to actively participate in a young woman's murder, then to sit in a hallowed space without so much as a shred of shame?

Finally freed from the gaol, Dylan reunites with his daughters. His grief-tinted joy makes me sick with guilt. He has no idea what's coming.

I glance up at Taliesin where he stands at the lectern. With Aledd gone, Taliesin slips deftly back in charge. He's slipped on the disguise he wears so well – white robes transforming him into the silver-tongued Halenprophet. All he needs to do is clear his throat, and the congregation falls silent.

'You listened to a false prophet,' he booms.

People shuffle uncomfortably in their pews, heads bowed.

'I – the conduit for Llyr – told you Catrin Morgan was no longer a suitable Salt Queen. Yet you did not listen. You took a girl to her death, and for what?' He blows out a shuddery breath, fingers curled around the lectern. 'As you witnessed, the sacrifice did not sate Llyr. He did not deter the tidewraiths.'

Taliesin's eyes skim across the congregation. He meets every single islander's gaze. Makes them culpable.

'Are you ready to listen, now?' he asks.

In unison, the congregation replies, 'Yes.'

He slams his fists down onto the lectern. People gasp. I knew it was coming, and still, I flinch.

'I spilled salt once more, to convene with our God – and Ffion Morgan is his choice.'

Taliesin's voice is so sincere that even *I* think he's telling the truth, even though I know it's a lie. If being crowned Salt Queen made Cat a martyr, it should do the same for Ffion.

Dylan thrusts to his rickety legs. '*No*,' he cries. 'Not another of my daughters!'

Lili, positioned strategically beside him, holds her father's hand. This is the cruellest part of it all – making Dylan believe a second Morgan girl must be fed to the sea.

'It is a testament to the beauty of your daughters, Dylan.' The tenderness in Taliesin's voice doesn't need to be forced. 'But this sacrifice will not be public. Llyr demands the sacrifice to take place within Point Beacon's walls, to cleanse the disrespect shown to him in our reliance on the lighthouse. Ffion's body will then be returned to the sea.'

This added fabrication is a result of Ffion feeling that being strung up and crowned was a 'bridge too fucking far'. We decided, in the absence of Lili's sensitive ears, that a quiet death in the lighthouse would be preferable. Ffion acted as if she wasn't scared of death, but I caught the way her voice cracked, and no amount of balling up her hands could hide the way they shook.

The islanders are confused at first. Why wasn't Catrin's death enough to please Llyr? Why must another Morgan girl die – and this time, inside the bowels of Point Beacon? Still, with the reassurance of both Halenprophet Taliesin and Ffion, the one set to be sacrificed, they come to terms with it easily enough. My stomach turns. It's never taken much for them to condemn a woman to death.

We move to the square, where the stage still stands. Ffion sits on it the same way Cat did. Stationed in the crowd, Lili and I reinforce the charade. We hold each other tight, shaking with wheezing sobs which might be real or might not. At one point, I whisper for her to hold me back as I lunge towards the stage, launching a final bid to save Ffion the way I couldn't save Cat.

People avert their eyes, disconcerted by my pretence of grief. Perhaps its efficacy lies in the fact it's not a pretence at all. It's a stain on my morality, but what Ffion is about to go through – no matter her willingness – isn't what pains me most. It's Cat.

It should reassure me to know that there's a part of her – no matter how small – that's still alive, but it doesn't. Not when I know we have to extinguish that part for good, if the island is to survive.

Mrs Llywelyn clutches her gaggle of grandchildren, glassy eyes fixed on Ffion. Perhaps she finally understands that one day, it'll be her own kin. That it was never going to begin and end with Catrin.

Eventually, we start the funeral march to Point Beacon. I'm allowed to walk at the front this time, Ffion and Lili beside me. Taliesin provides a barrier against the rest of the islanders. It's just as well, because I want to turn and curse them for the way they skip along behind us, talking among themselves as if this is just a trip to the beach.

They leave us at the lighthouse door. Ffion spares Dylan what her father believes is their final hug. The sisters, Taliesin and I retreat inside Point Beacon. The lighthouse groans, and when I glance backwards through the window at the islanders, I find them staring up at the tower, horrified. Mrs Llywelyn herds her grandchildren back across the heath; Mr Meyrick goes staggering home, blown by the wind. Gradually, the crowd dissipates.

'It's Llyr, isn't it?' I glance at Taliesin. 'He's what makes the lighthouse seem alive.'

Hot fires. Doors moving by themselves. Water heated just as I needed it.

Taliesin says, 'He thought you would be the one to stop her. Catrin, I mean. I think he wanted to earn your favour. Rhian and my father spoke about it often. I read his journals. He said that when you turned eighteen, Rhian wanted to send you and Cat to the mainland.'

'She could've still become a God on the mainland, couldn't she?'

Taliesin looks out the window. 'I think you're the only person she would've forsaken Godhood for. Away from Bronwen's influence, free to live her life by your side . . .' He tugs at his bottom lip with his teeth. 'I think, with you, she would've been content with being human.'

He might as well take a dagger to my heart. I suck in a breath to stop myself from crying. A watercolour tableau spreads through my mind: a cottage with a rose garden, Cat in a summer dress, Percy winding around her calves. I'm there somewhere, though I'm not sure in what capacity. I'm just grateful to be involved.

'Right,' Ffion slaps her knees, breaking my reverie. 'Based on my reading, the quickest thing would probably be to rupture my heart, or else to sever my jugular vein.' She traces it beneath the paper skin of her throat – that thrumming, vital beat. 'I think, if it's all the same to you, I'd rather go for the jugular.'

Taliesin makes a curious sound in the back of his throat. 'I'd go for the heart, personally.'

'When you're the one being murdered, we'll take that into consideration,' Ffion snaps.

I snort. 'Would you mind if we did it in the tub? It's just we'll never get the blood out of the grout if we do it here, and . . .' I trail off, the fiery focus of Ffion's glare forcing me into silence.

'You're so right, Guin,' she mutters. 'When I'm killing myself to protect you ungrateful lot, I should really prioritise the grout.' At my shrinking, she tuts and says, 'Yes, I'll die in the tub, if it'll make you happy.'

I briefly suggest that maybe she should take her clothes off to avoid staining them, to which she calls me both cheap and a pervert.

'But in exchange,' Ffion says, 'I want you to be the one that does it.'

'Oh, come on.' My protests fall dead in the air when I realise that Ffion is asking for much less than she's taking. Softly, I ask, 'Wouldn't you rather Taliesin did it? I'm sure he's more experienced with a blade.'

'*No*, believe it or not, I don't feel particularly comfortable with manipulation itself ending my life.'

Taliesin huffs with offence.

Ffion levels a finger at Taliesin. 'You said Cat'll be mature soon, but she's been a God for far longer than me. If that's the case, how am I going to mature quick enough to stop her from killing Llyr?'

He clears his throat awkwardly. 'You're the brains, and also the oldest. I can only hope it'll help you mature faster.'

'Hope,' Ffion mutters. 'Now that'd be a fine thing.'

Sensing we're all skirting around the precipice we need to throw ourselves from, I make up something about Percy feeling out of sorts, and assign Liliwen to take care of him. She takes it very seriously, and scoops him up onto her lap while she sits at the kitchen table, feeding him an incredibly expensive tin of sardines.

'Keep her busy,' I whisper to Taliesin.

He nods solemnly and takes a seat at the kitchen table.

With the distraction laid, I usher Ffion into the bathroom and settle her in the bowl of the tub.

The penknife feels both wildly violent and totally flimsy in my hand. I remember the way Cat's forearms tensed as she drove the butter knife through Gethin's chest – the conviction, the *heft* required to puncture it. Ffion's throat is nothing like that: it trembles like a captured bird beneath the point of the knife.

'This will work, won't it?' I ask, my voice breathy. 'You'll come back.'

'Yes,' she says. 'And if I don't, I'll be none the wiser.'

I lower the blade, resting it against the enamel tub. I look at Ffion where she lays and recall her as she was on the first night we met: windswept, barefoot. We've spent a decade as friends, and now I'm preparing to kill her. It feels wrong. Twisted.

'I'm scared, Ffion.'

She shuffles to a seated position. 'Me too. But for what it's worth, there's no one else I'd trust to do this.' Ffion swallows. 'You're a good friend, Guin. Always have been.'

'So are you,' I murmur.

Cat was always the stabilising pillar of my life. I pivoted around her, always keeping her in sight. At times, I was so blinded by her that I failed to truly appreciate the companionship offered by Lili, by Ffion. I think of all the books Ffion hefted up to the lighthouse after Rhian died. Of her acerbic wit, her wonderful brain, her kind heart.

I let out an unsteady breath and raise the knife again, pressing it flush against her throat. Her flesh balloons out around it, and the violence of what I'm about to do nearly makes me retch.

'Now is not the time for suspense, Guinevere,' she snaps.

I grit my teeth and apply pressure. Red drops of scarlet well to the surface, drops of dew on a spring morning.

'You've got to commit to it,' Ffion mutters. 'None of this softly, softly nonsense.'

'It's *hard*,' I reply.

'Oh, it's hard for you?' Ffion shifts, pressing her neck more firmly against the blade. 'Think how I feel, Guin. I'm on the bloody receiving end. Literally.'

'I don't want to kill you, okay?'

'I'll come back.'

'Still – I *don't want to kill you*.'

'Do you want Ynys Halen to be overrun by tidewraiths?'

'No,' I snap. 'I just wish I didn't have to slit your throat like a fucking pig.'

'Do it!' She's shouting now, the noise amplified by the bowl of the bath.

'If you've not noticed, I've never done this before ...'

'*Do it*, Guinevere!'

It takes nothing more than a jerk of my hand. A nervous reflex, really. One swift motion. A seam splits Ffion's throat in half. Blood – more blood than I thought possible – cascades down her throat. It's hot and pungent and it's *pissing* out of her. Urgent and fatal and oh my God, I think I'm going to be sick.

'Oh,' Ffion whispers. '*Oh.*'

She tries to stem the wound with her fingers, but it's useless, and I don't know that she really means to stop it anyway. This is what death looks like: pitiful and sad. Ffion fixes me with this desperate, animalistic stare – the eyes of an animal led to slaughter, beseeching its executor even though it's hopeless.

'Worse,' she chokes out. 'Worse than I thought.'

I curse beneath my breath. 'I'm sorry. So sorry.'

Her blood is filling the bath, now. It swirls in the bottom of the tub, refusing to vanish down the plughole. Ffion's trembling fingers find my own. She clutches hard enough that my joints begin to protest, but the pain pales in comparison to hers.

What if she *doesn't* come back? What if Taliesin was lying all this time, and I've just murdered one of my closest friends? What if her body stills, and cools, and doesn't warm back up again, and it's all my fault?

She starts to shake. Lets out those awful, rattling breaths Rhian uttered before her death.

'Come back,' I tell her. 'Please come back.'

I think she nods, or maybe it's just a reflex of her dying body. Her chest deflates, purging the air from her lungs. She's still staring at me, but her eyes begin to glaze over. I've never known whether to believe in the existence of a soul – an essence that makes us who we are, beyond the physicality of our bodies. But now, staring at Ffion, I see that whatever stitched her together is gone.

# CHAPTER 27

*If you dream of drowning, ask the Halenprophet for a tablespoon of salt. Scatter it beside your doorway in reverence to Llyr. Your nightmares will dissipate.*

—Local superstition

The blood in the bath is cold, now. It's still not draining, and I think Ffion's body must be obstructing the plughole, but I can't bring myself to move her.

I've not shifted so much as a muscle since I killed her. Lili's still in the kitchen, but Taliesin came in after half an hour. I watched the smell of it hit him – all rust and copper, billowing through the room like fog.

The flagstones are cold and hard against my weary joints. Taliesin throws a blanket around my shoulders, and after a few minutes, my teeth stop rattling inside my skull. I count down inside my head, starting from one hundred and promising myself that by the time I hit zero, she'll come back.

She doesn't.

'You told me she'd come back.' Tears bite at my eyes.

'She will,' Taliesin says. He sounds less sure than I'd like.

If Ffion doesn't wake up, I think I might just walk myself into the sea. I can't bear the thought of trying to nurse Lili through this.

Teeth gritted, I say, 'If you've killed her . . .'

'I mean, if either of us killed her, it was you.'

My nostrils flare. 'If you *instructed* me to kill her under false pretences, I swear to God you're next.'

'Got a taste for it, have you?' He feigns shock, one hand pressed against his chest. 'Didn't take you for a murderer, Guinevere.'

'You're the shittest spawn keeper this island has ever seen. You know that, don't you?'

'*You* try keeping track of three sisters—'

'Fucking hell, that was *awful!*'

Ffion bolts upright. Taliesin jumps out of his skin; I lean forwards, wrapping my fingers around the lip of the tub.

'I mean, *truly* awful,' Ffion continues. Her voice is far too loud for the claustrophobic confines of the bathroom. 'You know what people say about death being peaceful? They're wrong, or lying.'

Taliesin makes a gruff sound which might be something like triumph.

'You came back,' I breathe.

'Of course I did,' she mutters. 'I told you I would.'

Lili hurtles down the hallway and comes galloping into the bathroom. As the door rattles on its hinges, Ffion takes in a huge, gasping breath and promptly vomits – except it's not, you know, *human* vomit. It's an iridescent slick that coats the bottom of the tub.

Lili screams. I think I scream, too, but Lili's is so high-pitched that mine sort of fades into irrelevance.

Ffion wipes the back of her hand across her mouth. 'That burns.'

Liliwen launches herself at Ffion, arms flung around her neck. Ffion immediately stiffens, and I think that maybe having your sister latched onto you the minute you awake from undergoing the transition to Godhood is somewhat overwhelming. Still, Ffion pats Lili's back stiffly and tells her, 'It's all right, I'm here, don't get so worked up, little mite.'

'How do you feel?' I ask her.

She glances over at me with an expression that says, 'how the hell do you *think* I feel'. And then, without warning, she wraps her hands around the lip of the bath and hauls herself out. For a minute, I think she's about to be sick again, but then she pushes past us all and out of the lighthouse entirely.

I find her on her knees in the garden. Ffion groans, hands clawing at the soil. Her skin distorts, rising and falling like waves cresting beneath her skin. Suddenly, I realise the protrusions straining against her skin are her *bones*. They're shifting, lengthening beneath her skin.

'It looks like there's creepy crawlies under her skin!' Lili shouts.

'Not. Fucking. Helpful. *Liliwen*,' Ffion grinds out, her jaw straining. She collapses onto her side, writhing in the dirt.

To Taliesin, I whisper, 'Is this supposed to happen?'

He swallows. 'There are a lot of physiological changes that happen when a human becomes a God. Cat's still growing, too.'

Ffion arches her back and lets out this piercing scream that makes me curl in on myself. Her shin bones crack, grow, and mould back together; her shoulders widen; her knuckles pop from their sockets, shunted out of the way by newly long fingers and arms. When she opens her eyes, they're the same shade as Cat's: radiant blue, bordering on white.

She clutches at her throat, moaning. When she removes her hands, feathered gills slice across the surface. Ffion spits, and a handful of her teeth land in the dirt. She pulls out those that remain, trailing bloody saliva and roots of flesh. Sharp, jagged rows of fangs spring up in their place.

'She looks like a tidewraith,' Lili whispers.

Ffion shouts at us all to be quiet, except in much stronger terms. We stand there, watching her transform. By sunset, she's unrecognisable.

We cobble together a plan in what little time remains. Ffion can't fit comfortably inside the lighthouse anymore – she's at least seven feet tall now – so she sits with her legs swinging over the cliff edge, watching the sea. Waiting for Catrin.

Ffion listens to us through the open kitchen window, though she doesn't turn to engage. We lay tentative intentions. Step one: I will try to reason with Catrin. If I can convince her to show mercy and leave Llyr intact, I win twice: Cat lives, and so does Ynys Halen. But if I cannot, we'll have no choice but to meet her with teeth. Taliesin will distract her with gunfire, and we'll unleash our secret weapon. Ffion.

During all this, Liliwen will be tucked up inside the Morgan family home with Percy for company. She doesn't protest as much as I thought she might. We send her off, across the heath – pale skin, dark hair, a ginger ball of fury in her arms.

Once all is said and done, there's nothing left to do but wait. I watch Taliesin's finger as it traces the whorls in the kitchen table.

'What will you do, after this?'

He looks up, somewhat startled. 'Assuming we survive?'

'Assuming we survive.'

Taliesin leans back in his chair. 'I should stay. Have a litter of children who I can saddle with the burden of "Halenprophecy". Continue the family line. Make my father proud.'

'But you're not going to do that.'

He shakes his head. 'I've had enough of familial duty, I think. When they let me out of the gaol after Cat died, I was close to just setting sail and leaving this place behind.' He meets my gaze. 'But I felt I had a debt to you. So here I am, for better or worse.'

We sit in silence then, listening to the rushing of the ocean, the buffeting of the wind. I eventually grow so restless that I can no longer sit still. When I say I'm going out to stand on the beach, Taliesin doesn't protest. He simply smiles and tells me I'm the best bait we have.

# CHAPTER 28

*Never turn your back on the ocean. The waves love nothing more than a careless soul.*

—Island superstition

I knew she'd come out at night.

It's always been the time when she seemed most alive. Most like herself. I suppose it makes sense now, knowing where she came from. The deep dark, as Rhian used to call it.

She emerges from the ocean in one smooth movement. Water cascades from her lithe frame, landing like a transient rainstorm on the ocean's surface. She hovers there, more monstrous, more *beautiful* than I've ever seen her.

The terrible fangs have grown longer, more numerous. Where before her eyes would glint in the moonlight, they now exert their own light – twin beacons staring out from the centre of her face. I find myself transfixed, a moth to a flame. Her nails have lengthened into talons. She's taller than I remember, her legs grown long and sinewy. When the moonlight hits her just right, she turns almost transparent. I can see the network of her veins, the dark pulse of her heart.

But despite all that has changed, there's something achingly familiar about her. I know the scent of her hair, the shape of her lips, the sound of her laughter. I wonder if she knows how to laugh anymore.

She glides across the beach, the tips of her toes dragging through the sand. Her attention flits between me and Point Beacon at my back. I wave my arms in an arc above my head, desperate to be something she notices. It's the same thing I've spent my life doing – trying to be worth her focus. The stakes have never been higher.

'You can't do this, Cat.'

Cat blinks down at me, but I get the sense she's only registering my intrusion, not my words.

'If you kill Llyr, you'll kill everyone on this island.' I swallow down the alarm that surges through me as she glides closer, her bare feet skimming the grass. 'Point Beacon will stop working. The tidewraiths will overrun Ynys Halen. You'll kill us all. You'll kill *me*.'

She makes this odd, trilling sound – somewhere between a whale call and birdsong. Her eyes soften, the light inside them dimming until they simply smoulder, hot coals embedded in the soft, pale expanse of her face. She glides lower, almost meeting me at eye level. Cat cups my chin in her clawed hand, talons scraping my earlobe.

'Cat – protect Guin,' she whispers, her voice not quite of this world – echoing despite the lack of walls around us. 'Always.'

Trembling, I reach up to mirror her gesture. My hand looks

small and frail against the sharp line of her jaw. 'Please,' I whisper. 'Don't kill Llyr. Isn't his imprisonment punishment enough?'

She shakes her head. 'Life for life.'

I rub my thumb across her jaw, memorising its shape. 'We'll have to try and stop you. You know that, don't you?'

Catrin smiles sadly. Her eyes roam across my face. She begins to nod. '*Try*,' she says.

She sweeps her free arm towards me. It's so deeply elegant that I don't register its intent until too late. She doesn't even need to touch me to exert her force; it buffets me regardless. A blow to the chest so fierce it wrenches me off my feet. I bend in the middle, sent flying both upwards and backwards.

My spine cracks against Point Beacon. Bright, hot points of light burst across my vision. A metallic tang blooms on my tongue. I think some of my teeth have cracked, but when I probe my mouth, my tongue is too numb to feel anything. Groaning, I try to lift my hands. They stay welded at my sides, limp and useless.

Cat rises up over the cliff. Her heart flutters inside the cradle of her ribs. She reaches out towards me, and I flinch in anticipation of another blow. This long, plaintive sound passes between her lips.

*Crack*. Taliesin fires the rifle from somewhere behind me. Smoke fills the air, curling thick and acrid in the stagnant breeze. He places himself between me and Catrin. Through my fragmented vision, I can just about discern his outline – this breakable, insignificant barrier against the God in front of him. She seems to look down at me with regret for a split second, before clenching her fists and letting out a guttural howl.

'I tried!' I cry. 'I tried to save you!'

Behind Cat, Ffion rounds the coast. She rises into the air, hair billowing. Taliesin keeps Cat's attention with another round from his rifle. It penetrates her right arm, tearing straight through the muscle. I swear I can see daylight through the gap. Cat looks down at the wound with little more than mild irritation. She snarls, and rows of sharp teeth drop from her gums.

Ffion surges across the beach. Cat doesn't even hear her coming. The two Gods collide. Ffion smacks straight into Cat's back. I think they'd take Point Beacon right off its foundations, if not for the fact that Ffion's hands wrap around Cat's throat and keep her pinned to the spot. She writhes, but her strength is no match for Ffion.

'*Stop*,' Ffion snarls. 'You. Can't. Kill. Him.'

'Have to,' Cat growls. '*Need* to.'

'If you kill him, Lili dies. Guin dies.' Ffion's eyes dart towards the sea, where the tidewraiths must be watching. 'No more light. No more protection.'

Cat's eyes round, just for a second. The unnatural light in them dims. A single tear carves its way down her face, landing in a blotch on her chest.

But then she bares her teeth, furrows her brow, and roars, 'Revenge!'

Ffion lets out an anguished cry as she tightens her grip on Catrin's throat. I'm crying too, knowing that I'm about to witness my best friend's head ripped from her neck by her own sister. It's all so quick. So sudden. I thought she'd put up more of a fight, so it would feel less like a slaughter.

'Ffion,' Cat forces out with her last gasping breath.

And that pitiful, wheezing sound causes Ffion to falter. For all her wisdom, she cannot fight against the pang of familial loyalty.

Her grip loosens. Cat wrestles free. She turns on Ffion, hissing and spitting.

'You kill me,' Catrin drones. 'Protect Llyr.'

Cat tackles Ffion. The ferocity of their clash makes the cliff start to crumble beneath them, shingle and earth slipping down onto the beach below. Eventually, the landslide takes them with it. They plummet onto the sand, Cat straddling Ffion, hands at her throat.

I take the steps down to Sawtooth two at a time. Taliesin fires the rifle directly at Cat's back; I watch as she absorbs the bullets as if they're nothing. She's riddled through with holes, and it doesn't matter.

Catrin's arms tense the same way they did the night she killed Gethin. Ffion's eyes bulge from her head. Her arms thrash. One winds around Catrin's wrist and loosens her grip; the other snakes towards Cat's eyes, searching for something soft to gouge.

'They're both going to die at this rate!' I shout up to Taliesin where he stands on the cliff.

He looks down at me, a grim expression on his lips. By way of response, he reloads his gun and fires another round. Again, Cat does not react. She just presses her weight more firmly onto Ffion's throat, a low growl rumbling through her chest.

She won't kill her. She *won't.* Cat is the protector. Fiercely loyal to her family. She loves Ffion more than she craves revenge. She *loves* her.

But she's also a monster. I'm not sure the part of her that recognises familial bonds still exists. If it does, is it stronger than the part of her that is driven to kill Llyr by whatever means necessary?

'Catrin!'

The faltering voice carries down onto the beach, spoken from the top of the stairs. I turn, finding little Liliwen there, stood braced against the wind.

'Get out of here, Lili!' I shriek, incensed. I knew she'd relented a little too easy.

But Lili's bolting down the stairs, and Taliesin isn't fast enough to stop her. I stand with my arms braced, ready to intercept her, but she shrugs free of my grip and makes a beeline towards the warring Gods where they're laid.

'Catrin, you're killing her!' she shrieks.

A flash of something human passes across Catrin's eyes. She glances at Liliwen from the corner of her vision and snarls, '*Go.*'

Liliwen shakes her head, standing just short of the brawl. Cat's hands are still fastened tight around Ffion's throat. Ffion has gone very still, and very pale. She looks less like a God and more like something that washed up on the shore.

'Stop it, Catrin,' Lili demands, fists clenched at her sides.

She takes another step closer, and perhaps reflexively, one of Ffion's arms lashes out. It strikes Lili square across the stomach, sending her flying backwards into the sand. She lets out a yelp, all the air vacating her lungs.

I know what's about to happen, but I'm powerless to stop it. Times stutters to a jagged series of images: Cat's piercing gaze landing on Liliwen where she's sprawled in the sand. Looking back, then, to Ffion – the one she holds accountable for Lili's hurt.

Ffion locks eyes with me. I fall to my knees, one hand clamped over my mouth. Catrin lowers her head, bares her fangs, and sinks them into Ffion's throat. She draws back, metallic blood smeared across her lips. Ffion presses one hand against her wound, the same way she did when she was still human – and then Cat attacks again. Again. *Again.*

Ffion's screams echo across Sawtooth. I'm screaming for Catrin to stop, *please* stop, but she doesn't listen. Eventually, she pulls back, blood streaming from her teeth . . .

And Ffion's head is held between them.

Her eyelids flutter. The light in her eyes goes out. Catrin jerks her head to the side. Ffion's head arcs across the sky before falling to the sand and rolling to a stop.

I don't know if I'm screaming, or if Liliwen is, or if it's just the wind howling through the rocks. Ffion was *here*. She was alive, and incandescent, and powerful – and now she's dead. Irretrievably dead.

I vaguely register the tone of Taliesin's voice. He comes pounding down onto the sand. Herds Liliwen and me back up the steps, shouting something about a last stand.

From the cliff, I watch as Catrin sobs over Ffion's body. She takes her decapitated head in her hands, and seems to try to fit it back where it should be. When it doesn't take, she stands and lets out a sound that I can only describe as a lamentation. I clutch Lili to my side even though I'm barely able to keep myself upright.

Another sound joins Catrin's howling. The melody that's haunted my nights ever since I first moved into Point Beacon. A low, rhythmic humming. *Luh, luh, luh.* Only now do I recognise it for what it truly is. Bronwen's saying his name. Cursing it.

I watch as the leviathan – as *Bronwen* – hauls herself across the reef, eel-like tail thrashing to push her gargantuan body along. Jagged rocks beneath the surface open up wounds along the length of her body. She cries, but does not relent. The shallow water of Sawtooth beach barely conceals her hideous form, and suddenly, I'm grieving for her too. Cursed to spend eternity in a body that she does not recognise.

Bronwen hauls up onto shore. She slithers over to where Ffion lies, letting out a plaintive cry. Catrin inspects the slick, iridescent blood coating her hands. Bronwen wails again, and it snaps Cat out of the stupor she's in. She turns towards us, hair moving like silk in the air, and begins to levitate.

Cat glides up, over the cliff edge. Her shadow falls over us, over Point Beacon. She looks down at me with something that isn't quite indifference, but isn't quite love, either. I hold Liliwen tighter, and Taliesin moves to stand in front of us, rifle held aloft.

With a single swing of her fist, Catrin shatters the glass cage surrounding the lantern. Shards of glass rain down. We throw ourselves to the ground, hands braced over our heads. Another sound rings out – metal whining as it tears. I flip onto my back, and find Cat pulling down the crumbling widow's walk, leaving nothing more than a gangplank attached.

She pauses briefly to look at us. Reaches down as if to take my hand or crush me in her fist. But then she grabs something behind me – a jagged boulder. She heaves it down the length of the tower, gouging a gaping wound in Point Beacon's side. The walls give way, leaving a grotesque cross-section of my lighthouse.

I stuff my fist into my mouth and bite down. It's my home. My sanctuary and my prison. The place I grew to love Rhian. To love Cat. There are so many memories stuffed inside those walls, and she's laying waste to them. I'm glad Rhian is dead for this. I don't know how she'd cope, seeing Point Beacon this way. Decimated. Disembowelled.

When Cat reaches the base of the lighthouse, she gores a hole in the foundations. The cellar sees daylight for the first time. With the lighthouse peeled away like a snail's shell, Llyr must lie exposed – salt breeze ghosting across what remains of his skin for the first time in years.

Taliesin fires at Cat until he's only got a handful of bullets left. She doesn't so much as flinch. Even Liliwen's wails cannot reach her. She's a foxhound above a burrow, a shark scenting blood, a kestrel honing in.

Unthinking, I close the distance between us. Shove myself in front of the hole she's created. Catrin stares down at me, contempt burning in her eyes. I'm as entranced by her as I've always been.

'Stop,' I pant. 'Stop it, Catrin.'

She reaches down, talons poised to scar. 'Can't. Stop.'

'We're meant to be together,' I blurt out. She falters. 'You can't hurt me.'

'*Move*,' she hisses.

'I love you.' Tears stream down my cheeks. 'And I feel like neither of us were ever clear enough about what we meant when we said that. But I want you to know that I *love you*, Catrin Morgan. Even in this body, I love you. There is nothing you could do that would make me *stop* loving you. I don't know if that's right, or normal, but it's true.'

Sparkling tears roll down Cat's cheeks. Her chest flutters.

'And the worst part is I'm not sure if you ever loved me back.' The laugh that escapes me verges on hysterical. 'But it never mattered, you know? Because I was glad just to have a seat at your table.'

Her forehead pinches together in the centre, the way it always did, and pauses. She goes to her knees. The weight of her body shakes the ground, further disturbing Point Beacon's ruins. Llyr whimpers in the cellar. She cups my chin in her hand. The harsh light of her eyes dulls, and for a second, I can see her eyes as they used to be.

'Love you,' she murmurs, her voice a summer breeze as it skims my face. 'Love you always.'

I layer my small hand on top of hers. 'This won't solve anything, Cat. It will just multiply the suffering.'

Something lurches in the corner of my vision. I realise, then, that Bronwen has hauled herself up the steps. She drags her body towards us and stares straight at me. Her eyes are shrunken and receded. All the monstrousness that surrounds them fades: the slitted gills, the seaweed hair, the coral spine. Her eyes are a brilliant blue, just like Catrin's. They are deep and full of emotion – full of *tears*. And suddenly, I'm not eye to eye with the leviathan. I'm eye to eye with a woman.

Taliesin cocks his gun. Prepares to fire.

'Stop,' I tell him.

He lets the rifle fall to his side.

Bronwen slithers towards me and Cat. She's in so much pain. I can feel the weight of her trauma. This terrible, inescapable grief inside her. A stolen life. A man's cruelty. Her story rewritten, her suffering forgotten. She hums again, and this time I feel like she's imploring me. Begging me to look not with my eyes but my heart.

I glance across my shoulder, down into the ruined cellar where Llyr trembles. He's pathetic. Cowering against the moonlight, howling Bronwen's name into the wind.

'Revenge,' Cat whispers. 'For Mother.'

I swallow hard. 'It won't make you feel any better.'

A cruel smile curves her lips. 'How – do you know?'

My blood calcifies. I glance again down into the cellar. Llyr meets my gaze.

'Save me,' he hisses, his heart trilling. '*Save me.*'

But when I look at him, I do not see Llyr the God. I do not even see Llyr the man. I see *him*. Aledd. The man that killed my mother. The lines blur and blur until I cannot remember what Aledd looks like. Cannot remember whose fingers wrapped around my mother's throat. All I can think about is how revenge would've fixed everything. Would've fixed *me*.

I look inland to Ynys Halen. It's undergone the same transformation as Llyr – a shift in perspective which prevents me returning to the old one. I do not see my home, nor my community, nor my family. In fact, I do not see anything worth saving at all.

I glance down at Llyr. Back up at Bronwen. And then, without so much as a waver in my voice, I tell Cat, 'Kill him.'

Catrin tears Llyr's heart from the floorboards and places it between her teeth. With our eyes locked, she bites down. Searing white light explodes outwards, the same shade and intensity as Point Beacon's beam. Black blood erupts, dribbling down Cat's chin.

She goes for his face next. Tears it from the mortar and holds it up beside her mother. Bronwen writhes excitedly, opening and shutting her mouth until she's able to form a single word.

'*Monster*,' she hisses.

And then Catrin devours him whole.

# CHAPTER 29

A fleet of boats leaves Ynys Halen, bound for the mainland. Catrin chased us all the way to the harbour. I'm not sure what her intention was – only that her wailing set alight a grief so intense it cleared me of all thought. From our boat, I watch the tidewardens surge ahead. Predictably, they seized the biggest boat, leaving behind women and children they claimed to love.

We managed to gather most of them onto our boat. Osian took the rest, and looked to me with wide eyes as if I should thank him for it. I stand with my back braced against the bow's railing, watching Ynys Halen shrink. Dusk is falling, and tidewraiths are hauling themselves up onto the beaches. There's no sign of Catrin, nor Bronwen.

It feels as if a monumental tide is pulling us towards the mainland, towards *safety*. Tonight, tidewraiths are consuming Ynys Halen, and I'm not there to stop them. It's no longer my job. No longer my burden to bear.

'We were never going to stop them,' I say.

Sat with her back pressed up against the wood, Lili refuses to meet my gaze. She clutches Persnickety to her chest. Dylan sits beside her, his face pale. At the captain's wheel, Taliesin rolls his shoulders, setting the boat straight as it slices through the water.

'Maybe not,' he says. Then, almost to himself, 'At least we tried.'

Ahead, the vessel ferrying the tidewardens to safety lurches dangerously in the water before drawing to a complete stop. I glance across at Taliesin in questioning.

'I knew they'd take that one,' he says. 'Terrible shame about all the holes in the hull. I wonder who put those there.'

We glide past the tidewardens, watching as they desperately try to bail the water out. Their panicked shouts are lost to the wind. For the first time since we left Ynys Halen, Lili smiles.

I can taste possibility in the air, and I drink it down. I'll find a good apothecarist for Liliwen to study under, and a house for us both to live in. Somewhere with a thatched roof, and a pretty garden not blighted by sea spray and harsh winds. Inland, perhaps, away from the ocean's tug, protected from storms. Percy will sleep by the hearth. Maybe we'll get another cat to keep him company – a sleek, grey she-cat who loves me the way Persnickety loves Liliwen.

Maybe I'll allow Taliesin to visit. I might even let him take me to bed, if he puts in the effort. He's handsome, and has risked more to preserve my life than anyone else. When he looks at me, I get a strange feeling in my stomach. I think that could be a good thing.

But I laugh. What a funny story to tell myself. When really, Catrin Morgan still has her claws in me. If she is bound to Ynys Halen, so must I be.

I say goodbye to Dylan. Kiss Lili on the top of her head. Kiss Percy on the top of his, too, because he has always been a good cat, and I will miss his soft weight in my lap.

I take Taliesin by the shirt, knotting my fists in the fabric. He lets out a startled laugh and bows his head to meet me.

'Keep sailing,' I whisper.

Taliesin stiffens. 'What do you mean?'

I release him and run to the opposite end of the boat. Launch myself from the stern. A wave drags me under. For a moment, there is only the cold, dark desolation of open water – and then she rises from the depths, pale and terrible, her arms wide open.

Together, we descend into the dark.

# ACKNOWLEDGEMENTS

Thank you to my parents, for being my biggest fans. Even though I do find it slightly embarrassing when we go to a bookshop and you start talking – loudly – about my book being on the shelves, I wouldn't have it any other way. I am who I am because of you both, which is largely a good thing.

Thank you to my Cornhill friends, not only for your sage advice in difficult times – but for your thrilling reenactments of certain scenes in certain books, and generally being a force of light and positivity. Thank you to Kate, who stepped in at a critical moment to help drag this book to the surface. Thank you, in fact, to all of my friends - who have supported me not only through the writing of this book, but those that came before it, and those that will come after. Thank you to Maple, as always, for being the best companion a writer could ask for.

To my agent, Chloe Seager, who I sincerely believe is a guardian angel: I owe everything I have to you. We both know I'm prone to dramatics, but I mean it sincerely when I say that I am utterly in your debt.

To my fantastic editors: Charlotte Trumble, who first acquired this book; Louise Buckley, who later helped me hone it; and to Gemma Creffield and Antonia Desola Coker for ushering it over the line with their invaluable feedback. I am so grateful to you all.

At Simon and Schuster UK, thank you to managing editor Gail Hallett; copyeditor Moira Eagling; editorial assistant Odiri Ejaria; Karin Seifried in production; marketing wizard Sarah Jeffcoate; and publicist Laurie McShea. Thank you also to Pip Watkins for creating such a beautiful cover.

And as always, thank you to Phillip. Thank you for helping me weather the waves of this book, and for being my best friend (apart from the dog). I couldn't do any of this without your support.

Finally, thank you to you – the reader. The fact that you picked up this book means the world to me, and I'll never stop trying to repay you.